HEARTBREAK
FOR
HIRE

A NOVEL

SONIA HARTL

GALLERY BOOKS

NEW YORK   LONDON   TORONTO   SYDNEY   NEW DELHI

G

Gallery Books
An Imprint of Simon & Schuster, Inc.
1230 Avenue of the Americas
New York, NY 10020

First Gallery Books trade paperback edition July 2021

GALLERY BOOKS and colophon are registered
trademarks of Simon & Schuster, Inc.

For information about special discounts for bulk purchases,
please contact Simon & Schuster Special Sales at 1-866-506-1949
or business@simonandschuster.com.

The Simon & Schuster Speakers Bureau can bring authors
to your live event. For more information or to book an event, contact
the Simon & Schuster Speakers Bureau at 1-866-248-3049
or visit our website at www.simonspeakers.com.

Interior design by Michelle Marchese

Manufactured in the United States of America

1 3 5 7 9 10 8 6 4 2

Names: Hartl, Sonia, author.
Title: Heartbreak for hire / Sonia Hartl.
Identifiers: LCCN 2020044818 (print) | LCCN 2020044819 (ebook) |
ISBN 9781982167783 (trade paperback) | ISBN 9781982167790 (ebook)
Subjects: GSAFD: Love stories.
Classification: LCC PS3608.A787258 H43 2021 (print) | LCC PS3608.A787258
(ebook) | DDC 813/.6—dc23
LC record available at https://lccn.loc.gov/2020044818
LC ebook record available at https://lccn.loc.gov/2020044819

ISBN 978-1-9821-6778-3
ISBN 978-1-9821-6779-0 (ebook)

For Jen Hawkins, who knows me inside and out and loves me anyway. I'm lucky to call you my CP, even luckier to call you my friend.

CHAPTER 1

Dealing with the male ego was a lot like painting. Both required me to create an image, evoke an emotional response, and find the balance between indifference and trying too hard. They needed gentle strokes, the right amount of buildup.

Such fragile things.

Soft indie rock filtered out of a nearby speaker as I sat at the end of the fiberglass bar. Pixels—a pub with concrete floors, smooth white tables, and clean minimalist lines—catered to the up-and-coming tech crowd. Two women on the opposite side of the bar negotiated the sale of a search engine over martinis, while a guy at a nearby table double-checked the sales figures for ad space on a new social media platform before the rest of his party showed up. This was where people in tech came to network and make deals.

My target had big plans tonight.

I took a sip of my martini and twirled the tiny umbrella I'd requested between my finger and thumb as I went over my checklist for tonight. Chad Collinsworth, who sounded as douchey as his name suggested, had worked with my client for two years developing a dating app called Triple M (for mix, match, mingle). He'd worked in the register's office, so he'd handled all the filing and paperwork. My client had trusted him. A mistake, since right after they gained a relative amount of success, he blocked her number and disappeared. Turned out, Chad had not only listed himself as sole creator, but he'd also tricked her into signing away any rights to the app by slipping an affidavit in with all their other paperwork.

When she couldn't find a lawyer to take her case, she called Margo Pheffer.

I'd worked for Margo for the last two years at Heartbreak for Hire, an undercover operation that specialized in a variety of revenge schemes for jilted lovers, annoyed coworkers, and frenemies. For a price. Those in need of our services found us through word of mouth, Craigslist, and coded ads in magazines that catered to the women of Chicago. There were four of us Heartbreakers, each with her own specialty: Egos, Players, Cheaters, and Grifters. I handled the Egos, men in the workplace who needed to be taken down a notch, and I was generally hired by women who knew them on a professional level and hated them with the scorching rage of a thousand suns.

The pay couldn't be beat, and one day I'd have saved enough to buy my own gallery where I could surround myself with art and maybe even sell my own paintings, if I ever worked up the courage to show them. Until that day came, I'd happily give my clients the retaliation they deserved.

Chad walked into the bar and ran a hand through his game-show-host hair. He had the kind of face that just begged to have a drink thrown at it. He wore a navy suit, red tie, and smarmy smile, as if he'd been personally styled by the Young Republicans Club. The idea of flirting with this guy kicked up my gag reflex, but I was nothing if not professional.

Step one: get his interest.

His gaze met mine across the bar. I dipped my head and gave him a simpering smile. The tight red dress I'd chosen for tonight pushed my boobs up to my neck. My golden curls rippled down the length of my back. According to my research, he wanted a woman with an empty head and a full wallet. I fully intended to play the part.

Chad took a seat at a nearby table and checked his teeth in the reflection of a spoon. A waitress tried handing him a menu, but he shooed her away with a swish of his well-manicured hand. He thought he'd be meeting Tom Berry, the head of a software engineering company, here to negotiate the sale of Triple M. It had taken me two weeks of monitoring his social media interactions to put this con together. Posing as the real Tom Berry's secretary, I'd scheduled the setup. By the time Chad figured out he'd been had, my client would be well on her way to suing him for rightful ownership of the app.

After fifteen minutes Chad relaxed his posture and checked his watch as he drummed his fingers on the table. Any moment now he'd call Tom's secretary. I ordered a scotch on the rocks, then paid the waitress twenty dollars to give Chad the martini I'd sprinkled with edible glitter.

Now the real fun could begin.

Before the confusion could set in, I made my way over to Chad's table and set the scotch in front of him. "I think there's been a mistake." I let out a breathy giggle. "I'm so bad at this. I meant to send you the scotch and keep the Gold Rush for myself."

He smirked and picked up the martini, examining the glitter floating around in the clear liquid. "What exactly is a Gold Rush?"

A drink that didn't technically exist, but he didn't need to know that. "It's off-menu." I slipped into the chair beside him and took a sip of the martini, closing my eyes as if in ecstasy. "Made with edible gold leaf. Expensive, but delicious."

He perked up at the word *expensive*. Interest received.

Step two: feed his ego.

"I hope I'm not interrupting a date." I forced a blush. "I noticed you the moment you walked through the door, and I said to myself, 'You need to meet that guy.'"

He laughed like I was just the cutest. Darned. Thing. "What's your name, sweetheart?"

He asked it absently, to my boobs, like he genuinely could not give less of a shit. Typical Ego behavior. In the two years I'd been working for Margo, I'd yet to meet a target who did the bare minimum of looking me in the eye when he asked my name.

I took a sip of my drink, letting my tongue sweep my bottom lip while I stared at his mouth. Egos didn't respond well to subtlety. "My name is Anna."

I never gave targets any personal information, including my real name. My job as a Heartbreaker was to craft an image and play whatever part necessary to reel them in. Margo gave us all three rules when we started at H4H: never trust a target, never break character with a target, and never sleep with a target. She'd created the rules to protect us from the enemy, and considering our histories, none of us had a problem following them.

"Well then, Anna. I'm here for a business meeting." He leaned in closer, and I could feel a sneeze building from the fumes coming off his aftershave. "Not a date. How about that?"

How about that? Was he expecting applause? I thought about fuzzy kittens, long days at the beach, my ex getting swarmed by bees, anything happy to keep my expression from betraying my disgust. "That's good news for me."

"I'd say that's good news for both of us." He gave me what I'd bet he thought was his most dazzling smile. Very toothy. Like a cartoon shark. "Have you ever been to Monaco?"

I shook my head. Was that his idea of an icebreaker? Apparently, by the way he droned on about the places he'd traveled and the restaurants where he'd eaten and the people with whom he'd rubbed elbows. I did my best to look sufficiently awed.

"Wow, how exciting. It must be wonderful to have a job that lets you travel so much." I motioned for the waitress to bring him another drink. Not enough to get him drunk, but just enough to loosen his tongue. It was time to get this show moving along. "Do you work in tech?"

"In a manner of speaking." He glanced toward the door. Sweat beaded his upper lip as he glanced at his watch again. "What about you?"

Not bad. It had only taken him twenty minutes of puffing himself up to ask me a single question. "I won the lottery."

He swallowed too fast and beat against his chest as he coughed. "You did what now?"

I blinked at him, careful to keep my face blank. The lottery was a little over the top, but I needed to convince him I had money while simultaneously making him think I wasn't all that bright. This required the least amount of research.

"I won the lottery," I repeated just as earnestly, as if he hadn't actually heard me the first time. "My advisor said I should diversify my portfolio by getting into tech. That's why I'm here tonight."

"Really." He leaned back in his chair with an amused expression. He looked me up and down, like I was nothing more than a bubble-headed woman but he'd do me the favor of humoring me. "What kind of tech are you looking to get into?"

I took another sip of my drink and shrugged. "He set me up with a Tom Berry? I'm supposed to be meeting him here any minute now, but the decorators are redoing my condo, so I showed up a little early."

The front legs of his chair slammed to the ground as he sat forward. That had got his attention. "What business do you have with Tom Berry?"

Step three: make him chase.

"He's going to sell me a dating app." I picked up my drink and stood. "I should probably let you get back to your business, though. Call me sometime?"

I left a napkin with a fake number and walked to the bar with an extra sway in my hips. He'd need a good five minutes to pick his jaw up off the floor. While Chad spun that last bit of information around in his mind, I took my phone out of my beaded clutch and double-tapped the tracking app that Margo made us all install. Not only would it pinpoint my location for safety reasons if need be, but it was also a direct line to Margo. I'd informed her earlier today that I would need her to call me when she got the notification. My phone buzzed against the bar, and I answered.

"Hey, Tom." I kicked my heels against the legs of my barstool.

"You're ahead of schedule," Margo said. "Nice work."

Pride swelled in my chest as I glanced at Chad. His eyes narrowed as he watched me. "Oh no. That's too bad. . . . Sure. . . . Tomorrow then."

I hung up on Margo and settled my tab. Any moment now. Three, two . . .

Chad approached me with that humoring grin back on his face, though it was a little more strained around the corners. "I'm sorry, I couldn't help but overhear your phone conversation. Were you talking to Tom Berry?"

Step four: hold his interest.

I nodded. "It turns out he's not buying that dating app after all. But he said he has something else that might pique my interest. We're meeting for dinner tomorrow."

"I see." Chad swept a hand over his pale face. "Did he say why he's not buying it?"

"It was designed by a man. Not what we're looking for. I want an app that's women-centric, and I think it takes a woman designer to really achieve that, you know?" I let my fingers graze his hand. A casual touch to draw him in. "It's a shame. Dating apps are so big right now. I'd love to get in on the ground floor of one."

"What if . . ." He took a swallow of his drink. "What if I told you that you could cut out Tom as the middleman and still have your app designed by a woman?"

Step five: finish him.

I swirled my finger around the rim of my glass. "I'm listening."

"I own Triple M." He gave me the dramatic pause. My cue to be impressed.

"Oh my God." I bounced in my seat. "That's the app I was looking to buy."

"I know." He managed to pull off the perfect blend of mocking and superiority. A verbal head pat. "And there was more to the development than Tom is privy to."

This was the fuel that pushed me to do this job. Anytime I was inclined to feel guilty, I'd pull this moment out and recall the slight curl of his lip, his gaze clouded with equal parts disdain and desire. This was how he viewed women. They were either discardable or fuckable, but never worthy of respect. He was about to learn just how much his underestimation would cost him.

"Are you saying your app was designed by a woman? I have so many questions, I'm afraid I'm going to forget them before I

talk to my advisor. All this techy talk goes right over my head."
I unlocked my phone screen and turned on the camera. "Is it
okay if I record this?"

I held my breath as I waited for his answer. Thanks to Illi-
nois state laws, I had to have his permission to record for this
to be admissible in court. If he said no, I'd have to take a different, more unpleasant route. One that would require me to
continue pretending I enjoyed his company.

"Sure thing, sweetheart." He gave me a finger gun for good
measure.

"Yay!" I clapped my hands together and held them under
my chin. "Tell me everything about your company."

Chad proceeded to give me all the dirt on Triple M. How
my client had actually been the majority designer and pro-
grammer, while he handled the business end of things. Of
course, he painted a grandiose picture of his administrative duties, as if they were just as vital to the business, but he
made it perfectly clear my client had been the brains and the
muscle behind Triple M. It was the most glorious display of
self-incrimination I'd ever witnessed.

Once I'd gathered enough information to give my client a
fighting chance in a lawsuit, I set up a fake date for next week
to handle the sale. Unfortunately for Chad, he'd be getting
served papers well before then. After he left, I uploaded the
conversation to a movie player and e-mailed it to my client.
Per our agreement, I'd get 5 percent of whatever she made off
the sale of the app, which was expected to be around half a
million dollars.

I didn't typically make that much off an assignment, so

this called for a celebration. On my way home, I picked up a chocolate cake and a bottle of Malbec. Balancing both under one arm, I unlocked my apartment and pushed open the door, losing my grip on the cake in the process. The box hit the floor facedown with a dull splat. I dumped my purse by the door and picked up the cake. Most of the frosting stuck to the lid, but after I polished off the wine, I'd probably end up licking the box clean anyway.

"I'm home." I made kissy noises at my cat, Winnie, as she jumped on the back of the couch. Her black hair stood on end as she hissed at me in return. Her love language, or so I kept telling myself.

An evening of cake and wine with my angry cat. It didn't get much wilder than that. I stripped off my too-tight dress and left it on the floor. On my way to the kitchen, I peeked in on my latest painting. Soon I'd have the funds to start my gallery. Soon I'd be able to reclaim my nights and weekends for myself. Soon I'd have to muster up the courage to show my work.

Soon.

CHAPTER 2

Still riding high on my success with the dating app scammer, I took on a few smaller-scale assignments, the kind that required me to humiliate targets rather than maneuver them into incriminating themselves. At a thousand dollars, humiliation was the cheapest—and most popular—option on my pricing list.

I hoped that tonight's paycheck would allow me to carve out time to do some painting this week. I'd been playing with my latest canvas for the last month now, and I'd finally hit a breakthrough. All I wanted was a full, uninterrupted day to lose myself in my art.

I ran a finger over the pink, floral-scented card stock that held the info on my latest target. Markus Cavanaugh was an adjunct professor at the University of Chicago with lofty career goals and the ambition to match. He wore sweater-vests and argyle socks, and his hobbies included metal detecting and watching historical documentaries. He liked bullet-point outlines and a well-organized office, and hated animals dressed like people. In short, this guy was no fun.

Markus spent his Tuesday nights at the Reading Lounge, a snooty bar with dark paneled walls, stiff leather chairs, and top-shelf scotch on the rocks. The kind of place where a professor would feel right at home. I knew of it, though I'd never been. On purpose.

My phone buzzed, and I grabbed it from my purse. Selena, the woman who had hired me for the evening, chirped in my ear: "Quick change of plans. He said he was going to Finnigan's Hobby Shop before the bar, so hold off on the Reading Lounge for at least an hour."

"I know Finnigan's." It was my favorite place in the city outside my apartment. "I'll just do the meet-cute early."

"Are you sure about that?" So much haughtiness in her tone.

To say I didn't like my newest client would be an understatement. She'd talked down to me during the interview, then proceeded to call me every other hour with questions and suggestions as if she didn't fully trust me to pull this off. Even though I felt bad for her—Markus had dismissed her research in front of their colleagues and made her work look like a joke, all because he couldn't stand being bested—dealing with her had been difficult and exhausting. I was so ready for this assignment to be over.

"It'll be okay." I aimed for reassuring, though I feared my voice came out more biting. "He'll be a ruined man when he walks into work tomorrow."

"Maybe I should call Margo and tell her this was a mistake."

Closing my eyes, I rubbed the lids and took a deep breath so I wouldn't scream. "If that's what you want, but I'm already on my way out."

"Fine, just know if you mess up, I expect a full refund."

I clenched my jaw and hung up before I said something I'd regret.

I needed to get going anyway if I was going to catch Markus at Finnigan's. In our initial interview, Selena had said he had a thing for smart women, so I wore a cherry-print cardigan, cat's-eye glasses, a knee-length skirt, and three-inch heels with a rounded toe. My outfits were always carefully crafted to snag the target's attention as quickly as possible. I only had one night to make an impression. I had to make it count.

"Be good, Winnie." I gave my cat, wearing her pink angora sweater, a pat on the head. She hissed and swiped at me. "I'll miss you too."

I grabbed my purse, locked the door behind me, and took the elevator down from my eighteenth-floor apartment. As I stepped onto Michigan Avenue, a strong wind swept down the street, threatening to undo the tight bun I'd spent an hour trying to contain. Wisps of curly blond hair escaped and blew around my face. The scent of exhaust and woodsmoke with the first hints of fall lingered in the crisp air.

Finnigan's Hobby Shop was only a block from my apartment, with the Reading Lounge another two blocks over from there, so I opted to walk. My smart heels clicked along the concrete as I breathed in the pulse of Chicago. The city came alive at night as young professionals shed their suit jackets in favor of slinky camis and rolled-up sleeves. A woman rushed past me, changing her boring gold posts for dangling silver earrings. No doubt on her way to a real date.

I hadn't had one of those in over two years.

By choice. An important distinction I had to make whenever those wistful feelings threatened to make me sentimental. I had my career, my cat, control. The Three C's of avoiding that hopeless cycle of loving someone who didn't love me back.

The warm glow of Finnigan's greeted me as I pulled open the heavy oak door, and a charming bell chimed above my head. I loved it here. I'd spent more Friday nights than I could count loading their adorable wicker baskets with fresh art supplies.

Markus had been impossible to find on social media—he probably had a self-inflated username, like TheProfessor-Cavanaugh or something—so I had no pictures to reference, only Selena's description. I was supposed to be on the lookout for a guy with dark-brown hair, wearing a blue checkered button-down and a navy sweater-vest.

I allowed myself one longing look at a new set of oil paints before I found my target in the last aisle on the left, by the metal detectors. He had his back to me, giving me a chance to evaluate him before I made my move. Dark hair that curled slightly on the ends brushed his collar. He had broad shoulders tapering down to a lean waist and a tight butt that just begged to be squeezed. Good grief. No wonder this guy had an ego.

Nothing prepared me for when he turned around though. My breath caught as I took in his strong jaw, pouty bottom lip, and dark eyes the color of gathering storm clouds. Eyes that currently assessed me as my heart raced and I stood frozen like a posable doll.

Library Barbie, meet Hot Professor Ken.

I gathered my wits and remembered the role I was supposed to play. This wasn't a real meet-cute. This guy was a serial bragger, an entitled prick, and a narcissist unfairly blessed with a pretty face. His dark eyes took me in from head to toe, and I willed myself not to flush under his unhurried gaze.

I gave him a nod, then squeezed past him in the tight aisle, as if I'd come here for a reason other than getting his attention before our chance run-in at the bar later. He cleared his throat and continued to peruse the books on dig sites around Chicago. I watched him from the corner of my eye as I pretended to do the same, and when he moved to grab what he'd been seeking, I shot my hand out. My skin prickled with awareness from the brush against his as we reached for the same book.

"I'm so sorry." I ducked my head and blushed. Not entirely the act I'd intended it to be.

"Don't be." His storm-cloud eyes lit up with interest. "It's nice to have some company. I'm usually the only person in this part of the store."

"Yeah." I glanced at the shelf, as if it would reveal some secret language of the metal detecting world. "I've been looking for a new dig site for ages, but you were here first." I shoved the book into his hands. "You should take this one."

"No, I couldn't." He moved to hand the book back to me. "I only came in here on a whim, this isn't even my regular store."

"So did I." I pushed the book back at him with enough force to have him raising his eyebrows. So help me if I got stuck buying the world's most useless paperweight.

I let my hand fall to my side and casually tapped the upper left corner of my phone. The nifty little app had gotten me out of more than one tight spot. A second later, it buzzed.

"I have to take this." I let regret flood my eyes as I glanced at the book. "But it was nice to meet you . . . ?"

"Mark." His lips pressed together when he said his name, making the pouty-shape more prominent. A little shiver went down my spine.

"Mark," I repeated before I answered my phone and rushed out of the store.

"Everything okay?" Margo asked.

"Close call with my lack of metal detecting knowledge." I looked through the windows, watching Mark pay for the book I'd narrowly avoided buying, and groaned. "I need to do some quick reading before I go to the bar."

"It's not like you to be unprepared. Are you sure you don't want me to—?"

"I don't. I'm fine." It had taken me a year and a half of heartbreaking for Margo to loosen the reins and let me have solo control over my assignments. I didn't like anyone meddling in my work, and Margo was a classic type A. We'd finally come to terms, though we both agreed the tracking app was a necessity. "I'll handle it before I get to the bar."

"Don't screw this up." The line went dead.

As far as pep talks went, I'd had worse.

I ducked into the corner CVS and hid in the tampon aisle

while I googled "metal detecting near Chicago." Once I'd read enough to comfortably fake my way through a conversation, I headed to the Reading Lounge.

The brisk Chicago wind once again played hell with my no-nonsense bun. I took the cement stairs leading down to the entrance of the bar. While the leather chairs by the fireplace and the cozy private cubbies certainly looked inviting, I pulled up a stool at the bar where I'd be most visible. The place had a ton of nooks for small gatherings or reading while having a drink. Low voices hummed in the air, giving the place an intimate feeling, different from the other loud and crowded bars in the city. The rich mahogany bar and dark wood walls with low-light sconces added a touch of class. My earlier assessment of this place had been way off, and I had to admit I'd only avoided it because I avoided all places where academics like my mom gathered. But the Hot Professor had great taste.

I ordered a Maui Wowie, complete with a ridiculous umbrella, and waited. As soon as the waitress appeared and asked the bartender for a whiskey sour, I made my move.

"Is that by chance going to a good-looking guy in a navy sweater-vest?" I asked.

The corner of the waitress's mouth lifted. "A friend of yours?"

Definitely not. "Can I make you an offer?"

Five minutes later, the waitress had an extra twenty in her apron and my Maui Wowie on the way to Mark. His whiskey sour sat in front of me as I pretended to be too engaged in my phone to notice his drink. I had dig sites around Chicago pulled up on the off chance he'd look at my screen. He leaned against the bar next to me, radiating the kind of warmth that made him feel like part of the atmosphere.

I allowed myself two steady heartbeats before I met those intense eyes. Two heartbeats to remind myself of who I was and what I was doing here. I was a spider. A devourer of ego-maniacs. Karma personified. And I would not be deterred by a strong jaw, pouty lips, and whatever he was packing beneath his academic attire.

"The metal detector." His low voice held the tremor of a growl, like he was giving me a preview of exactly what he'd sound like when he came.

"The other metal detector." I averted my gaze before he could see every dirty thought written there and tilted my chin toward the drink in his hand. "I didn't take you for a Maui Wowie guy."

"It seems the waitress mixed up my order with someone else's."

I allowed myself a glance at the whiskey sour before me and willed my expression into one of surprise. "Did you order this?" I scooted the glass toward him. "Because I think you got mine."

A seductive smile curved his lips. "What are the odds?"

I shrugged and took my drink from him. "Since fate seems determined to throw us together twice in one night, we might as well make the most of it." I patted the stool next to me.

"No, thank you."

Okay, then. We were off to an excellent start.

"Suit yourself." I turned my nose up and faced the front of the bar. Years of doing this had taught me that I couldn't show interest. Guys like Mark wanted the chase.

"It'll get really crowded up here in about an hour. I have a more private seating area in the back, if you'd like to join me." He offered me his hand.

I cocked an eyebrow. "Why not?"

My palm tingled as I slid it against his solid grip. The scent of light rain and moonlit nights enveloped me. It had been too long since I'd touched a guy I found attractive, and it took everything in me not to melt into the ground. I really needed to figure out the art of one-night stands. Clearly, I had a lot of built-up tension.

"I told you my name," he said. "But I didn't get yours before you ran out of the store."

We walked past the fireplace and around the corner. This bar was way bigger than it looked from the outside. Near the back, in one of the little sectioned-off cubbies, were two leather chairs. Facedown on the low table was the metal detecting book.

"I'm Anna." I picked that one often, for simplicity's sake.

He pursed his lips as he took a sip and set his glass down next to the book. "That's funny, because the clerk at Finnigan's seems to think your name is Brinkley. She wanted me to let you know they got a new set of oil paints in yesterday."

Well, shit.

CHAPTER 3

————————————————➤

reathe. Breathe. Don't panic. The game wasn't up yet. I plastered a coy smile on my face and crossed my legs. I didn't miss the way his gaze fell to the hem of my skirt as it inched higher up my thigh. "Okay, fine. My name isn't Anna, but a girl can't be too careful in the city. Too many creeps have access to Google."

"Fair enough." He tapped his lips. "Though I do wonder why the fake name when you're the one who's been tailing me all evening."

I waved him off. "Coincidence. But if you still want to discuss metal detecting, I did some quick studying on the off chance I'd run into you at Finnigan's again."

He threw back his head and laughed, deep and throaty in a way that made my toes curl. "I appreciate the honesty."

"I've never actually gone metal detecting before, but it seems like an interesting hobby. How long have you been doing it?"

He relaxed, leaning back into his chair. "I started when I was a teenager. My grandfather got me into it, thought it would keep me out of trouble."

"So you've been at it for a while." I rested my hand on his arm. He'd rolled up the sleeves of his collared shirt and he had incredible forearms, so it wasn't a hardship to move into the casual touches phase. "Is it something you do for work or pleasure?"

"Pleasure." The word rolled off his tongue like warm honey, and the way he looked at me when he said it had me squeezing my thighs together. Good Lord. I needed to get my shit together. "I'm an adjunct in the anthropology department at UoC, but part of me still wants to be Indiana Jones when I grow up."

He definitely had the sexy professor look going on, and though he had more smolder than Indy, he also would've looked excellent with a wide-brim hat and a whip. But those types of fantasies didn't belong in my head. Librarian Brinkley wouldn't approve.

"Relatable. I still want to be Georgia O'Keeffe when I grow up."

"You want to paint giant vaginas and call them flowers?" He put a hand on his chest. "Because same."

I burst out laughing. "They are not giant vaginas."

"They absolutely are." He pulled out his phone and tapped on it before turning it toward me. He scrolled through tons of O'Keeffe's paintings. "I mean, come on."

"Okay, fine. I'll give you that one. This is my favorite." I touched the iris painting on his screen, running my finger down the opening of the bud and back up again in slow motion. Crude, but effective. "The up-close details are lovely."

"Yes. Lovely." His voice had a strained edge to it as his darkening gaze met mine.

Holy hell. I was so turned on right now. What was wrong with me? This was a target. An Ego who put down a female colleague's work so he could step over her to get more classes. Not a prospective hookup. The quicker I finished this, the quicker I could get out of here and take a painfully cold shower.

"Good to know where I can find inspiration if I ever need it." I swallowed half my drink in one gulp. Where was that waitress when I needed her?

"I . . ." He cleared his throat and rubbed his hand over his face. The poor guy was very cute when flustered. "I can't believe how interesting my Tuesday night just got."

"Are you saying you don't discuss vaginas with strangers on a weekly basis?" I lowered my lashes. "Because I find that hard to believe."

"It's one of my best icebreakers. I'm a blast at parties."

"I'll bet."

He needed to stop being so charming.

"Enough about vaginas. There's a sentence I never thought I'd say." He gave me a playful grin. "What about you? You said you wanted to be Georgia O'Keeffe when you grew up. Is that something you ended up pursuing?"

I rarely had a target who asked me anything about myself, and it threw me for a loop. Usually it was a chore to get them to look at my face rather than my chest. If he'd just show a hint of that ego, it would make my job much easier. I could deal with Egos. They practically drew a map directing me to their buttons and invited me to press them.

"I'm an aspiring artist, so I guess you could say I'm pursuing it." I had no idea why I told him that. I never shared anything about myself with targets. Librarian Brinkley wasn't an artist, aspiring or otherwise. She liked knowledge and writing essays and five-page outlines, all the boring things that made her a perfect match for Mark.

"I think that's really cool."

"You do?" I didn't talk about my painting with anyone other than my best friend, Emma, who also worked at H4H. I'd been burned by too many people before. "A studious career man such as yourself, you don't think it's a silly pipe dream?"

"I think passions are always worth pursuing." He paused, studying my face in the way that only academics who studied people for a living could. "I don't think it's silly at all. More important, I don't think *you* think it's silly."

How long had it been since I'd talked to someone outside my immediate circle about my art? And how much longer than that had it been since my aspirations were taken seriously? I'd have to noodle what all that meant at a later time. But for now, I needed to stop enjoying myself with the man I was supposed to be sabotaging and get to work. Though if I was being honest, I'd have to admit that the more of myself I let filter in, the less this felt like a setup.

I always played a part on assignment, always kept a healthy distance between myself and my character. After my breakup with Aiden, and the careless indifference of my former friends, I didn't care to open myself up. Maybe this evening with Mark was my subconscious's way of telling me to let the past go and move on. Or maybe I just really needed to get laid.

"Not everyone feels the same way." My mom's cold and dismissive voice crept into my mind, and I shoved it out again. "And how do you pursue your archaeological passions while climbing the academic ladder?"

"I have my hobbies." He nudged my foot with his own. "I'm glad I ran into you again. What were you doing in the metal detecting aisle anyway?"

"I was checking out the new oil paints." Not technically a lie. I had looked them over for a second. "Then I saw you."

"And?"

"You looked like someone I wanted to meet." I glanced away, as I'd done hundreds of times in hundreds of bars before. The setups changed, but the push and pull remained the same. Get his interest, make him chase, leave him wanting more.

"I noticed you right away too. I'm glad you made the first move, because I'm not sure if I would've had the guts to approach you." His genuine tone, the earnestness on his face had me reconsidering how I wanted to end this evening. If we'd run into each other by chance one day at Finnigan's, maybe I could've tried this for real. Regret stabbed through me as I once again reminded myself that I didn't do casual dating and I'd been hired for a different sort of game.

"I doubt you have trouble approaching women." I swept a hand up and down. "With all of that going on."

He blushed—actually blushed—and if I'd thought he was

sexy before, I was definitely in trouble now. "It's not that easy meeting new people in the city."

"Tell me about it." I'd tried dating after Aiden, but it took so much energy, and most men I'd matched with on Tinder felt too much like work. Literally. "The bar scene is a nightmare, but I like it here. This place seems way more my speed."

He looked around, as if just becoming aware that we were in a public place, though the private cubby we occupied wasn't nearly as public as the main bar area. "This is more my speed too. I come here most Tuesdays. It gets busy out front, but I can still have a drink and feel like I'm making an effort to go out. Even if I keep to myself."

I wanted to touch his hand, a small physical connection that said I understood, but it was time to get this setup moving again. "It reminds me of the library at Northwestern."

He tilted his head. "You went to Northwestern?"

I had. A sore spot in the series of disappointments known as my life, but he didn't need to know that. "I work there." I paused. "I was practically raised in their library too."

Why had I told him that last part? I'd picked the Northwestern library specifically because I knew it so well, in case he was familiar with it. He only needed to think I worked there, nothing more. But I couldn't seem to stop the truths from coming out. My mother had been so determined to make me follow in her academic footsteps that while other kids spent their summers chasing down ice cream trucks and braving the freezing waters of Lake Michigan, I spent mine in the library with my mom as she tried to get me interested in her research. It was where I'd first discovered books on art and realized what I really wanted to do.

"I spent a lot of time at the library as a kid too." He ran a thumb over his pouty bottom lip. "Is that where you picked up an interest in art?"

"Yes." Screw it. I'd already blown my studious librarian persona, and I still had his interest. Part of being a Heartbreaker involved leaning into the curves when a date went off-track. I relaxed as more of myself bled into the character I was supposed to be playing. "Working at Northwestern pays the bills, and that's okay for now. One day I'd like to have my own gallery though." One day would be within a few months if I kept saving my killer commission from H4H. "Immersing myself in art is all I've ever wanted to do. I'm not confident enough to show my own paintings yet, but I'd love to showcase other types of work from local artists, like sculptures, beadwork, photography. A mishmash of different media all in one place."

"Are you thinking of staying in Chicago? Or trying a larger market, like New York?"

"Chicago is my home, and the art scene here is pretty amazing. It doesn't feel as cold or competitive as the New York market. There's a real sense of community here." And I'd officially talked about myself too much. I needed to steer this ship back toward him. "What about you? Was Harvard or Yale ever your academic goal?"

"Nope. My family is here. I enjoy teaching at UoC and living in Chicago for much the same reasons you do. I'd like to have a full-time position though."

He went on to share the specific areas of anthropology he connected with most. His area of expertise was modern culture, though he also had a passion for history. His enthusiasm for teaching was evident, though it felt a bit distant. As if the act of teaching meant more to him, but he had to hold back and play the part of the distinguished professor.

I knew all about playing parts.

Two hours later, which went by way too fast, I paid my tab with the waitress. She gave me a wink as she discreetly pocketed the second twenty I gave her for her silence. I should've moved this evening along faster, but I didn't want it to be over just yet.

"Can I take you out this weekend?" he asked.

His easy question jarred me out of this temporary fantasy where I was just a woman in a bar having a conversation with a man I found interesting. It couldn't go past this point. The thought made me inexplicably sad. I should've maneuvered the conversation while we were talking about his work and gotten him to say something disparaging about his position while I discreetly recorded him on my phone, but in the end, I didn't have the heart to do that to him. Emma would call me soft. Margo would probably try to elbow her way back into overseeing my assignments. I'd just have to say he hadn't gone for me. Not every target fell for the bait.

"Where do you want to take me?" I asked.

"Anywhere you want."

"So eager to please." I rubbed my thumb and finger up and down the stem of my glass, aware of the way Mark tracked the movement.

"I'm always eager to please."

"Hmm." I took a last sip of my drink. "Give me your number and I'll call you later this week to make plans."

As much as he intrigued me, as much as I wanted to see him again, I was a professional. Mark couldn't be for me, but it wouldn't hurt to get his number. I'd probably end up deleting it tomorrow when I was thinking more rationally anyway.

We stood, and I stumbled before I found my footing after sitting for so long. Mark put a hand on my shoulder to steady me, and I looked up at his storm-cloud eyes. His gaze once again dropped to my mouth—as it had been doing all night. I swallowed. This was so, so bad, but for some reason, I couldn't recall why.

CHAPTER 4

Forgetting my role, my job, what I was supposed to be doing here this evening, I pushed up on my heels and caught his bottom lip with my teeth. I'd been wanting to nibble on it since I first saw him at Finnigan's. He groaned, cupping the back of my neck as he dragged my body flush against his. He was rock hard. Everywhere. My hands roamed over him, as if I were desperately searching for a soft spot and coming up empty.

He backed me into the corner, tilting my head back to kiss me deeper. Heat pooled in my core. As my lips parted to let him in, a moan soon followed. His tongue, so gentle, brushed against mine before becoming more demanding. Wanting more, taking more, I dug my nails into his shoulders, going straight through that ridiculous sweater-vest. I needed to get closer.

He ran his hand under my skirt, gripped my thigh, and hauled me up against him. Right there. Oh God. Exactly where

I wanted him. I was panting, literally panting. My hips ground against him, and I was on the brink of having an orgasm right in the middle of the bar.

Suddenly he broke away. I might've whimpered. Not my proudest moment, but dry-humping a guy I was being paid to manipulate in a public bar left little room for pride.

He ran a hand through his hair. "Christ. I just mauled you like an animal in the bar I come to every week. I'm so sorry."

"I'll accept your apology if you do it again." That sounded dangerously like begging, which I had personal issues with, but screw it. I'd been too close to let him quit on me now.

He huffed out a shaky laugh. "I live a block from here, if you want to keep this going."

I nodded. It was wrong on so many moral and ethical levels, not to mention it broke Margo's cardinal rule—but no one had to know. I could do this one thing. One time. Just let go and take because I wanted to. It had been too long since I'd had a man's hands on me, and while I managed to get by on my own, I missed the feel of being pressed beneath a hard body.

He took my hand, practically dragging me out of the bar. As soon as we stepped outside, he hoisted me against the stair railing, fitting me against him again. I attacked him with my mouth, dragged my lips up his throat, sank my teeth into his neck. I lost all sense of self and reason and became a writhing ball of need. My entire existence homed in on the pressure between my legs. The urgency of release. Just as I began to build once again, he pulled back.

"One block," he said. His eyes were the color of tornadoes,

and all I wanted him to do was rip right through me. He took my hand again, and I had to sprint to keep up with him.

We managed to make it the full block without tearing each other's clothes off. No small feat. I recognized his building as one I passed whenever I walked to Emma's for girls' night out. We took the stairs because he lived on the second floor and I doubted we would've made it out of the elevator. As soon as we hit his front door, I buried my fingers in his thick dark hair and yanked him against me again.

He fumbled with his keys as I rubbed him through his pants. The door flew open behind me, but he had a steady hand on my back to prevent me from falling. I didn't even have a chance to look around as my hands and mouth brought us both near the edge.

His apartment was dark. I could barely make out the shapes of furniture in his open living room. The backs of my legs hit a bench by the door, and I sagged against it as he dropped to his knees. His hands trailed under my skirt.

"Is this okay?" His voice reminded me of rich bourbon over gravel, smooth and dirty.

"Yes," I gasped. "It's more than okay."

He pushed my skirt up until it bunched around my waist. Hooking my lacy thong over his thumbs, he tugged it down. "I've been dying to taste you all night."

I clenched a fist. Trembles raced up and down my spine. I would explode if he didn't put his mouth on me. "Please."

He trailed kisses over the inside of my thigh, breathing me in as he took his time torturing me. "God, you're beautiful. Better than painted flowers."

"Don't make me laugh right now, I'm barely keeping it together."

His chuckle turned into a hiss of pleasure as I sank my fingers into his hair and tugged him closer. He pushed my legs farther apart, fully exposing me, and dragged his tongue right up my center. I shuddered around him.

"So fucking sweet." He put a finger inside me, then another, pumping in and out as he licked me again. "I bet it'll be even better when you come."

I moaned. I couldn't even form words. I pushed against his mouth, gasping as I rode his tongue. He buried his face in me, like he couldn't get enough.

"You're so close." His thumb circled my clit, and I nearly blacked out. He kissed the inside of my thigh. "Come for me."

White spots clouded my vision as everything in me gathered down to that one point where Mark continued to work me over with his mouth. Something buzzed against my hip. *What the hell?* It had been a long time since I'd had an orgasm that wasn't self-induced, but I didn't recall it feeling like that.

It buzzed again, and I straightened up. My purse. My phone. Shit.

"What's wrong?" Mark squeezed me behind my knees.

Emma and I always called each other to check in after an assignment. It was an extra layer of protection and gave us both a chance to vent. If I didn't answer, she'd call Margo and demand she activate the tracking app. She was overprotective that way. Mark's apartment would be swarming with police within minutes. And I couldn't answer the phone in front of him. I'd have no way of talking myself out of that one.

I pushed my skirt down. "I need to leave."

"What?" Mark sat back, his sex-glazed eyes clouding with confusion. "Did I do something wrong?"

"No. You were great. This was . . . great." My phone buzzed again. I grabbed my purse and hauled ass out his front door. "I'll call you," I yelled as I let it slam behind me.

I made it to the stairwell entrance before I heard his door open behind me. Without looking back, I tore down the stairs. One of the heels on my cheap shoes gave out. I crashed against the railing, gripping it to keep from falling. My purse flew out of my hand, scattering the contents across the stairwell. I scooped them all back in as quickly as possible, then kicked off both my shoes and ran.

"Brinkley! Wait!" Mark was following me down the stairs. "Is everything okay? Let me help or apologize or, shit, I don't know."

The buzzing from my purse became a scream ringing in my ears. My pulse pounded in my throat. If I answered it within Mark's hearing range, it would be all over for me. Why had I gone back to his apartment? There was no way this could go anywhere. I didn't have time to date. I didn't even have time for a quick little fling.

I skidded out of his building and rounded the corner. My gaze darted around the alley. I was trapped. Without thinking, I dove behind the dumpster and crouched down. I prayed to every god I could remember by name that he wouldn't look back here.

"Fuck." On the opposite side of the dumpster, Mark slammed his fist on the lid. "I'm such an idiot."

I didn't dare move as his defeated footsteps trailed away. I was shoeless and thongless, and I'd accidentally bumped my leg against a splatter on the wall. Something slimy slid against my ankle. On my list of Piss-Poor Life Choices, this currently ranked number one.

My phone buzzed again, and I forced my breath to steady as I answered it. "Sorry I missed check-in," I said. "I'm just leaving the bar now."

"I was about to call Margo," Emma said.

"I couldn't risk answering the phone in front of him."

Emma paused for long enough that I pulled my phone back to make sure she was still on the line. "Call me when you get home."

I hung up, heaving a sigh of relief as I slunk out from behind the dumpster and took the ultimate walk of shame home. And because the universe enjoyed mocking me, every corner showcased proper and normal couples in love. Outside a corner bakery, a guy with a shock of red hair kissed a girl with dark curls. The next street over, a guy so pale he was practically translucent got on one knee before a woman who had a face like a fish.

"Get out now, before he really screws you over," I said as I passed them. Judging from both their expressions, I was very lucky I didn't get punched.

By the time I made it to Finnigan's—limping after I'd stepped on a discarded bottle cap and who knew what else on the filthy Chicago sidewalks—my bun had come half-undone and strands hung over my forehead in a tangled mess. And that slimy thing I'd felt on my ankle? Rotten coleslaw. The stench of it trailed me all the way back to my neighborhood. If I were a self-portrait, I'd title it *Woman Gives Up*.

So, of course—of course!—I had to run into the one person I never wanted to see again. The man who had broken me so completely, I didn't paint for months. The reason I hadn't had a proper date in more than two years.

"Brinkley?" I cringed at the sound of his voice.

I gritted my teeth in what I hoped passed for a smile. "Hello, Aiden."

He looked the same as he had the last time I saw him. Same sandy-colored hair, same thin mouth, same condescending expression. The woman at his side clung to him like a partner in a three-legged race. It was a shame I didn't have a bottle of Boone's Farm wrapped in a brown paper sack, that would've really set off my whole ensemble.

"How are you?" His voice was laced with faux concern, purposefully, so he could make certain I knew he pitied me. The Midwest version of "bless your heart."

"I'm doing very well, thank you. A few of my paintings recently sold for six figures, and I started dating one of the Cubs." I might've oversold myself there, but Aiden had a way of bringing out the absolute worst in me.

His eyes narrowed. "Which Cub are you dating?"

"Jeter."

"You mean Derek Jeter, former shortstop for the New York Yankees?"

Okay, so I knew jack shit about baseball. "No. The other, less famous, but still highly paid Jeter of the Chicago Cubs. Google him and cry."

"We should go, babe." The woman attached to his hip tugged on his shirt.

"Agreed." His gaze passed over me with polite indifference. "It was good seeing you again. Send my regards to . . . Jeter."

If karma were kinder, he would've caught me wearing a slinky cocktail dress and making out with my six-two, Mack truck boyfriend outside our private helicopter, while he developed gangrene on his nuts from a routine shaving accident. But that wasn't the way the world worked. At least, not for me.

CHAPTER 5

I slammed the door of my apartment, peeling my clothes off and leaving them behind in the hall as I headed toward the shower. Catastrophic didn't even begin to sum up the night. I could never go to Finnigan's again. In fact, it might be best if I moved out of Chicago altogether. Possibly the United States too, just to be safe. Running into Aiden had truly been the cherry on top of the enormous shit sundae I'd scooped myself into.

Hot water poured over me, washing away the lingering stench of coleslaw à la mode. If only I could reach inside my head to scrub my brain too. I'd thrown away the job with Mark when I needed the money, all for the temporary feelings I'd caught just because he listened and treated me like a human being. It sounded so pathetic laid out like that.

Worse, Selena would get her thousand dollars back and get to gloat about how I couldn't land her target. She'd be so smug. It nearly made me want to lie, but I had no proof I'd done my job, and that's what most clients wanted.

My first mistake had been getting personal with Mark. I never should've told him about my plans for the future. I never should've let it matter that he didn't find them absurd. This couldn't happen again. Staying in character made it easy for me to treat men like a job, and forgetting my place had put me into one hell of a mess.

Winnie climbed into my lap, hissing as she headbutted my hand, demanding attention. I picked up my phone and debated keeping Emma out of the loop, but she'd see through me eventually, and I needed someone to talk to.

"I messed up," I said as soon as she answered.

"I knew it." She clicked off *The Good Place*, which had been playing in the background. Emma Yoo was the kind of Netflix binger who only watched one show at a time, until she'd seen every episode; then she'd move on to the next. "Tell me everything."

Emma handled the Players for H4H. While my clients sought revenge against coworkers they couldn't stand, Emma's wanted to take down coworkers who had also been romantic partners, men who had played them to get ahead in their careers. Her list of services had a much higher base price since her assignments tended to be longer and more involved; she spent weeks in her clients' companies to gather information on her targets' duplicitous behavior, until she had enough ammo for the women to take to HR. Not only did she ruin any hope for these men to remain employed at those particular jobs, she also scorch-earthed any chance they had of working in their field ever again.

She'd lecture me—I braced myself for it—but she wouldn't sell me out to the other Heartbreakers or hold it over my head. I trusted her with my life. She made all the right sympathy noises in all the right places while I talked, and when I mentioned Aiden's name, she did a pretty solid impression of Winnie by hissing into the phone. That was why she was my best friend. She wouldn't just help me hide the body. She'd take part in the actual stabbing.

"That decides it," Emma said. "We finally have an excuse to murder Aiden."

I laughed, but it sounded as tired as I felt. "I don't think that's necessary. The girl wrapped around him like a python probably thought I was homeless though, so that's one more humiliation I can take to my grave."

Emma gave a noncommittal grunt. I wasn't kidding about the stabbing thing. "Here's what you're going to do about Mark. Tell your client you couldn't get his attention, give her the refund, and let it go."

"I know." I'd already decided to give Selena a refund, even though it burned me. "You won't say anything to Margo, right? I finally got her to let me handle assignments without her input, and I don't want her using this as an excuse to take over again."

"Please," Emma said. "I can't believe you just asked me that."

"Sorry." I really should've known better.

"How could you, though?" Emma's tone went sharp. Here came the lecture. "He was a target. A *target*. For fuck's sake, B. You know better than this. He screwed over someone he worked with bad enough for her to want to drop a thousand dollars on revenge."

"He didn't really strike me as a typical Ego though."

"Why? Because he was hot? Because he was smooth? Those guys make the best liars. They undermine women until they don't even know themselves anymore. Do I need to remind you that Aiden was hot and Jacob was a smooth talker? That's how both of us ended up fucked sideways and working at H4H in the first place."

"Em. Calm down. I made a mistake. It won't happen again."

Her heavy breathing came through the line. "I don't want you to get involved with someone we already know is an asshole. You deserve better."

The worst of her temper had passed. She'd gone easier on me than I'd expected.

"Maybe this means I'm ready to . . . date again." I hesitated on those last two words, afraid Emma might laugh at the suggestion, even though I knew she'd do no such thing.

"You should try going out. See how it feels. Anything is better than going home with a target." Emma took a deep breath. "I don't mean to lecture."

"Yes, you do. But I needed to hear it." Needed to remember that men, especially the men we were hired to take down, would always screw us over in the end. "You keep me sane."

"One of us has to be." She sighed. "Sorry you didn't get your orgasm though."

"I am too. It was nice while it lasted." He hadn't acted like the other Egos I'd dealt with. Admittedly, I didn't know him at all, but I couldn't wrap my head around him stomping on a coworker. He seemed passionate enough about teaching and driven enough to excel without resorting to putting down his colleagues. Especially since women had a hard enough time in the boys' club of academia. But making excuses for him in my head wouldn't do me any favors. "Guess I'll have to fall back on plan B, moving to Hollywood and marrying Chris Evans."

"Haven't you been keeping up with TMZ? He just got engaged to a Korean woman. Not me, sadly. Her name is Susan something-or-other."

"Welp. Plan C, then. Die alone and become cat food for Winnie."

"On the bright side, the price of your paintings would go through the roof." Emma gave me kissing noises before she hung up.

I gathered Winnie in my arms, where she started hissing and flung out her claws to get away. We had a deeply intense love/hate relationship. At least she let me dress her without much fuss. She stuck her butt in the air and flounced out of the room.

God. I couldn't believe I'd run into Aiden. For the first six months after he ended things, I'd had nonstop fantasies about running into him on the street. I'd be wearing something low-cut and clingy, my hair would finally have the perfect beach waves I never could get right in real life, and I'd be on the arm of some faceless stud. But he was hot. And huge. He'd make Aiden look hung like a circus mouse. I'd toss my head and laugh at something witty my faceless beefcake said, and Aiden would shrivel into a little lint ball and roll into the sewage drain. Sometimes, in these fantasies, he would beg me to come back. Apologize for all the ways he'd hurt me.

"I tried, Brinkley. But you're too much of a mess."

I shut the words out of my memory. The things he'd said to me after I found him in our bed with one of his fellow psych majors. It wasn't just that he was naked with another woman, or that it was in our bed, or that they'd ruined the sheets I'd just bought with my money, but he was holding her. He never wanted to hold me after sex. He just wanted to get it in and roll over. According to him, it was because I was cold, rigid, completely dull in the sack. Trying to please me wore him out. He had no energy left for cuddling. Every ugly word he'd ever said had cut away pieces of me until there was nothing left.

It was at that final meeting, at a restaurant of his choosing, that he'd said those last words to me as I handed him the key to our apartment after I'd moved out my stuff. That was where Margo had found me, crying into a chicken Caesar salad. She'd taken Aiden's vacant seat and offered me the opportunity to make bastards like him pay for a living.

I didn't want to take her up on the offer at first, but pulling my life together after Aiden had proved to be more difficult than I'd imagined. I took a semester off school, thinking I'd use the time to figure myself out again. Have that whole *Eat, Pray, Love* experience, minus the praying and love. Every time I tried to pick up the pieces though, I'd hear Aiden telling me I was a mess. I'd hear him cutting down my early paintings and calling them prosaic. I'd hear him making jokes with his friends about his poor, dumb girlfriend who couldn't hack it in psych and took the easy way out by majoring in art theory and practice, and how it was a good thing I was hot so I could end up working in pharmaceutical sales.

The rest of our friend group had naturally gravitated toward Aiden. As psych majors, they had all their classes together, they held study groups, and they'd been hearing his insults for years without speaking up to defend me. Even Eliza, who had been my roommate since sophomore year after my first roommate dropped out to follow One Direction on tour. Eliza had introduced me to Aiden at the end of junior year. I didn't get to keep her in the breakup.

Once one semester turned into two, and it became obvious I wasn't going back to school, my friends had stopped making excuses for why we couldn't hang out and just ghosted me completely. We still followed one another on social media though, so I got to see their lives move on without me. That was when I called Margo.

During the first year of H4H assignments, I saw Aiden in every setup. I'd taken pleasure in tearing apart the big egos of small men who thought of me as an object designed for their amusement. They soon learned differently.

But as those old wounds started to heal, I wanted something more for myself. I wanted to create and bring joy back into my life. I didn't want my tombstone to read *Here lies Brinkley Saunders. She pissed off a lot of shitty men.* The gallery began to take shape in my mind, and it had become my singular goal and focus for the last year.

I wandered into the master bedroom, the space I'd turned into an art studio because it had the most windows and best light. A few hours with a blank canvas would clear my head. I picked up my brush and dabbed it into the turquoise, the same color as Aiden's eyes. More than two years of avoiding him in this city of three million people, and I had to run into him on the one night I came off looking worse than the last time he'd seen me.

"I tried, Brinkley. But you're too much of a mess."

I set the brush down, turned off the lights, and walked out of the room.

⤬

There was something truly depressing about going out alone. It should've been empowering to strut into a club like I didn't need anyone to have a good time, but being surrounded by groups of friends and couples in the party atmosphere made me feel more isolated than the Sunday nights I spent with ice cream, Winnie, and Netflix. But I wanted to give this a try. The only way I met men anymore was when I was hired to take them down, and the last thing I needed was to go home with another target.

I took a seat at the bar, resenting the skimpy black dress I'd squeezed into. This was supposed to be a painting and yoga pants night, damn it. The upper floors of Belly Shots—three levels of red walls and pulsing lights designed to ooze sex—were known for being a meat market, and I shuddered to think of the horrors a black light would reveal in the private VIP rooms that took up most of the top two floors. That was why I'd be sticking to the bar on the first floor.

A guy with trim blond hair and a well-cut suit approached me. He had nice teeth. This could be promising. "Hey, pretty lady. Can I get you a drink?"

Pretty lady. I tried not to cringe. "Sure. I'll take something fruity. Bonus points if it has a tiny umbrella." I loved those umbrellas.

Instead of ordering from the bar, he walked away and returned with something frothy and pink in a mason jar. Any bonus points he'd earned for the umbrella would have to be deducted and then some for the roofie he'd likely slipped into the pink concoction. I set it aside on the bar.

"Aren't you going to drink that?" He leered at my cleavage, because God forbid he make the effort to look at my face. "I went to a lot of trouble to get your umbrella."

While working for Margo had made me a lot more jaded, it had also honed my survival skills. I handed the drink back to him. "Nice try, but if you want to drug me, you should try to be a little less obvious. Your moves are straight out of the pamphlets sent to every college girl her freshman year."

"Bitch." He took his drink and left. Was it something I said?

I went back to leaning against the bar with my bored-and-ready-to-mingle expression. Wednesday nights weren't exactly hopping, but the thought of hitting the bar scene on Friday night exhausted me. Most of the people in the club had come with a significant other—a little break after work to pretend they were still part of the hip singles scene without actually having to be a part of the hip singles scene on the weekends.

This wasn't going to work for me. I wasn't ready to date, and Mark had been an anomaly. If I got the urge to go home with a target again, I'd just book an extra appointment with my therapist. I grabbed my purse off the bar and prepared to give up for the night.

I looked across the room and saw that my roofie creeper had found a new target. He actually tried to press my pink cocktail on her. He must've only brought one pill tonight. She couldn't have been older than twenty-two, and the guy was all up in her personal space. She had that deer-in-the-headlights look, frozen with fear and not sure how to make an exit.

I marched over to her table and threw my arms around her. "Go with it," I whispered in her ear. Then louder: "I'm so glad I finally found you. It took me forever to find this place."

"Excuse me." The guy tapped me on the shoulder. "We were having a conversation."

I cut him down with a withering glare. "Not anymore, you're not." I took the girl by the arm. "Come on, sweetie. Your UFC boyfriend is waiting at the bar up the street."

As soon as we stepped out on the sidewalk, the girl turned to me. "Thank you. I didn't think I'd be able to get out of there without him following me."

"No problem. Girls in this city have to look out for each other, right?"

"Right." She gave me a relieved smile. "Though I wish that UFC boyfriend was real."

"Don't we all." I waited with the girl until her Uber driver pulled up, then headed back to my apartment. I hadn't found a guy worth talking to, but at least my brief experiment had confirmed that Emma had been right. Hooking up with future targets wouldn't be an issue.

CHAPTER 6

The next morning, I grabbed an Uber to work and took the elevator up to the twenty-fourth floor, where the Heartbreak for Hire office was located.

Aside from myself, there were three other Heartbreakers. Emma was head of Players, Charlotte Diaz took care of the Grifters, and Allie VanHousen ran Cheaters. Margo had hand-selected us to form H4H, finding us at restaurants, bars, or coffee shops all over the city, alone and in tears after a horrific breakup. Right when we were primed to enter this business. Because there were only four of us, we'd grown close. Not only did we get to live out our revenge fantasies, but the commission we made on assignments would fund all the dreams we hoped to accomplish one day.

I barely had time to turn on my laptop before Margo summoned me to her office. I had a meeting with Selena in fifteen minutes to give her the refund, and I hoped to have her out in less time than that. Closing my laptop again, I got to my feet and headed down the hall.

When Margo told me to come in, I pushed open the door, then stopped short. Margo sat at her desk, cozy as could be, across from Selena. I narrowed my eyes. This was my client, and Margo had promised she wouldn't interfere. She'd been doing so well the past few weeks too. I should've known she'd crack soon.

"What's going on here?" I took a seat. "You're early, Selena."

"I couldn't wait to see you and gush about what a great job you did. Mark looked like absolute shit yesterday." Selena wore a wide grin, which didn't give me any sort of satisfaction.

"He did?" I asked. Margo cleared her throat, and when I glanced at her, she gave me a quick jerk of her chin. "Okay. He did."

None of this made sense. I'd assumed Mark wouldn't have loved my exit, but as far as Margo knew, he hadn't gone for me. Why was she acting like all had gone as planned?

"I'm so pleased you found our services helpful." Margo poured a cup of tea for Selena from her frilly pink pot and passed her a gold-filigreed cup. "I do hope you'll pass the word along to some of your friends, since we can't exactly advertise this sort of thing."

"Certainly." Selena flipped her sleek blond hair over her shoulder. I could spend all day under a hot iron and still never get my hair that straight. Her salon bills must've been astronomical. "If only I could've been a fly on the wall when you destroyed him."

She would've been one unhappy fly if she'd witnessed what I'd actually done with him. I didn't care for Selena as a person, but when she salivated with delight over Mark's misery, she reminded me of those kids in school who pulled legs off crickets and tied strings around cats' tails just to see what they would do. The way she took pleasure in it all went well beyond that of a contemptuous coworker. I looked her over as I considered what real score she had to settle.

"Brinkley is our best." Margo handed me a cup and gave me the kind of motherly smile I never got from my own mom. "She's been with me for two years and rarely strikes out."

I glowed under the unwarranted praise. Margo was all business, but she always talked us up to the clients. Maybe it was just because it was good sales practice, but it was more than I ever got growing up, or from my disastrous three years with Aiden, so I lapped it up like a kitten with a bowl of milk.

"I'm going to recommend your services to the other adjuncts in my department." Selena's eyes sparked with malice, and for a moment it was like looking in a mirror. A really harsh mirror with bad lighting that showed all your pores. "Half the assistant professors are like Mark."

If she meant assistant professors who gave great ladyhead, I'd have to seriously consider a career change. "Can I ask you a question?" Margo shot me a warning look, but I ignored her. "Mark seemed okay during our meet-cute. Not like the typical narcissists I deal with on a weekly basis. Is there something we should know about your relationship with him?"

Selena's smile turned feral for an instant, before melting back into her earlier pleasantry. "I assure you. He is a complete jerk-off."

Touchy.

Margo cleared her throat. "Which is why we were happy to assist you in bringing him down a peg. Men like that need to learn they don't always get what they want."

"Yes. Of course." I buried my grimace behind my teacup. I had no idea why I'd even asked Selena about her relationship with Mark. It wasn't my job to defend him or poke at her personal business. It wasn't my job to do anything other than make him feel terrible, and apparently I'd succeeded at that without even trying.

"You were very effective." Selena crossed her legs as she turned toward me. "Care to share how you broke him so fast after just one meeting?"

"Trade secret, I'm afraid." I smiled, but I'm sure my eyes were like ice chips. Everything about Selena rubbed me the wrong way. She carried herself like a tiger. While I generally respected women who gnashed their teeth and flashed their claws to get ahead in a world that constantly tried to hold them back and keep them sweet, she had an unnecessary cruelty about her. As if she didn't just use those claws and teeth on the men who stood in her way.

"If we're all done here, I'll walk you out." Margo stood, brushing a hand down her slacks, the ironed crease so sharp I was surprised she didn't slice open her hand.

Selena followed, but turned back to me before exiting the office. "It was so nice to meet you, Brinkley. I was pleasantly surprised you managed to pull this off."

I plastered on my *see you in hell, but I'll bring a muffin basket* expression, and she turned around and left. What an odd little duck.

I leaned my head back and stared up at the faux-tin tiles on the ceiling. Margo had outfitted her office to be what she considered an inviting space for women. It was a cross between shabby chic and Palace of Versailles. Lots of pink. Lots of gold. Lots of doilies. The light-teal wallpaper had a shiny French design, and every chair was covered in the same cabbage-rose fabric. It had the mothy scent of a grandmother's attic.

Margo's clipped gait echoed off the marble tiles of the hall as she made her way back to the office. She shut the door with a firm click. "What the hell was that?"

"I could ask you the same question." I rubbed my eyes. In any other job, I couldn't talk to my boss that way, but Margo and I had never really had a normal working relationship.

"I was saving your ass from having to pay out a refund. Now you."

I knew I had no business questioning the client. We weren't supposed to care about their reasons for hiring us. "Selena bugs me. She was a pain in the ass during the interview process, and I don't think that guy she hired me to take down was anything like she described."

"Why do you think I didn't want you to give her the refund?" Margo passed me a tin of thin little cookies that reminded me of Listerine strips. "Not only did she pay the thousand, which is seventy-five percent yours, she's also going to refer her coworkers and friends."

"How did you know she wasn't going to want proof?" I asked.

"Because she came to my office first to let me know how well my staff is performing." Margo gave my hand a quick squeeze. "I didn't butt into your assignment. Though I do wonder why your target looked so terrible the next day if he hadn't taken the bait."

"Indigestion?" I sipped my tea.

No way would I tell Margo what had really gone down. I didn't need to put my job at risk. At worst, she'd fire me for breaking the rules. At best, she'd mother-hen me or start inserting herself into my assignments again. Neither option appealed to me. For the first time, I felt like I had true control over the direction of my life, and I intended to hang on to it.

"Mmm-hmm." Margo pursed her lips. "Aside from work, how is your social life?"

"What social life?" Last night's attempt had been a bust, and I had no desire to repeat the experience anytime soon. "Unless you count girls' night out with the other Heartbreakers."

"I know you're still in a delicate state. Even though the work you do for H4H is helping, what Aiden did to you will continue to linger." Margo put one of the thin cookies on her tongue, where it dissolved almost instantly. "However, I can respect that you might be overworked."

I didn't like the way she said "overworked." Like it was a rotted tooth or an infected hangnail. Margo considered work and life to be synonyms. I hadn't had a single vacation in the two years I'd been working for her, and I'd never complained. The first year work had kept the grief at bay, the next it had helped fund my future, but I was tired. My evening with Mark had made me realize just how tired I was of not ever having anything close to normal relationships with people.

"I don't mind the work. Really."

"I know you don't mind doing your job. That's why I trust you the most. You're my most dedicated Heartbreaker." Margo set her tea aside on one of the white crackle-paint end tables and patted my arm. "I'm working on something. I hope I can count on your support?"

"Oh?" Whenever Margo was "working on something," it usually meant adding another department to H4H. Last year she'd hired Allie when she started the Cheaters division, which required Allie to do to the Cheaters what they'd done to her clients. She would take on several clients at once, get them all hooked on her, promise them exclusivity, and have them all "accidentally" show up to the same restaurant. Then she stood back while all hell broke out. She was the only Heartbreaker whose clients got to watch the live show. "Please don't tell me you're adding an Abusers division. I can't support that."

"Goodness, no." The shocked look on Margo's face reassured me that she wouldn't go there. "We've already dismissed the idea for Abusers. I won't put my girls at risk in that way. This is more about . . ." She twirled her wrist. ". . . sharing the workload."

"That doesn't sound so bad." I didn't want a full vacation. The hours helped me put more money away for the gallery. But having a little more time during the week to paint would be nice. Maybe we were getting an assistant. We'd all been begging for an assistant to help us with the research end of things. It was incredibly time-consuming to dig up enough information on a guy to craft a persona around. "Whatever it is, I'm sure it will be brilliant."

"I hope you'll all be pleased." She tapped a few keys on her computer. "This is a recent idea though, so it will take me a few weeks to put it all together. Just hang tight until then."

"I always do." I crossed my legs and picked up my next file off her desk. "If we're done debriefing Selena's case, I'd like to get going on my next assignment."

"Yes. Have a look-see." Margo waved her hand at the folder. "Your next target is a used car salesman. A real sleazeball, according to the word of the three coworkers who pooled their money for this one."

I looked over the sparse file. It didn't come with any pictures or stats. I got his name, where he worked, who'd hired us, and why they needed our services. The rest was legwork I had to accomplish on my own, which was why an assistant would've been nice.

This one was a jackass salesman who took commissions from his female coworkers because he made most shoppers feel like presence of penis and car knowledge went hand in hand. He constantly bragged about his sales numbers, cut other people's throats to get to the top, then spent his weekends sucking up to the big bosses by treating them to their favorite strip club.

I'd have my own interview with the clients later to gather intel, but I liked going in with some ideas for the setup beforehand. "By chance, did these women mention what might get the salesman's attention?"

Margo gave me a catlike grin. "Ever seen *Jersey Shore*?"

Maybe I needed a vacation after all.

CHAPTER 7

Lunch with my mom usually resulted in a battle, and this time I wouldn't go in unarmed. She'd look for weaknesses and pick at them until I cracked. Most of our meetings consisted of screaming matches and storming away. That's why I had to look like I had my shit together, so she couldn't nag me about my never-ending flaws. I was a wall. A fortress. A strong, independent career woman who didn't need a man or a master's degree.

I wore a pressed gray suit and bright-red lipstick. I'd swept my hair into the tight librarian bun I'd worn the night of my meet-cute with Mark. Curly tendrils framed my face, the ones that always managed to escape my bobby pins.

I hooked the strap of my most professional purse over my shoulder and pushed open the door to the psychology wing at Northwestern. My mom loved to have me meet at her office, her little way of reminding me how I'd failed and why she took it personally. The Great and Powerful Dr. Saunders didn't do well with failure. Not for herself and especially not with her offspring. Lately she'd been pushing hard for me to go back to school, even though I'd told her time and time again my interests lay elsewhere. She acted like having a bachelor's degree was akin to having a GED, and she feared that my lack of impressive credentials meant I'd probably spend my golden years greeting people at Walmart.

I knocked and opened her office door, my posture already going ramrod straight, as if my entire body knew it had to go into tense mode starting now. "Are you ready?"

"Darling!" Mom stood and clasped my hands like I was one of her colleagues. I'd gotten more affection from Winnie the day I forgot to feed her. "I was just talking to Dr. Faber, and did you know he's retiring at the end of the semester? Time sure does fly."

Here we go. "Good for him."

Dr. Faber was a kind old professor with candy-floss hair who had worked in the anthropology department for over forty years. I'd known him my entire life. Mom didn't really have friends, she had colleagues and associates, but I'd say Dr. Faber came as close as she got to a friend. Mainly because it didn't benefit her in some way to be nice to him.

A few of my former friends had taken classes with him, since anthropology and psychology had a lot of crossover. We used to think his spirit would haunt the halls forever. He used to come to Sunday dinners back when Mom and I had Sunday dinners, a connection the people in my life had tried to exploit on more than one occasion. The world of academics was full of users. At the time, I'd been too naïve to see it, but those days were long gone.

"His office will have an opening." She had absolutely no subtlety. "You could finish your master's. A couple of your old professors would still give you a recommendation if you wanted to consider teaching while you finished your doctorate."

I let out a long sigh. "We've talked about this. Several times. I'm not going to finish school and I have no desire to work in academia."

"You're only twenty-seven. I had no idea what I wanted at twenty-seven."

I once again sidestepped the fact that she'd had me at twenty-seven. I fell under the category of those things she didn't know she wanted. Which was a joke, considering where she'd procured the sperm that made up half my DNA. That had been all her choice.

As a child, I used to dream that I hadn't come from a sperm bank, that instead my father was a prince who had to keep me secret for royal reasons until he could whisk me away to his castle made of gingerbread and blank canvases. A land where I'd never have to pretend to take an interest in behavioral science. In my adult life, I still wondered what that other half of me was like. If it wasn't for our last name, no one would even know I was related to my mom. Where I was tall and skinny, she was short and stocky. I had curly blond hair; hers was straight and brown. My eyes were a light blue, while hers were the shade of dark chocolate. The only things I seemed to have inherited from her were her high cheekbones and full lips, the latter of which were usually turned down in disapproval. At my expense.

"Can we not do this today, Mom?" I pinched the bridge of my nose, already feeling the headache forming there. "I like my job. I'm painting again. Let it go."

She huffed. "An administrative assistant at an insurance company is beneath you."

Yeah, she had no idea what I did for a living. I'd never be able to live it down. She probably wouldn't even have an issue with me using men to exact revenge for the clients who paid me. Her problem would be the possibility of other people finding out. She wanted me to be a mini version of her, a plastic little academic bobblehead who nodded yes and didn't cause a fuss or a scandal. Appearances were everything.

"I like being an administrative assistant," I said. "It's not as glamorous as what you do, but it pays my bills. It gives me time to paint until I can open a gallery."

She waved that off. My artistic aspirations were a sore spot. She thought art was one of those fanciful careers kids dreamed of while playing dress-up, but never actually pursued. Like being an NFL quarterback or a fairy princess. When I'd changed my major from psychology to art theory and practice my senior year, she'd screamed and ranted for a week solid, threatened to stop paying for school and have me tossed out of Northwestern so I couldn't take advantage of the 50 percent reduced tuition, and attempted to have my spot in the master's program denied.

Our relationship had never been great, but the moment I defied her and tried to be my own person, it imploded. She went from treating me with distant fondness to outright hostility. We'd basically been having one long fight for four years.

It had all been for nothing anyway.

A year into my master's in art theory and practice—a highly competitive program that only admitted ten students per year—everything with Aiden fell apart, and I dropped out of school. After all she'd done to block my way into graduate school, I managed to do the one thing she hated more: drop out with a bachelor's degree in a useless field that barely qualified me to flip burgers at McDonald's. When I told her I'd gotten a job at an insurance company to cover for what I actually did for Margo, it still wasn't good enough. She couldn't resist flinging every one of my mistakes in my face whenever she got the chance.

My breakup with Aiden wasn't the only reason I'd had years of therapy.

"Pipe dreams aside, many students face burnout." That's all my gallery would ever be to her. A pipe dream. The by-product of academic burnout. I didn't even want to invite her to the eventual opening. It would put a damper on everything I'd worked to accomplish. "Your grades were good enough before the end that you would be welcomed back, even if you wanted to continue on with that completely useless degree. At least it would be something."

"I have something now." I turned out of her office and started down the hall, not caring whether she followed me or not. "Why can't you just believe me when I say I'm happy?"

"Because you're my daughter." My mom's voice trailed behind me, though there was still a good distance between us, and my shoulders scrunched under the judgmental glare that scraped against my back. "I know you're not happy."

I closed my eyes and counted to ten while I waited for her to catch up. If I was going to survive this lunch, I needed to let whatever she said roll right off me. I'd worn my battle armor, damn it. I wouldn't be bowled over so easily.

"Can't we enjoy our lunch?" I tried very hard to keep the exasperation out of my voice. "We don't get to see each other nearly enough."

"And whose fault is that?"

"I'm busy. You're busy. Let's just—"

I caught sight of a familiar profile and broad shoulders. Shoulders I'd dug my nails into while he had his head between my legs two short weeks ago. Oh God. Of all the places and times to run into Mark. What was he even doing here? He headed toward the anthropology wing across the courtyard. Acting on instinct, I grabbed my mom's arm and pulled us behind some nearby bushes. Their color had already started to turn, and some of the leaves had fallen, but they camouflaged us well enough.

"Brinkley, for heaven's sake. What are you doing?" My mom's tinny voice carried across the courtyard, and Mark's shoulders stiffened as he paused.

"Be quiet," I hissed at her. Maybe it was the panic in my expression, but she had the good sense not to open her mouth. For once.

Slowly, with horror movie timing, Mark turned around. I hadn't been prepared for the full effect of seeing his face again. It was a gut punch. My gaze strayed to his pouty lips, my skin flushing at the memory of what that mouth had done to me. Everything about him made my pulse race. Not just his looks, but the way he'd made me laugh, the attention he'd paid me when I talked, as if he actually found me interesting and cared about what I had to say, and the way he'd made me feel after just one evening in his company.

But we wouldn't, couldn't, ever be more than that.

"Please don't tell me Aiden damaged you so badly that you're now hiding from perfectly fine-looking men," my mom whispered.

"Hush." I waved a hand in front of her face to make her stop talking.

Mark looked around the courtyard, his eyes narrowing as they skimmed past the bush that concealed us, but he didn't linger. Shaking his head, he turned around and lifted a hand to wave at a wisp of a woman with thin hair pulled back in a simple clip. Her boxy brown suit made her shoulders stick out like pointy wire hangers. Eve. I barely recognized her. I'd gotten too accustomed to seeing her face layered under Instagram filters.

Eve had been part of my friend group with Eliza. She was the one who always pushed my connections, who always angled for an invite to Sunday dinner, who always asked if I would go with her to casually stop by Dr. Faber's office so he knew we were friends. She was the first one who stopped talking to me after I dropped out and was no longer useful.

Of course she'd be acquainted with Mark. Academia was a tight little circle.

"There's Eve Fillion," my mom said, as if I wasn't the one who'd introduced them. "I must say hello before she catches us hiding back here."

Eve's ears perked up, and her gaze swung toward our happy little bush. It was like she'd developed doglike hearing for her own name. "Dr. Saunders? Brinkley? What are you doing?"

"Great. Now we look utterly ridiculous." My mom straightened the lapels of her suit jacket. "Lost an earring," she called. "It rolled into this shrubbery, but I've got it now."

With nowhere to hide, I slunk out from behind the bush and followed my mom across the courtyard. I could feel Mark's stare boring into me as I kept my eyes on the sidewalk. I didn't know what to say to him. *Sorry I ran out while you were going down on me? Sorry I didn't call? Sorry your coworker— whom I can't stand, by the way—hired me to hurt your ego?* None of those things would make either one of us feel better, and it couldn't fix the damage done.

If I didn't look at him, maybe he'd eventually disappear.

"Brinkley, hello." Eve turned her body toward my mom—a subtle, yet clear, dismissal of my presence. I muttered something back, but it wasn't like she would've acknowledged me beyond the polite greeting. I had nothing to offer her.

"It's so good to see you." My mom did the typical handclasp with Eve. "We must get lunch next week."

"Yes, I'll send you an e-mail. We have some catching up to do between our departments. I haven't been over to your wing since I discussed my most recent paper with Dr. Hirst." Good to know Eve could still exploit that network I'd built for her. "Which reminds me, I was sorry to hear your latest paper was passed over for publication."

My mom's smile sharpened, as if she could taste the meat of the gazelle who thought she could run with lions. "And I was sorry to hear you were passed over for an assistant professor position. Though I admire your grit, persevering after four attempts. Weaker people than yourself might've given up after the second time."

"Three." Eve's plastic-coated smile wavered. "It was three attempts."

"Yes, of course, three. I don't believe I know your friend." My mom put on her brightest smile, which would only dim if she discovered Mark wasn't someone worth knowing.

Meanwhile, I'd been waiting for a handy sinkhole to open up and swallow me straight into the ground. Neither Mark nor I had said a word while my mom and Eve clucked around us. If I had to stand there for another second, I'd run into the nearest building and pull the fire alarm.

"How rude of me." Eve fluttered her hands. "Dr. Saunders, this is Dr. Cavanaugh. He's an adjunct at UoC, and we're what you'd call friendly competition."

My mom elbowed me in the ribs, probably because I hadn't spoken a single word, or even looked up from the sidewalk. "Remember when you and Eve used to be friendly competition with each other? Those were the days."

We'd never competed. We would've had to want the same things for that to happen.

"I didn't know you used to run track, Eve," Mark said.

Her expression clouded with confusion. "I didn't."

"My mistake." Mark flicked a piece of lint off his sleeve. "I was under the impression that Brinkley was a runner."

"Okay, well, this has been fun, but we really need to get going." I dug my nails into my mom's wrist and dragged her away.

I pulled her behind me for twenty feet before she yanked me back. "They've gone inside now. Care to tell me what that nonsense was all about?"

"Just a guy I used to know and didn't really want to see again." I left her there and headed for the safety of the parking lot, in case Mark wanted to come back for round two.

Once I made it to my mom's car, I shuffled my feet outside the passenger-side door, beckoning her to hurry up. She took her sweet time, like she was out for a Sunday stroll and had all the time in the world. If I'd told her there was a student who wanted to argue for a higher grade on a poorly received research paper chasing her, I bet she would've moved faster. She unlocked her eco-friendly Prius from ten feet away. I slid into my seat, resting my head on the dashboard. I guessed I could add my mom's office to places I could never go again.

"Do you want to talk about it?" My mom rested an unsure hand on my shoulder, as if the smallest gestures to show she cared were so far out of her comfort zone that she didn't know how to act. It made me feel worse than if she hadn't touched me at all.

"No." I couldn't explain it even to myself, let alone the person who believed I filed papers and sorted insurance claims for a living. "Just drive."

CHAPTER 8

The following week, Margo asked us to come in late and go straight to the conference room we used for quarterly meetings first thing in the morning. I sat between Emma and Charlotte, with Allie on the end. Our initial training had started in this room, where Margo had run a three-week course on how to execute the Five Steps of Heartbreaking, after which she brought each one of us to a bar to observe us in action before she let us take on assignments of our own. A low hum of anticipation buzzed between us. Our consensus seemed to be that Margo would be adding another department. We prayed it wouldn't be Abusers. She'd promised me she wouldn't, but no one put it past her to try.

"How did lunch with your mom go on Friday?" Charlotte pulled her long dark locks over her shoulder and picked at the ends. As the Heartbreaker in charge of Grifters, she took on the fewest assignments, but she made the most money per client by taking a percentage of recovered assets. She often spent up to six months working a single target. Despite the extreme levels of stress she was under in Grifters, Charlotte was a calming presence, the person I went to when I needed a strong dose of positivity.

"As well as can be expected," I said.

Though my mom hadn't probed me for more information about Mark, she did harp on about Dr. Faber's impending retirement. The fact that I didn't have the proper bachelor's to be accepted into the anthropology program, nor the master's required for teaching, didn't faze her. She'd forever hold out hope that I'd eventually come to my senses and follow in her footsteps.

"Sounds like she gave you another push toward going back to school," Allie said.

"That never changes, but now she's added a teaching opportunity to the mix."

Emma smirked beside me. I'd called her the minute I got home and told her about my run-in with Mark and Eve. I trusted Allie and Charlotte to keep my dirty little secret, but I wasn't quite as close with them. Emma was the only one I'd allowed into my Mark drama.

Water under the bridge though. I barely even thought about him anymore. Selena had paid her fee, and if I avoided Finnigan's, opting to drag my ass to the art supply store a full six blocks from my apartment, I never had to see Mark again. Now if I could just get my dreams to cooperate. I'd woken up on more than one night, tossing and turning and shaking with the memory of how his mouth had moved over me.

"Whatcha thinking about?" Emma singsonged. "You're about eight shades of pink."

I elbowed her in the side.

"Where's Margo?" Charlotte asked.

I shrugged. She'd been very insistent about us all showing up at 1:00 p.m. on the dot, yet it was now 1:15. It wasn't like her to be late. "I'll go see if she got held up in her office."

I left the conference room and turned the corner toward Margo's office, but the sound of construction on the opposite side of our floor had me changing directions—to where the Heartbreakers' offices were located. Margo's office had been designed like an old southern belle and a puffy pink unicorn had had a baby, but our personal offices were much sleeker and more modern. We all worked out of what amounted to little glass boxes. Our walls, our desks, even our filing cabinets were all chrome and glass. There was nowhere to hide.

Margo, wearing a pink hard hat with lace trim, stood between two burly men as she pointed at my office. The three of them had a blueprint spread out on one of the glass desks, talking in low voices, but it was clear they were in the middle of a project. Emma's office already had a second desk set up.

I tapped Margo on the shoulder, and she jumped, her silver bob swaying under her chin. She glanced at her watch and frowned. "Looks like I lost track of time."

"What's going on here?" I swept my hand toward Emma's office. "Are we getting an assistant? Is that the big surprise?"

A funny quivering rumbled in my stomach. One assistant was all we needed for the four of us, but it looked like each of us was getting a second desk in her office. I sincerely hoped she wasn't hiring more Heartbreakers. I needed every penny from Egos to save for my gallery.

Margo gave me a secretive smile as she hooked her arm through mine. "Let's go back to the conference room, and I'll explain everything there."

I didn't like the sound of that.

Ignoring the weight that had settled in my gut, I let Margo lead me away from the construction. Whatever she had up her sleeve would be revealed in moments anyway. A hush fell over Emma, Charlotte, and Allie as we entered. Margo made her way up to the pink podium, and I settled into my seat between Emma and Charlotte.

"What did you find out?" Emma whispered.

"You have a second desk in your office," I said. "It looks like we're all getting them."

"Really?" Emma's face lit up. "Are we each getting our own assistant?"

If only. I had a strong feeling Margo had something much worse up her sleeve. I put a finger over my lips to shush Emma as Margo's gaze fell on us. Charlotte fidgeted in her seat. Out of the four of us, she had the most bizarre way of organizing, and the idea of having to share her weirdly chaotic space with an outsider must've made her queasy.

Margo tapped her cotton-candy nails on the podium. "Listen up, girls."

We fell quiet at once.

"Business is going well. But we are unique, and if we want to stay ahead of the game, we need to make adjustments when adjustments are due." Margo smiled at us, though there was a strained edge to it. "I'm hoping this will be a change you'll understand in time."

"I don't like change," Charlotte said under her breath. I was inclined to agree.

"For the first time ever . . ." Margo paused for dramatic effect, looking each of us in the eye with steely resolve. Like it would be the last time she saw us before sending us off to war. ". . . Heartbreak for Hire is going to employ male Heartbreakers."

A weighted silence hung over the conference room, as if every single one of us had simultaneously stopped breathing. She'd hired men to be Heartbreakers? No. No way. There was no possible way Margo could think that was a good idea. Men didn't belong at H4H. The whole reason we'd taken this job was that Margo had promised us an all-female environment. We had all been trampled on by men, either in the relationship or the career department, and Margo had offered us these roles as some kind of pseudo-healing from the ways we'd been wronged.

"I can't fucking believe this," Emma said.

I figured she'd be the first to speak up. Emma had joined H4H after having been passed over for a partnership at the advertising firm where she used to work. Jacob, the guy she'd fallen in love with, had gotten the promotion. After he used her to steal her ideas. This blow must've hit her especially hard. She'd never wanted to leave advertising, but she couldn't stand to work with men after what she'd gone through.

An angry buzz hummed between us. We all had stories similar to Emma's and now felt betrayed by the one person who'd sworn to look out for us. This was worse than adding an Abusers department. This was inviting snakes into our bed and asking us to cozy up to them.

"Calm down, ladies." Margo kept a serene smile on her face. I had a strong urge to throw one of my ankle boots at her. "The men understand that this is a women-first organization. Trust me when I say they won't get special treatment."

"Fucking bet." Emma crossed her arms. Her small eyes were narrowed in disgust, and her delicate features were all scrunched up. She was fierce when angry, like a tiny fire-breather.

"This won't be happening all at once. They need to learn the Five Steps of Heartbreaking first, and they'll need to train with you in the evenings. But I think you should meet them before you make any snap judgments." Margo gestured to a side door.

At her cue, a guy built like the Jolly Green Giant strolled into the conference room. He had to have been at least six and a half feet tall, with a very attractive face and light-blond hair. His expression was guarded as he took in the women shooting him death glares.

"This is Liam Oosterhouse, and he'll be the male Heartbreaker in Grifters," Margo said.

Beside me, Charlotte made a small noise that sounded a lot like choking. Her warm skin paled to a light brown. I squeezed her shoulder, just to remind her to breathe.

"Next we have Charles Woodwyk, in Cheaters." Margo gestured toward the door again, where another meaty piece of muscle entered, this one with bronzed skin and a devilish grin.

"Kill me right now," Allie muttered. She was almost as small as Emma, and just as strong-willed, with strawberry-blond hair, big brown eyes, and a light sprinkling of freckles across her alabaster nose that stood out like peach paint splatters.

"And for the new male counterpart in Players," Margo said as Emma growled beside me, "we have Nick Stafford."

"He'll be lucky if he ends the day with his balls attached to his body," Emma said, casually tucking a lock of her shoulder-length black hair behind her ear. Allie gave her a fist bump as Nick turned a light shade of green. Good.

"Hold down your breakfast." Margo patted Nick's arm. "She's more bark than bite."

Emma bared her teeth.

Margo fiddled with the patterned scarf around her neck. "Moving on." She looked at me, and I willed down the bile that had risen in my throat. "Egos welcomes Markus Cavanaugh."

The side door opened, and in strolled Mark, looking out of place in his herringbone sweater-vest and khakis. The apprehension on his face quickly melted to a piercing glare as he looked directly at me. My heart stopped as a roaring rush pounded in my ears.

No. This had to be another dream. My subconscious couldn't send me delicious images of Mark moving over my body forever. At some point, even my own mind had to turn on me. That's what I got for eating chocolate in bed and bingeing on reruns of *Gossip Girl*.

I blinked, but he wasn't going away. This couldn't be happening. Maybe he had an evil twin. That had to be it. I'd entered an alternate dimension where I was trapped on the set of a soap opera. I was about to wear the same outfit for three months straight and get one of those kids who aged ten years overnight. This must be the part where I'd find myself in a love triangle with Mark and Evil Mark.

I pinched myself, willing the nightmare to fade. I'd wake up with a half-eaten Cadbury egg stuck to my face, and all would be right in the world again.

"Stop doing that." Emma smacked my hand. "This is really happening."

Mark smoothed out his expression, pretending to listen to Margo, but halfway through her speech, his storm-cloud eyes met mine across the room. A sizzle of electricity passed between us, even as the razor-sharp smile he gave me could've cut through diamonds. None of the goofy charm or kind interest he'd possessed at the Reading Lounge was present. He raised an eyebrow as his gaze settled on my shaking hands, the only outward sign that I was losing it.

Fuck my life.

CHAPTER 9

clenched my fingers together. My hands wouldn't stop shaking. The walls in the spacious room pressed in on me, squeezing the oxygen out of my lungs. Margo made some speech about the future of the company and expansion plans, but I didn't hear a single word. Emma whispered something to me. I didn't hear her either. The only thing I heard was the speed at which my blood rushed to my brain. I bent forward, shoving my head between my knees. Puking all over the conference room floor would only add to my living nightmare.

Emma rubbed my back. "We'll fix this."

I sat up. It was too late to fix anything. This must've been what lab rats felt like the first time they had mascara tested on them. On my opposite side, Charlotte murmured words of comfort, while Margo told the men she wanted a private moment with us and excused them with the same flourish she'd used to introduce them. But not before Mark sent me a scathing glare meant to shred me to ribbons. The kind of look that promised a reckoning.

I swallowed the lump in my throat.

"Charlotte, Allie, Emma, Brinkley." Margo waved a beckoning hand at us. "In my office, if you will. We have some things to discuss."

"You're damn right we do," Emma grumbled. She took my arm, squeezing it lightly. "Are you okay? You look like you're about to pass out."

"I need to talk to you." My lips felt like paper as I spoke. I desperately needed water. Or something stronger. "This is really bad."

"I know," Emma said. "But we'll present a united front and nip this bullshit in the bud before it goes any further."

I couldn't say anything else, for fear of Charlotte and Allie overhearing. Emma had never seen Mark and we all avoided sharing targets' full names, so she had no idea how bad my head was spinning. I still wasn't entirely sure this whole situation was real. How had he ended up here if he was an adjunct at UoC? Adjunct teaching didn't pay all that well, and wasn't always full-time, but from the way he'd talked at the Reading Lounge, teaching was his passion. He'd never mentioned a desire to take on a side gig screwing over women. But then again, why would he? As far as he knew, I was some girl he met in a bar, brought home, and almost got lucky with. He had a lot of nerve to look at *me* like he was pissed. Everything about him had been a lie.

The four of us shuffled into Margo's office, and as the door clicked shut behind us, Emma was the first to speak up. "How could you?"

Margo folded her hands over her desk, that serene smile still in place. "This is a business decision. And it's not going to affect you as much as you think."

Emma opened her mouth and the glint of the fire-breathing dragon that lived in her heart surfaced in her eyes, but Allie held up a hand to cut her off. "What do you mean, this won't affect us? You're bringing men into this office, and you swore up and down to all of us that this would be a women-only establishment. You promised us this would be a safe environment, and you broke that promise."

"Have I?" Margo asked, the picture of innocence. Like a vampire who hides her fangs so she can score an invitation into your house.

"Why now?" Charlotte asked. "Why at all? What purpose will men serve?"

"Fair question." Margo poured us all tea, which I refused in case she tried to drug us into accepting this. I wouldn't put anything past her at this point. "I'm glad one of you has an interest in what the terms of this arrangement will be."

"What terms?" Emma asked.

Margo leaned forward. "They are to remain beneath you, for one. Brinkley." I flinched when she addressed me. "Wouldn't you say it's a different kind of empowerment to have a man taking orders from you? Learning from you? Answering to you?"

"I don't know what you want me to say." I picked my words carefully. Margo had asked for my support without telling me what it would be for, and now that I knew, it was as though I'd stepped into a minefield, with only wrong moves ahead of me.

"None of you like change. Emma, Charlotte, Brinkley, don't you remember the fuss you three threw over the Cheaters department? You said it was too risky. The guy who hosted that show got stabbed. But then I reminded you, what is the ultimate humiliation for a man?"

"Calling out his mom's name during sex," Allie said.

"Getting a tramp stamp while drunk on spring break," Emma said.

"Having to order customized condoms in extra small," Charlotte said.

"Hearing Maury Povich say 'you are the father' on live TV," I said.

"Okay, none of those." Margo's lips thinned, the only sign she showed of her wavering patience. "The ultimate humiliation is being thrown over for another man."

"I think calling out his mom's name is way worse," Allie said.

We nodded in agreement.

"Listen." Margo slammed her teacup down with a sharp clink. "I was right about Cheaters, and I'm right about hiring male Heartbreakers. They will earn less than you because they will work *for* you. After their training is complete, and if this venture becomes successful, on top of your regular commissions you'll earn fifteen percent of their share as their direct managers. Congrats, ladies. You're their bosses now."

For once, Emma didn't have anything to say. Neither did Charlotte or Allie. I had a lot to say. Too much. But nothing I could vocalize. Although the new source of revenue would bring my gallery that much closer to fruition. If only I didn't have to work with Mark. If I could get rid of him somehow and have another man take his place . . .

I shook my head. Just because Margo held the dangling carrot didn't mean we had to be her asses. We'd been sold on H4H because it was supposed to be a female-driven enterprise, a chance to heal old wounds while we doled out the revenge we couldn't ever take for ourselves. And yeah, we got paid. But it hadn't just been about the money for us. We'd bought into Margo's empowerment spiel. All the way. If we trained men to break women's hearts, what did that say about our mission?

What did that say about us?

Emma held up a finger. "And what if we still don't like this?"

"Then I'll find someone to replace you." Margo looked each of us in the eye to impress on us that she meant business. "Either way, the men are staying. You can get on board and reap the benefits, or you can get out of the way."

"Can we have a day to think all this over?" Charlotte asked.

Margo waved a hand. "Sure thing. Take tomorrow off. Think things over. But I expect a response from you on Wednesday morning. The men will be here on Friday evening, and you all have new assignments. You'll be able to bring them along to start their training." We all murmured in unison that we'd have an answer by then, and stood as a unit. "Brinkley, can you stay a minute? The rest of you are free to leave."

Emma gave me a look to let me know she'd wait for me. The four of us had things to discuss, and we had to do it somewhere else. Preferably a place that served alcohol. I couldn't be the only one who needed a drink.

As soon as the door closed again, Margo turned her piercing gaze to me. "You weren't as vocal as I expected. That's not like you. How are you feeling about this change?"

"I don't know." I still didn't fully understand how Mark had gone from adjunct-in-anthropology to apprentice-in-heartbreak, but his career was the least of my worries. I had to do what I'd been doing best for the last two years: look out for myself. "I need to think it over."

"Is there anything you want to tell me?" She slid a delicate plate of cookies over to me.

I stared down at my knotted fingers. "No."

Not only did I fear losing my job, but I also feared losing face. Margo was more a mother to me than my own in ways I'd been hungry for two years ago, and I didn't ever want her to look at me like I was a disappointment. I never wanted to be anyone's disappointment again.

"Okay then. We'll circle back to that later." Margo sat back. "I appreciate your not leaping down my throat right away. I know this is going to be a hard adjustment, but I hope you'll believe me when I say your well-being is always my first priority."

"Why men though?" I asked. "Why couldn't you just hire more women? You've always told us men are the enemy, and now this?"

Margo gave me a sad smile. "Every company has to find new ways to grow or it will flounder and sink. Our old business model can't survive. It's not punchy enough. But I promise, this environment will still be safe. These are your employees as much as they are mine, and you might find you have more in common with the men than you think."

"It feels wrong. Maybe because it's *all* wrong." I didn't want to voice it, but that nagging feeling wouldn't go away. We did well by women, I believed that with every fiber of my being, but at what expense? Mark hadn't been so bad, but it was the first night I'd stepped out of character and taken off my blinders. What if others hadn't been terrible either, and I just couldn't see it? I feared I'd become so jaded that I could no longer see the bigger picture.

"No." Margo reached out for my hand across her desk. She'd always given her approval without question. No matter what I did or felt, she was always on my side. For that alone, I owed her everything. "We're not wrong. Remember your clients, the ones who have been so grateful for our services. Remember how Aiden made you feel so powerless? Remember how weak you were when I approached you in that restaurant?"

Every time she brought up what Aiden had done to me, old memories threatened to choke me. The time I'd rented a cabin on Lake Michigan for our anniversary brought a fresh wave of shame to my mind, like a slimy coating that never quite washed away.

"I have finals coming up—how could you be so stupid?"

I'd presented the key and accompanying note to him in a gift-wrapped box, while I wore nothing but scraps of lace under a short robe. I'd tried so hard to be a fantasy for him that the only fantasy I ended up creating was the belief that he'd ever loved me. He'd scorned my gift and given me the silent treatment until I was on my hands and knees begging him to forgive me, when I knew—*I knew*—I'd done nothing wrong. Still, I'd begged, because I couldn't stand the stony silence and disapproving glares.

"I have finals coming up—how could you be so stupid?"

Margo waved a hand in front of my face. "Brinkley. You in there?"

"Yes, sorry." I straightened my spine and folded my hands neatly in my lap, willing them to stop shaking. Aiden was gone. He no longer had the power to hurt me.

"There now." Margo's comforting tone soothed the last of my frayed edges. "I'll have no more talk about what we do being wrong. Not when it's been so integral in empowering women, and in allowing you and the girls to take back what had been stolen from you."

She was right. Of course she was right. I put those thoughts of guilt and shame away. We only hurt men who truly deserved it. I still didn't approve of Margo's latest business idea, but it was clear I wouldn't get through to her, so I'd have to see what the other girls wanted to do about it. "What made you want to hire the men in the first place?"

"Ah." Margo picked up her tea, but her cup didn't quite mask the smugness in her expression, which left me feeling even more uneasy. "That came to me in an interesting way. Not one I'll be sharing today though. You've already had enough to process."

On that cryptic note, I made my exit.

Emma pounced on me as soon as I shut the door. "What did she say? Did she try to justify her choices? What do you think of the management kickback? Do you think she only offered that to placate us?"

"Slow down." I laughed. "We need to get out of here and get a drink first."

"Please. We're five steps ahead of you. Allie and Charlotte are reserving us a table at the Reading Lounge as we speak." She gave me an evil grin. "I believe you're familiar with it?"

"You're going to regret that joke," I muttered.

✕

Emma got us an Uber, which we skipped so we could walk when I told her Mark was *the* Mark from ladyhead-gate. She raged in her own Emma way, which included finding a shallow grave for him next to Aiden, but she also worried. Running into him at Northwestern had been unpleasant. Working with him in the same office would be a nightmare.

"Didn't Margo do a background check on these guys?" Emma asked. "Wouldn't she know Mark was a target?"

"I don't know."

"You could explain the situation to her." Emma hopped over what looked like a puddle of vomit on the sidewalk. "I bet she'd dismiss him right away."

"And risk both my job and getting the same scathing judgment from Margo that I already get from you?" I couldn't.

Even when she made me incredibly angry, I cared about Margo's opinion. I'd come to rely on it. "No, thanks. For better or worse, I'm stuck with him."

"Maybe he'll leave on his own now that he's seen you?"

I could only hope.

Half an hour later, Emma and I crowded into a booth at the Reading Lounge. Around the corner from where Mark had lifted me against the wall and worked his body against mine. Just being in here brought every second of that night to the forefront of my mind, including my humiliating escape. I'd never eat coleslaw again for as long as I lived.

"Classy joint. Sorry." Emma winced.

"Told you you'd regret that joke." I waved over the waitress, the same one from my night with Mark. Her eyes lit with surprise, but she didn't say anything. I'd tip her generously again for her discretion.

As soon as the waitress returned with a round of vodka cranberries, Allie raised her glass, clicking it against ours. "To not giving a fuck about the promotion."

"To taking down those bastards anyway," Emma said.

"So, we're in agreement?" Charlotte asked. "We don't want men at H4H?"

"They don't belong. The extra money isn't worth this." I gave myself a single second to think longingly of my gallery. Still so far beyond my reach, but getting closer every week. "Ethically, we can't stand by it. Our company has always been women-only. It's why women have felt comfortable hiring us."

Everyone agreed. Though we didn't consider ourselves moral by any standards, we cared about women. We wanted to help our clients. In the world at large, men still had the upper hand, and in our own twisted way, we considered what we did an evening of the odds.

"What are we going to do though?" Charlotte asked. "I can't afford to lose this job, and Margo said she'd get rid of us if we don't get on board."

"Simple. We murder them," Emma said. "The fish in Lake Michigan will make quick work of their bloated bodies."

I resisted the urge to roll my eyes. "Anyone else?"

"We ditch them." Allie shook back her strawberry-blond hair. "Tell them to show up at locations across town from where we actually are. We can't train them if they don't show up. And Margo can make her threats, but she can't fire all of us."

"I like it," Charlotte said.

"I like it too," I said.

We traded rants back and forth as the drinks flowed, and the more we drank, the more worked up we got. Margo couldn't bring men into H4H. We had to protect what we'd helped her build. Six hours and countless vodka cranberries later, I could no longer feel my face, but I felt confident in our plan. Or as confident as one could feel when the room tilted.

"I love ooo," Emma slurred. "My Ooooober is here, but I can't leave yet. Not until you know how mush I wuv ooo."

I patted her cheeks and slurred something back. Wow, the room was really spinning now. I slung my purse over my head like a necklace. I might've called it a cowbell and made moo-ing sounds. That part was fuzzy.

My feet dragged up the sidewalk, and I'd never been more grateful I'd chosen to wear one-inch ankle boots instead of five-inch heels. I had three blocks to walk until I made it to my apartment. Then I could land face-first in Winnie's fluff and pass out. Maybe she'd harvest my eyeballs while I slept. Then I'd never have to see Mark or the way his features twisted in disgust when he looked at me again.

I leaned against a building and tilted my head toward the sky. Two blocks to go. Everything that wasn't numb tingled. I really wanted to make out with someone. Anyone would do. I'd reached *that* portion of the liquored-up phase. The street looked vaguely familiar, but not in the way it should look familiar when I was only two blocks from my apartment. I weaved in front of the building as I squinted at the number.

Of course.

Not only had I gone the wrong way, but I'd ended up in front of Mark's apartment. My drunk ass needed an intervention. But, since I was here, and I still really wanted to make out with someone, why not make out with Mark? That seemed like a grand idea in my vodka cranberry–addled brain.

No. *Bad, Brinkley.* I wanted to give him a piece of my mind. How dare he look at me today like I was full of shit? He was the one who'd pretended to care so much about teaching.

He wasn't going to show up at my work and judge me. I'd tell him exactly where he could stick that look. I took the stairs, barely hanging on to the railing as I used it to propel me around corners. I looked for the cheap shoes I'd kicked off when I ran from him, but someone must've swept them away. I stood in front of his door, full of righteous indignation and ready to rage. Or make out. I'd be lying if I said I'd completely taken that off the table.

One way or the other, we were going to have this out. If only his door would stop moving so I could knock. I ended up rapping my knuckles against the wall. Good enough.

Heavy footfalls sounded from the other side, and he opened the door. All of his faces held a mix of annoyance and surprise.

"You have, like, three heads right now." I weaved in front of him. "As soon as I find out which is the real one, I'm either going to punch you or kiss you, so hold still."

It was the last thing I remembered.

CHAPTER 10

———————————➤

I peeled an eyelid open and had instant regret. Sun streamed in through the window like a laser beam determined to punish me for my night of debauchery. The room was too bright. It made everything hurt. I must've stumbled into my apartment and crashed on the couch. Groaning, I pulled the blanket up to my chin. It was soft and smelled lightly of rain and moonlight. Not like my blanket . . .

I sat up, gripping my head as the room spun and my stomach churned.

This wasn't my apartment.

Everything in the room was white. White walls, white couches, white end tables. I looked down. Oh God. Even the T-shirt I wore, which definitely wasn't mine, was white. I squeezed my eyes shut and opened them again. I was either dead and in some kind of void before my spirit moved on, or I was about to be and was in the apartment of a serial killer.

The only spot of color was a potted plant with waxy leaves perched on the white coffee table.

"Hello, little friend." I pinched one of the leaves and shook it in greeting. "Are you going to be joining me in the afterlife?"

I always knew I'd be spending eternity with a plant.

"You're not dead yet," a familiar voice said. "Though I'm betting you feel like it."

I whipped my head up, then cringed when the sudden movement sent the room spinning again. Mark stood before me with a cup of coffee in his hand and an amused smirk on his face. His feet and chest were bare, and holy shit. Even though my head throbbed and my teeth had a fuzzy peach-skin texture, a slow lick of lust rolled through my core. I'd felt his hard body through his shirt, but my best fantasies hadn't done him justice.

My gaze skimmed his broad chest, well-defined arms, and the ridges in his stomach muscles. I pressed my lips together, and he cocked an eyebrow. Smug bastard. And damn him for having a reason to be. Plaid sleep pants hung low on his hips, highlighting those perfect V-muscles that tapered down below his drawstrings. I wanted to run my tongue over every inch of his—

"Penis funnel." I clamped a hand over my mouth. Those words were *not* supposed to leave my brain.

He choked on the sip of coffee he'd just taken. "Penis what?"

"You know." I covered my eyes as I gestured toward his waist. "Those muscles. The V. It's like a funnel leading to your . . ." *Argh.* I peeked at him between my fingers. "Anyway, it would be really awesome and helpful if you put on a shirt right now."

"Oh, I don't think so." He set his coffee on the counter behind him and prowled toward me. "This is my apartment. If you don't like it, you're free to leave."

I looked around the stark white living room. "You're not going to murder me?"

A deep chuckle rumbled from his chest. "Not today."

"Cool." This wasn't at all awkward. I still had no idea how I'd gotten here, but I'd worry about that later. For now, I just wanted to go home and drown my head in a vat of bleach. "If I could have my clothes back, I'll be on my way."

"I washed your dress last night. It's in the bathroom." He jerked a thumb over his shoulder. "You can change in there."

"Why did you wash—?" Nope. I would not admit that the details of last night had escaped me. "That was nice of you."

He shrugged. "I didn't want my apartment to smell like vomit. I had to wash it after you threw up all over yourself. That was after you yelled at me and called me a liar, then tried to kiss me. In case you can't remember."

My cheeks burned. I'd thought running into Aiden while I was covered in garbage would be my worst humiliation. This morning had just told that night to hold its beer. "You're really enjoying this, aren't you?"

"A little bit." He shot me a cocky grin that made my blood boil.

Lifting my chin, I mustered as much dignity as the situation allowed. I wrapped the blanket around my waist and stood. I had to squeeze past him, and he didn't even do that fake lean where you look like you're trying to get out of someone's way while not really moving at all.

"First door on the left down the hall," he called.

I made quick work of changing his T-shirt for my sweater-dress, and I definitely didn't linger over the way his rain and moonlight smell clung to the fabric. To add insult to injury, he'd also washed the lace thong he'd removed from me the night of our disastrous meeting. My dress didn't have any pockets, because it had clearly been designed by a man who hated women, so I had no choice but to put them on over my other underwear. I'd die a thousand deaths before I walked out of the bathroom holding them in my hand.

After rummaging around in his drawers, I found a tube of toothpaste and finger-brushed my teeth. My mascara had smeared beneath my eyes in my sleep, and my hair hung in tangled knots, one of which was crunchy with dry vomit. Awesome.

After I tilted my head under the faucet to wash out the remaining puke, I took advantage of my location to snoop. The vanity drawers held his shaving kit and some washcloths. White, of course. I opened his medicine cabinet and found only Tylenol and allergy pills. What a disappointment. I'd been hoping for Rogaine or Viagra or something equally embarrassing, but at least I didn't find a collection of serial-killer trophy teeth, so I'd probably live through this.

No tampons or an extra toothbrush or any of the other telltale signs of a woman spending a fair amount of time here. It annoyed me that I was relieved.

"If you're done going through my stuff, I brewed you a cup of coffee," Mark called from the kitchen.

"You wish I was going through your stuff," I yelled back as I peeked under the vanity sink. Nothing but a refill bottle of hand soap and a can of Ajax. Perfectly normal. Damn it.

I smoothed out my hair as best as I could, though it was a lost cause, and exited the bathroom. I perched on one of the white leather stools tucked under his kitchen counter. A steaming mug of coffee sat in front of me, and I breathed in the nectar of the gods. With one sip, the pressure behind my eyes loosened.

Mark stood on the other side of the counter in the kitchen, his arms crossed over his chest. He still hadn't put on a shirt. "Find anything of interest in my medicine cabinet?"

"No. I'm just going to assume you keep your collection of anal beads and fingernail clippings in your room."

He threw back his head and laughed. The warm, rich sound traveled down to my toes. "You have a lot of nerve, I'll give you that."

"Can you blame me?" I glanced at the living room over my shoulder. "I mean, what's with all the white? Does it make it easier for you to locate the blood splatters?"

He heaved a long-suffering sigh. "I just moved in last month and I'm having issues with the storage facility currently holding a good portion of my things hostage."

"Oh. I guess that makes sense." I took another sip of coffee as I tried to gather my courage. "So . . . about last night. I don't know how I ended up here, but it's probably my fault."

His lips quirked with amusement. "Probably?"

"Fine. It's very much my fault. But it's also at least half your fault."

"How is it half my fault that you showed up at my door, drunk out of your mind? I'm pretty sure it's one hundred percent your fault and I'm the injured party here." He pointed at his bare chest, which only drew my eyes to the hard sculpting of muscle I'd been doing a decent job of ignoring. "In more ways than one."

"What do you want? An apology?"

"That would be a good start."

"Well, too bad." I was being childish and, admittedly, a giant ass. I wasn't pleased about him working at H4H, but causing a drunken scene and throwing up in his apartment wasn't the most mature way to handle things. Still, I couldn't bring myself to say I was sorry. I'd promised myself I'd never apologize to another man after I spent the better part of three years groveling for Aiden. "You're not going to get one."

He shook his head. "Why am I not surprised? When it comes to doing the right thing, I should've known you wouldn't be capable of even the bare minimum."

That *tone*. My headache came roaring back full force. "Spare me your moral high ground. Yeah, I was paid by someone who hates your guts to break your ego, but have you forgotten you just got hired to do the exact same thing?"

"Believe me, I don't think I'll ever forget finding out why you ran out on me." His eyes burned with a temper that matched my own. "I'll admit, you excel at your act. A-plus bullshitting."

"Oh, please." I rolled my eyes. "Like you're any better than me. I actually believed you were passionate about your career, but I guess you'd rather roll around in the mud with the rest of us bullshitters."

He rested his arms on the counter across from me. "I am passionate about my career, but adjunct spots are cutthroat. They expect us to write articles, create exams and submit them for approval, hold office hours, and all the other things professors do, on part-time pay. They gave a promotion to someone who published a well-received paper on modern dating rituals. Eerily similar to the one I'd been working on for months, using all of my data. I'm assuming the same person who hired you. Still think you don't owe me an apology?"

Shit. I knew there had been something off about Selena. That nagging feeling I'd had the other day, the questions around whether or not we were really doing the right thing, began to tap at the back of my mind again. Still, he could hardly blame me for her actions. "It sucks you're having issues with UoC, but that's academics. And it's even less my fault than the other stuff you want me to be sorry for."

"You're a real piece of work, aren't you?"

"And you're not any closer to getting that apology you seem to want so badly."

His pupils dilated as his gaze skimmed my lips. "You have no idea how badly I want it."

I shifted on the stool, suddenly very aware of the heat at my core. A slow smile spread over his lips, and he took a step back. I'd fallen right into his sexy *fuck-me* trap like a goddamned amateur. I did this shit for a living. I wasn't about to be schooled by my subordinate.

I sauntered around the counter to the kitchen. He stood stock-still as I approached him and walked my fingers up his chest. I pushed up on my toes and got a rush from feeling his breath hitch as I whispered in his ear: "Guess you'll have to tend bar now like everyone else who needs a second job in this city."

He reeled back. "Why would I do that?"

"You can't work at H4H." I could feel my hysteria rising and couldn't do anything to choke it down. "Our brief history aside, it's a female-only business and should remain that way. Men already have so much power in the world. Why can't you just leave this one corner alone? Why do you have to come in and take everything?"

"I'm not taking anything except a job that was offered. I'm sure you're used to thinking the sun shines out of your ass and every slight is personal, but this isn't about you."

His steely gaze, the drip of condescension in his voice, brought on a painful flashback to the days when I'd been with Aiden, when he practically made a sport of chipping away at my confidence until I became a shell of a person. No matter how hard I'd tried to please him, it was never enough. He'd stepped on my fingers while I was crawling like a dog begging for his affection. I'd never go back to that again. I'd barely survived it the first time around.

Mark must've seen something in my expression, because he laid a hand on my shoulder. A jolt of electricity ran through me, making all my nerves tingle in the most traitorous way. I got a small amount of satisfaction from knowing I wasn't the only one when he snatched his hand back and rubbed it on his sleep pants.

"How did you end up at H4H anyway?" Of all the men in this city, Margo had hired this one. I was well past believing in things like fate and coincidence. There had to be a reason.

"I found your note card. The one you dropped the night you ran out of here. It had all kinds of interesting information about me. And for the record, I don't live for bullet-point outlines, and my social media accounts are all private."

I felt the blood drain from my face as my vision blurred around the edges. This couldn't be true. There had to be another explanation. "You found the cheat sheet. And, what? Decided to use it as an employment opportunity?"

"I was a little freaked out when I found it. Even you have to admit I had every right to question what the hell had gone on that night. The 'cheat sheet'"—he air-quoted—"as you call it, had a number on the bottom. I called and got Margo."

"You told her I'd been in your apartment." God. I could only imagine what she thought of me, going home with a target. It was like she'd taught me nothing over the years. Maybe she wanted me to train Mark to be my replacement when she fired me.

"Nope. I thought Margo was your mother and didn't think that information would go over well." He grimaced. "I asked her a bunch of questions, we got to talking about the business, and one thing led to another."

My fault. It was my fault the guys had been brought on. And Margo knew. She knew he'd been my target, and she'd hired him anyway. This was what I got for giving her unquestioning support and loyalty.

"I'm done here." I spun around and hurried for the front door, well aware that I'd just shown my hand and folded whatever game we'd been playing, but I couldn't think in this apartment. It was too white, and there was too much Mark.

My purse and boots sat on a white bench by the door. The bench where Mark had hitched my skirt up to my waist and buried his face between my legs. My face flushed with the memory. The quicker I got out of here, the quicker I could stew in my mortification. I held the wall in his entryway, weaving on one leg while I tried to maneuver on my boots without sitting.

Mark joined me, glancing between me and the bench. He ran his thumb over his lower lip. "Leaving so soon?"

I flung open the door and stepped out of his apartment, but I couldn't leave without making a parting shot. "If you don't quit H4H, I'll tell your bosses at UoC what you're doing as a side gig. My mother is the queen bee of academic politics, and I know damn well how important appearances are."

"No, you won't. Because if you try to run me out of UoC, I'll tell Margo I nearly had you screaming my name while I licked your pussy so good you were seeing stars." He gave me a lazy grin. "See you on Friday, boss."

And with that, he shut the door in my face.

CHAPTER 11

Margo owed me answers. I'd done everything she asked of me for two years straight. And then not only had she gone behind my back to hire men, but she'd gotten the idea from one of my targets. Was this some kind of sick punishment for asking for more autonomy? Did she really think she could treat me this way? I wouldn't be pushed around. I wasn't weak or helpless anymore, and Margo should've known better.

Before heading into the office, I needed to shower and change. I walked into my apartment to find that Winnie had clawed her way up the drapes again. She mewed pathetically while she hung on by her nails at the top of the window. I plucked her off and received a hiss for my trouble. Though if she'd given me any sort of affection, I might've thought she was dying.

My phone buzzed, and I dumped out the contents of my

purse on the couch to search for it. After I plucked it from a small pile of receipts for way too many vodka cranberries and an order of fried pickles I had no recollection of eating, I answered.

"Hey, you." Emma's voice came through the line, along with a mix of city noises. She must've been up on her roof again, desperately trying to get the last rays of natural sun before the long winter washed her out. "Feeling like shit?"

She never got hangovers. I really should've hated her for it. I kicked off one of my ankle boots, and it hit the wall with a dull thud. "I just got home."

"Shut the fuck up." The sound of Emma's sunglasses clinking against the concrete rang in my ear. "You went home with someone? Who?"

I rubbed the bridge between my eyes, the headache still hovering just there. "I ended up at Mark's apartment."

"B. No." Disapproval coated her voice. "It was bad enough when he was a target, but now he's the enemy. You're Julia Roberts. You're sleeping with the enemy."

I had enough running through my mind with Margo's betrayal, I didn't need Emma's lecture on top of it. "First of all, I don't know how I got to his apartment. And we didn't sleep together. I woke up on his couch, we got in an argument, and I left."

Which made it the second time Mark had gotten the upper hand. What was it with this guy? I wasn't perfect, far from it, but I kept it together okay. I went to work, paid my bills, didn't go looking for trouble or bad relationships. I flossed. But the minute I got within radius of Mark, I boarded the Hot Mess Express and couldn't seem to get off this train. I became the kind of woman who had to walk home wearing two pairs of underwear.

"I'm just looking out for you," Emma said. "That's what we do, right?"

"I know." Even if Emma's lectures occasionally annoyed me, it was only because the two of us looked out for each other when no one else did. "Anyway, listen to this. . . ."

I explained how the men had come to be at H4H, and Emma immediately offered to go to Margo's office with me, even though we had a rare day off. As much as I loved Emma, she'd probably make a big dramatic scene. I needed to proceed with caution.

"Are you sure you don't want me to come with you?" Emma asked. "I have a few choice words for Margo myself. How could she set you up like that?"

"I can handle her." I paused. "Plus, I'm not going straight home from the office. I thought I'd check out some rental space in River North for my gallery while I have the time."

"Have fun," Emma said before letting me go. She used to come with me on my gallery hunts, but when I never made a down payment, or even looked into funding, she began to lose interest. She appreciated my art. She just didn't believe I'd ever put the money down and make it a reality. Most days, I didn't believe it either. But I still put money away, telling myself—always telling myself—just a few more months.

After I showered and changed into leggings and an oversize sweater, I took an Uber to H4H. I'd thought about putting on a power suit, the type I reserved for lunches with my mom, but Margo would see right through that. I wanted to appear calm. Casual. As if I'd just dropped by to pick up some info on my latest assignment. If I could catch her off guard, she might be more likely to spill her reasoning behind this new transition.

Margo looked up as I entered her office. "I thought I told you girls to take the day off."

She looked so composed in her puffy pink office, so harmless, that for a moment I wondered if Mark had lied to me about how he'd gotten hired at H4H. "I had to grab a file."

"I'm so glad. Please, have a seat." Margo immediately plugged in her electric kettle.

Tea was so much a part of her aesthetic, it had become a comfort to me as well. I'd recently gotten my own kettle and was experimenting with bagless teas. I still preferred coffee while painting though. As she set up her box of various teas, I plucked at a loose thread on my sweater, crossed and uncrossed my legs, and shifted in my seat.

"You seem nervous." Margo passed me a cup of hot water and a green tea bag. "Is there another reason why you came by the office today?"

The glint in her amber eyes threw off my plan to approach the subject delicately. She already knew that I knew. "I wanted to ask about the men. How you came to hire Mark specifically, when he'd been one of my targets."

"I wondered when you'd get around to admitting you already knew Markus." Margo leaned back, her expression reminiscent of a cat who'd finally trapped a tricky mouse. "So unlike you to lose one of your cheat sheets like that."

What did she expect me to say? I certainly wouldn't be telling her anything about the night I'd been paid to embarrass Mark. "It was an accident."

"I'm sure." The look she gave me suggested otherwise.

Before she could corner me into admitting anything, I deployed a guilt tactic I'd learned from the best. "How could you let him convince you to hire men? You let a man make new rules without even consulting us. How do you think that makes us feel?"

Margo's eyes hardened, even as they widened in concern. "I didn't let the men make rules, and I think bringing them in will be good for all of you."

"You keep saying that, but you won't say how. You just expect us to go along with it." Exactly what I'd been doing for two years. Even when I'd been given autonomy over my own clients after repeatedly asking, Margo had still found a way to pull the strings.

"I think it's time for you girls to get accustomed to working with men again. You can't do this job forever, and eventually you'll all want to date again, have normal lives. This is my way of easing you into it, while still making sure you hold the power."

I shook my head, wanting to deny what she said, but at the same time wanting so badly to believe it. Fear and resentment had ruled my life for so long now, I hardly knew who I was without them. Yet I wasn't sure if I wanted to find out.

"Didn't I ask you to take a chance and trust me two years ago?" She reached across her desk to pat my arm. "I'm asking the same of you now."

"I'm trying, but it feels like you're going against everything you told us to believe."

She grasped my chin, turning my face from side to side as she tsked. "You're so pretty. Men love to take advantage of a pretty face, but you already know this. Look at what Aiden did to you. If you don't learn how to exert power over men on a professional level, you will always be a silly, pretty little toy. This is making you stronger. Don't forget, unlike the other people who have let you down in the past, I'm always thinking of you."

⤬

I left Margo's office no better off. Somehow she'd once again gotten me to agree she had our best interests in mind—I even walked to the elevator believing it—but as soon as I stepped outside, that unsettled mood hovered over me again. As if I'd just been maneuvered out of my own thoughts and feelings.

A walk through River North's gallery district always cleared my head. I took in bright abstract art displayed on white brick walls, black-and-white photography of natural wonders, intricate beadwork hanging from thin wire rods. This was where I belonged.

I grabbed a latte at the Other Chicago Bean, a kitschy little coffee shop that smelled like incense, sold local art, and had polka-dot tables and chairs. It also shared a wall with the space I'd been eyeing for a few months.

At only fifteen hundred square feet, the space was a bit small for most businesses, which was likely why it hadn't been snapped up yet. It was on the corner, so windows walled three sides, and its wide-planked honey oak floors gleamed in the afternoon sun. I suspected the space might've been a book-store before it was vacated, as the exposed brick wall it shared with the coffee shop was lined with built-in shelves with enough room to display tall children's books. It wasn't huge, but the openness made the space feel larger.

"You going to stand out here all day staring at this place again?" Ava asked. She had a short cap of vibrant pink hair, three nose rings, and a tattoo of a phoenix rising out of her generous cleavage. She'd been a year ahead of me in the MFA program and was making a splash in the art world with her metalwork. "Been waiting for you to make a move on it."

This was my third trip to this location in two weeks. I should've known it wouldn't go unnoticed. "I'm still in the planning stage."

I'd been in the planning stage for two years now.

"That line got old eighteen months ago." Raised by parents who'd followed the Dead until the passing of Jerry Garcia, Ava had been born and bred into nonconformity. The exact opposite of my own building blocks, but we'd somehow be-come friends. The only one I had left from my Northwestern days. "This space isn't going to stay available forever."

"It's not big enough." Lie. It was perfect.

Already I could envision pottery and glasswork from local artists lining the shelves. Large canvases could be set up with displays all around the windows, drawing people's eyes as they passed by on the street. Cases featuring beadwork and stands with metal sculptures could be dotted all around the open floor plan. Everything I wanted and had been working toward came alive in my mind. I could see myself there, carving out a name in River North.

Panic clawed at my throat. Not yet. I needed more time. I wasn't ready for the kind of commitment it would take to run a business.

"One day you'll have to let go of your fear. If you don't, your art will suffer. You will suffer." Ava squeezed my shoulder before she went back to her studio across the street.

Every time I told myself today would be the day I'd take that next step toward my dream, self-doubt shoved me two full steps back. I wanted a place in this neighborhood. I wanted to prove I could do more than break hearts for a living. I wanted to bare my soul in colors and textures and light and be told my work was worthy and important.

A pretty young woman with silver hair smiled at me as she balanced an armload of easels while she pushed open the door to a glass and pottery studio with her back. I didn't know her, which depressed me more than the idea of failing at my nonexistent business. I used to be a fixture in this community. There had been a time when I'd spent every free moment down here connecting with other artists, sharing in the joy of creating, and looking toward the future.

That was years ago. Now I'd become comfortable working for Margo. I relied on H4H to be an outlet for whatever I couldn't put down on a canvas. I'd gotten stuck in a cycle of resentment and revenge.

And I didn't know how to find my way out again.

CHAPTER 12

Friday morning, Emma cornered me in my office. She took the chair that would soon be occupied by one Markus Cavanaugh and kicked her feet up on his glass desk. On her way into work, she'd taken the trouble to walk through the dog park and now tapped her heels until flecks of poo landed on the glossy surface. She lacked prudence that way.

"Do you think he's going to show?" Emma spun Mark's chair from side to side.

"Yes." Of course he'd show. He'd made it pretty clear how far he was willing to go to keep this job. "But I can't think about him right now. I just got a new assignment on Wednesday that I'm scheduled to launch tonight."

"I got one too." Emma's lip curled. Since her assignments lasted much longer than mine, she needed a full week to gather intel. I only needed a day or two for the simple ones, enough time to capture their interest without needing to hold it. "A pilot who used his dick to secure a job at a larger airline, then anonymously leaked nudes of the upper-management lady he was banging so she'd quit before he had to admit he'd been playing her."

"Jesus." I didn't envy Emma's job in Players, but it was cathartic for her to bring assholes like that down. "Let me guess, his kink is stewardesses?"

She tapped her nose. "They are predictable. And who will you be playing tonight?"

"Food critic for a chef." We didn't refer to targets by name with each other, only occupations. Though none of us would admit it, we didn't always enjoy hurting them. Dehumanizing our targets was a coping mechanism Margo had taught us. It made the reality of breaking a human being for pay an easier pill to swallow. Even if they deserved it. "The restaurant staff is tired of being his verbal punching bag. I did the meet-cute last night. Scored an invite to an exclusive event tonight."

"Nice work." Emma gave me a fist bump.

"Margo wants me to start training Mark by bringing him along to observe so he can see me in action."

"He's seen you in action." Emma wiggled her eyebrows.

I shoved her chair with my foot, so it went rolling back against the glass wall. "And you're the only one who knows that. What are you going to do with Nick?"

"Ditch him, I guess. Since you all vetoed murder." She took out the sanding file she carried in her small wristlet and sharpened her nails into points. "Margo wants me to train him by getting him involved in my setup so he gets accustomed to acting without a script. She wants him to play my friend, thinking it will drive the pilot crazy, questioning what kind of friends we are, how close we are, and whatnot."

If the pilot was an insecure jerk, and he definitely sounded like it, that would actually be a brilliant way to both speed up declarations of exclusivity with the pilot and train Nick. I didn't say so to Emma though. I still firmly believed Emma could handle Players on her own. She was so smart and beautiful and witty, she had Players eating out of her hand inside a month. If only she could see herself the way the rest of the world did, then maybe she wouldn't need this job anymore.

Emma left to get started on the in-depth research she'd need to win over the pilot enough to have him confessing his sins. I tucked my thin folder of material on the chef into my to-do box and headed over to Margo's office. As soon as I pushed open the door, Mark turned his head. I froze. I was supposed to have another hour to prepare for his inevitable arrival. He wore a different tweed jacket than the one he had on the day I saw him at Northwestern, because of course he had multiple tweed jackets. He probably had a dozen of them.

"I thought the men wouldn't be arriving until later today," I said.

"I called Markus in early." Margo poured us both a cup of tea. "Since you're launching your new assignment tonight, the timing is actually quite perfect."

"I was just finishing up my research." Didn't Mark still have his day job? There had to be someone else at UoC or in the Chicago area he could terrorize for an afternoon.

Margo waved a hand. "I already looked through your latest

update. It'll be brilliant. And I'm not just saying that because you don't like me interfering in your assignments. Now, off you go. Please show Markus to your joint office."

The cheeriness in her tone did nothing to alleviate my sour mood. I stepped into the hall, and the heat of Mark's body as he walked behind me made the hairs at the back of my neck stand up. With every one of his footfalls, my shoulders scrunched just a bit more. By the time we got to our office, all my nerves were tightly wound.

He moved to sit down, and I had to hide my smile as he paused at the brown crusts on his desk. Taking a tissue, he swept them into the trash. "Classy."

"A little welcome-to-the-team present." I turned my back on him and fired up my computer. "You can just meet me at the restaurant at seven."

"Which one? Shouldn't I know something about tonight?"

"Anchor Grill. The place with all the shiplap." I didn't dare look at him. The air already snapped and sizzled the moment we got near each other. I had a feeling if I faced him, he'd see the truth written under the deception. But I'd promised the girls I'd do my part.

The chef did own Anchor Grill, but he wouldn't be there. He'd just opened a new place in Lincoln Park called the Butterfly Lounge, and he'd invited every food critic in the city for a special tasting tonight, including—under a pseudonym and the lie that I'd be the new critic for the *Sun-Times*—myself.

"Is that Jethro Felango's place?"

"Friend of yours?" I peeked over my shoulder and smirked. "Why am I not surprised?"

"Not a friend." Mark leaned back in his chair as he gave me that look I so often saw from my mom. The look that suggested I was a simpleton who couldn't possibly appreciate the finer things in life. "I just make it a point to familiarize myself with up-and-coming restaurants in the area. They're a good place to network."

I rolled my eyes. "You must be the poster child for academic ass-kissers at UoC. Aside from your impressive sweater-vest and tweed jacket collection, you've also managed to perfect that snotty air of pretension without even trying. Well done."

Mark steepled his fingers. "Some of us have goals in life. We don't all live for figuring out which outfit is most likely to ruin some poor sucker in a bar."

"Go ahead and take your cheap swipes at me." I lifted my nose. "I don't need or want your approval. I know exactly who I am and what I'm capable of."

"Do you though?" He gave me a meaningful look as he rubbed his bottom lip.

Without another word, I grabbed my folder with all the info about where I'd actually be meeting the chef. I walked out the door and didn't feel an ounce of guilt over sabotaging Mark's chances with H4H before he could even get started.

※

The Butterfly Lounge was the kind of place built for tall champagne flutes and short cocktail dresses. The walls and ceiling were composed of large arching glass panels that encased a greenhouse full of butterflies of all species. The only tables belonged to the booths that ran along either side of the space. The center had been left open for socializing, and waiters carrying trays of wine, champagne, and exclusive appetizers encouraged a networking atmosphere. Its first week open it had become a hit with stockbrokers, lawyers, and respected professors. Jethro Felango had created a mingling ground for wealthy professionals.

I'd contoured my eyes to look bigger, my nose narrower, my lips thinner. I'd donned a shoulder-length black wig with fringed bangs, a tight white top, and sleek black pants with built-in butt pads. My look had changed enough that the target wouldn't be able to recognize me if he passed me on the street later on. According to Jethro's staff, our chef had quite the ugly temper when criticized. He kept it under wraps with the food critics though, and was considered something of a darling in the Chicago restaurant scene. Since I fully intended to push his buttons, this promised to be a quick evening.

Inside the restaurant, I grabbed a glass of wine and popped a lobster toast hors d'oeuvre into my mouth. Might as well take advantage of the fine dining before I ripped it to shreds. After a reasonable amount of time spent pretending to mingle—where I just stood in various circles and laughed in all the right places—I ducked into the coatroom to call Margo.

"Mark didn't show," I said as soon as she answered. "I gave him the address and have been here by myself for the last hour."

"That's funny, because—"

Before I could hear the rest of her response, my phone was plucked out of my grip. I spun around, and Mark's steely gaze settled on me. His cold expression was completely at odds with his bleached-blond wig, which looked as though it had been pieced together by dozens of discarded Barbies. I had to bite the inside of my cheek to keep it together.

"Everything is fine here. Turns out going to the wrong restaurant was my mistake," he said. He hung up and tossed my phone back to me. I fumbled to keep from dropping it. "You almost had me there."

"Is this your idea of a disguise? Was the clown shop having a discount on plastic hair?"

"I saw you at the entrance and figured I needed to go incognito too, so I slipped into Walgreens across the street and grabbed a Halloween wig. It was the best I could do on short notice without any help from you."

"How did you know it was me?" I thought I'd done a pretty good job of masking my identity, and it was an insult to my art and makeup skills that he'd recognized me so easily.

"I could pick out the way you move from a mile away."

Hmph. I crossed my arms. "How did you even get in?"

"Told the doorman I was your date. You'll have to do a lot better than lying to me about your location if you really want to shove me out of this job." He took my arm, hooking it through his. "Now, let's go work the room."

"I'm not working anything with you." I pulled out of his grip and stormed away.

His laughter at my back had me cursing him as I wound my way through all the major food critics in the city. I took my seat and the lights dimmed, illuminating the tiny fiber bulbs embedded in the greenhouse plants, giving the entire room the vibe of a bioluminescent rain forest. Mark slid into the spot across from me.

"Can you at least lose the wig?" I whispered. "You look ridiculous."

"I'm sorry, were you talking to me?" Mark looked around with mock surprise. "I thought we were still doing that thing where you pretend I don't exist."

"Never mind." It was like dealing with a child. "Just sit there and don't say anything. This should be over soon."

He mimed zipping his lips and tossing the key over his shoulder, which was just corny enough to be almost adorable. The corner of my mouth threatened to tug upward, but I kept a stern frown on my face as the first course arrived.

I took one bite of the risotto and shook my head, pushing the plate forward until it clinked against my water glass, drawing the attention of the other diners. "Bitter. Trying too hard."

The food critics sitting closest to me eyed each other, and a few others whispered to one another before jotting down notes. Years of playing the academic game had taught me some finite rules about human nature and self-proclaimed experts. Everyone in the room was afraid of being exposed as an impostor. The more vocal I became in my disdain, the more the other critics would follow my opinion or risk the accusation of an unsophisticated palate.

Mark's eyes gleamed in the luminous light as he quietly ate his risotto without a word.

Next when the roasted lamb and mint sauce came out, I repeated the one-bite process, but this time I sent the plate back with the waiter. "Tell your chef this is unacceptable. Overcooked." As soon as the waiter hustled away, I turned to the critic next to me, a short man with a turtle head and round glasses. "What a boring, uninspired menu. No new flavors here."

He dabbed at his lips with his napkin. "I quite agree."

"Looks like people are paying for the ambience, because they certainly aren't shelling out three hundred a plate for the food." I tapped my foot and checked my watch. Any moment now.

The critics began murmuring with one another, and above the din, a crash rang out from the kitchen. There it was. I'd been starting to get worried he wouldn't respond.

Jethro marched out of the kitchen. His angelic face, which had turned an impressive shade of purple, contorted with rage as he pointed a finger at me. "How dare you."

The other critics had begun to shift uncomfortably in their seats. I didn't bat an eyelash and kept a bored expression on my face. Mark rose from his seat, blue and purple light dancing off his sad excuse for a wig, as Jethro towered over me, spewing obscenities.

The moment Jethro got in my face, Mark pushed him back a full foot and stood between us. "I wouldn't come any closer if I were you. The lady is entitled to an opinion."

The threat on my behalf, while considerate, was hard to take seriously when he looked like he was auditioning for the circus.

Jethro wiped his mouth with the back of his hand. "She is here on my invitation and she disrespects me in my place of business."

I patted Mark on the shoulder. "It doesn't matter. My work here is done."

With that, we both walked out of the restaurant. Jethro couldn't see past his own anger. If he had, he might've noticed his Darling of Chicago façade crumbling around him. Critics might be an insecure group, but they stuck up for their own and wouldn't tolerate abuse from a chef. By this time tomorrow, Jethro's professional image would be in tatters.

I supposed I should've felt good about that, but for some reason I just felt empty.

CHAPTER 13

>>> ———————————————————→

Over the next week I completed a few more successful assignments. My biggest score was a dentist who referred healthy patients to a specialist for kickbacks and then fired the dental assistant who tried to expose him. After a few drinks and some light flirting, I'd managed to record him bragging about his cabin on Lake Michigan, paid for with healthy teeth. I got an up-front fee for the recording, and I'd get a portion of the money from the wrongful termination suit. Mark was supposed to join me for another night of training and observation, but he'd gone to the wrong bar. Oops.

The other girls had also ditched their male counterparts, giving them wrong locations or simply refusing to fill them in on assignments. The men had received zero training from us, and if we kept this up, we hoped they'd just quit out of frustration. So far, Margo hadn't said anything. Either this was some kind of test, or she was playing with us.

On Friday, Margo called me into her office. I'd just gotten a new H4H assignment for the following night, and I brought along my research folder since I had a feeling she wanted to give her two cents on how it should be handled. I'd listen, then politely reject her suggestions. I already had a few ideas on how I wanted to work this one.

Instead, I walked into an ambush.

Mark gave me a slow smile. From an outside perspective, it might've looked like a greeting. In reality, it was a challenge.

"Good afternoon, Margo." I took the seat next to Mark, shifting the chair away from him a few inches. Petty, but necessary, since I couldn't give him the middle finger.

"It seems like Markus and the other men have had a little trouble with training this week." Margo passed me tea, as if this were a friendly chat, but I considered sniffing it for arsenic. "They haven't been able to make it to a single assignment to train."

"What a pity." My exaggerated pout wasn't fooling anyone.

"We're having dinner tonight at the Gilded Swan. All eight Heartbreakers. My treat."

"Fancy." The Gilded Swan served French cuisine, and a dinner for nine would likely cost a month's rent. I'd never been, but I'd looked longingly at the desserts online. "Might be too hip for the professor over here."

Mark looked down at his argyle sweater-vest. "Are you saying I'm not hip?"

Margo managed to turn her choked laugh into a cough.

"I'd love to go," I said. "But I'm launching my new assignment tonight."

Mark gave me a sharp look. I might've forgotten to tell him about this one.

"All of your assignments are pushed back until tomorrow night." Margo's eyebrows drew together in annoyance, and she swept a hand over her silver swing of hair as she regained her composure. "The nonsense that's been going on ends tonight. I'm also becoming fully involved in your assignments again until you prove you aren't a child in need of babysitting."

A lead weight settled on my chest. Margo was done indulging our tantrums. We'd known it was only a matter of time before she dropped the hammer, but this was the first time she'd spoken to me like that. It both shamed and scared me. I didn't have a clue what I'd do without this job. It had been my whole world for the past two years.

I'd have to play along until I could get with the other girls and we could come up with a plan to sabotage the men in less obvious ways.

"You know the basics of my next one." I set the folder on Margo's desk. She wanted involvement, but we'd see if Mark could stomach the reality of what we did at H4H.

"I'm sure Markus would like to know too," Margo said.

I spared him half a glance before filling him in. Jesse James—yes, he'd had it legally changed—owned the Stir-Up, a honky-tonk bar in the heart of Chicago with live country music and dancing. For twenty bucks, customers could pay to have any waitress of their choice ride the mechanical bull. Jesse didn't bother to split the take with the girls forced to ride that thing upward of ten times a night, so they'd pooled their tips to teach him a lesson.

I was going to take a lot of pleasure in ripping him to shreds.

"From what I've been able to gather from the waitresses, his weaknesses are his receding hairline and the fact that he's never ridden a horse, yet fancies himself a cowboy," I said. "His father was a bit actor in some westerns. It's one of the first things he mentions to people."

Mark shifted in his chair. "How much info did you gather on me?"

"Enough," I said.

"Is the bar owner fame-hungry?" Margo asked. "Might be an angle to work."

"I don't think so. He has one of those walls for signed celebrity pictures, to show off who's been to his bar, but he never auditioned for so much as a commercial. I think he likes fame by proxy." I flipped open my folder. "Both his ex-wives were Dolly Parton look-alikes."

"You're going to need bigger boobs," Margo said.

Mark sputtered and beat on his chest as he started coughing.

"Problem?" I smiled pleasantly at him, venom dripping from every syllable.

"I don't think . . . you're . . . you shouldn't . . ." He glanced at my chest and back up, his cheeks pinkening. "Is that necessary?"

"They're called falsies, sweetie." I patted his cheek. "And yes, in some cases, they are necessary. Don't be surprised if you have to stuff a sock in your pants one day."

He swallowed hard. "Right."

He had that look in his eye. The *what the hell did I sign up for?* look. I was pretty sure I'd worn the same expression the

day Margo handed me my first assignment. It took time to de-
velop a taste for our work, and not everyone was cut out for
the ways we had to objectify ourselves in the name of revenge.

I'd learned that the more elaborate the costume, the easier it was to separate myself from the assignment, and my
background in art had given me skills in contouring, allowing
me to work repeat venues without being recognized. Falsies,
wigs, press-on nails, fake lashes, jeans with built-in butt pads,
I'd done them all. Sometimes simultaneously.

Mark paled as Margo and I went on to discuss conversation prompts, outfit choices, and how best to stage the meet-
cute. Real glamorous stuff. Margo took notes on what I'd put
in my cheat sheet, the main points I'd need to keep in mind.
She vetoed a cowboy hat, pointing out that it would smush
my hair, and it was necessary to go big there. She told Mark
to observe me from the bar for most of the evening, until I
needed to use him. She wanted me to pretend to leave the bar
with Mark while we made fun of the bar owner on our way
out the door.

After we'd gone over the plan twice more, with Margo as-
serting her opinions and me pretending to consider them, I
stood and stretched. "I need coffee."

"Me too," Mark said, looking like he just needed an excuse
to get away.

"Why don't you two go together and discuss the logistics
of tomorrow?" Margo said. "I know Markus is observing for
training purposes, but it would be nice if he could contribute.
I like this idea of using him to crush the cowboy."

His lips thinned. It hadn't escaped him that Margo had

basically referred to him as one of my props in an elaborate role-play. *Welcome to the world of objectification, Mark. Women have been enduring it for centuries.*

He followed me to the elevator. The warmth of his body was so close that, if I stopped short, he'd bump into me. His hard body would press against my back, and he'd grab me around the waist to keep me from falling, bending me over, and . . . Nope. Not having a fantasy about my sworn enemy today.

I really needed coffee.

As soon as the elevator door closed, he hit the emergency stop. This was how at least a hundred pornos started, but he didn't look like he wanted to ravish me. In fact, he looked like someone had just backed over his cat.

"Give me a minute." He ran his hands over his face. "How do you do this?"

"It's a dirty business, and it's only going to get worse."

"How?" He looked at me like I was his teacher and he was my patient student.

"Jesse James sounds like a terrible person and an even worse boss. I won't mind taking him down. But some-times . . ." My gaze traced the curve of his lips. "Sometimes you actually like your targets. But you have a job to do, and you can't have it both ways."

The air had gotten too tight. I hit the green button next to the emergency stop, and the elevator started again. His hand brushed mine, and I looked up into his stormy eyes.

"Have you liked many of your targets?" he asked.

The elevator stopped, and the doors whooshed open. "Just one."

I stepped out and hurried through the glass door. He took his time following me down to the Starbucks on the first floor of our building. While he looked over the muffins, I ordered a tall skim latte. My name had been spelled *Boinkly* on my cup. That was a new one. I took my favorite window booth and people-watched until Mark joined me. There wasn't much we had to plan for the Stir-Up, since I really didn't want him helping in any way, but I'd sit down here and drink coffee and act like I was fine.

"I think we should call a truce." Mark sat across from me with a frozen mocha and a muffin. "Though I do think you still owe me an apology."

"It's not a genuine truce if you're asking for something from me."

"Fine." He held up his palms in surrender. "No apology. Just a truce."

"Okay." I could pretend to make nice. "Truce."

"Good." He gave me a smile I hadn't seen since the night we met. Genuine and full of the kindness he didn't have to fake. "How long have you worked at H4H?"

"Two years." Two years of my life spent baiting and trapping men, and what did I have to show for it? Half a master's degree, no dating prospects, and a cat I was pretty certain was just waiting for me to die so she could feast on my remains. I had a plan for the future, but the here and now wasn't all that great. "I'm sure you won't be here once something permanent opens up at UoC."

"That ship has sailed. I'm hoping I'll be a better fit at Northwestern. I had an interview the day you saw me there."

He tilted his cup toward me. "A friend let me know a professor from the anthropology department is retiring at the end of this semester, so I jumped on it, even though I was told the process could take months and the competition is tough."

"Good old Dr. Faber." My mom would be annoyed I'd missed my opportunity, since she somehow believed I could complete an advanced degree in a field I hadn't studied by the time next semester rolled around.

"You know Dr. Faber?" His eyes narrowed.

"He's a longtime family friend. My mom is head of the psychology department, and they've been close for years. I almost got my master's in art at Northwestern." Which was akin to saying I almost won the lottery or almost cleaned my apartment. Almost was worse than nothing at all. The failure lay in the attempt. Talking about school made me itchy. Or maybe it was talking about my mom. I turned the conversation back to him. "Did you always want to be a college professor? Or do you just like teaching in general?"

"Teaching is the only thing I care about. I hate university politics." He took a sip of coffee, and I had a feeling the bitterness in his expression had nothing to do with his drink. "If I had my way, I'd teach in my old community, maybe middle school, where I could run an after-school program."

"Why don't you just do that then?" Middle school teaching jobs had to be easier to come by than assistant professor jobs with tenure tracks. "Isn't it your life?"

"You'd think." He frowned at the name on his cup. *Marc Withakay*. The baristas were in fine form today. Then he frowned at me, as if he'd just realized who he was talking to, the person who had been sabotaging him all week. "Forget I said anything. It's not nearly as dramatic as I made it sound."

"I grew up around academics. They are vicious and back-handed. They'll smile to your face while they twist a knife in your back, and if you do manage to survive, it's only because you've sliced the throats of anyone you could possibly care about in your rise to the top. Enjoy the lonely view."

He cocked an eyebrow. "Speaking from experience?"

"Yep." Eve, Eliza, and Aiden had all had a hand in my fall from grace, but I'd learned the bitter lessons best from my mom. "It's not like I need to tell you any of this."

"I understand the consequences." He stared out the window with a faraway look.

"Why are you doing it then?"

"Why do you care?"

I opened my mouth to reply and promptly shut it again when I couldn't come up with an answer that sounded reasonable or genuine.

"That's what I thought." He stood and tossed his cup in the nearby trash bin.

It wasn't like his lofty career goals were my business anyway. Though the look in his eyes stirred something in me. The resignation. I knew the feeling all too well, and I nearly reached for his hand out of a misguided sense of empathy. Which probably would've just embarrassed us both.

CHAPTER 14

M y Uber driver stopped in front of the Gilded Swan, and I managed to exit without flashing my goods to the street. The strapless plum dress I'd squeezed into left little to the imagination. Emma stood outside the restaurant, looking stunning as always in a black cocktail dress with lace trim. She had her back to Nick, who scowled in her direction. A cigarette dangled from her lips.

"Em, what the hell?" I took the cigarette out of her mouth and stomped it into the sidewalk. "You don't smoke."

Nick whipped his head in our direction. Emma took my arm and pulled me closer. "I know I don't," she whispered. "But Nick is such a health nut. It annoys him."

"Can't you find other, noncancerous ways to do that?"

"I don't inhale." She poked at the crushed cigarette with the toe of her shoe. "It doesn't matter anyway. I'm over this."

A stone sank in my stomach. I'd told her about Margo

cracking down on me with regard to training Mark, but Emma had seemed wholly unfazed by all of it, almost as if she was looking forward to the confrontation. I just hoped she wouldn't do anything she'd regret.

"We're all over this," I said. "We just need to stay united."

"No." Emma laid a hand on my shoulder. "I mean, I can't keep doing this. As soon as Margo brought in the men, it made me start thinking—" Before she could finish, Allie pulled up with Charlotte, and Charles, Liam, and Mark soon followed. "We'll talk later."

Mark had managed to dig up a suit, much to my surprise. The gray jacket he wore fitted over his broad shoulders, then tapered down to his trim waist. He'd paired it with a baby-blue shirt and a patterned tie with threads of blue and gray. He looked like the cover of a glossy magazine. I wanted to unfold him and tack him to my wall and practice French kissing.

Emma cleared her throat and nudged me. It wasn't fair that he got to walk around looking like that. He should've at least been given elongated nose hairs or a twitchy eye.

The rest of our dinner party greeted one another at the curb. Liam grabbed Charlotte's attention immediately, and she laughed at something he said, as if the two of them were in their own private world. Emma narrowed her eyes. *Uh-oh.* I waved the girls over to us, hoping to defuse the issue without involving the guys.

"You're looking cozy with your partner," Emma said to Charlotte.

"He's a funny guy. Is it a crime to laugh at jokes?" Charlotte snapped.

Even Allie did a double take. Charlotte rarely got short with anyone, and never with one of us. I bit my lip and glanced at Liam, who was watching Charlotte with his heart in his eyes. She had that kind of effect on men in general, but I hadn't expected it from this one, considering Charlotte had been telling us she'd done her part and ditched him on assignment.

"Whatever." Emma frowned but didn't push it. "Let's get this shitshow over with."

The guys followed us into the restaurant. Deep burgundy and gold silk papered the walls. Plush velvet couches around a six-foot-high fireplace formed a cozy waiting space beside the reservations desk. Gilded mirrors hung from steel wires embedded in the ceiling, and potted plants screened the tables from each other. Margo already had a table waiting in an indoor courtyard.

Mark pulled me aside before we entered the courtyard. "You look beautiful."

What was this flattery? A new tactic? "I had no idea you even owned a suit."

"I own lots of suits," he said. "They aren't my favorite, but there are times for them."

Margo would keel over from shock when she got a load of Mark, since—in her words—he'd walk into Nordstrom and walk out with a sweater-vest from the clearance rack. I personally found the Hot Professor look appealing, but I'd never say so to his face.

He slipped a loose curl behind my ear, and I shivered as his finger traced the shell. He bent closer and whispered, "Want to share an Uber when we leave?"

"What?" My eyes narrowed, even as my fingers and toes were tingling.

"Share an Uber. We live in the same neighborhood, and it's cheaper. Wouldn't you agree?" His wide-eyed innocence didn't fool me for a second.

"Fine." I put a hand on his chest, resisting the urge to curl my fingers, and pushed him back a full step. "But why do you have to make everything sound so scandalous?"

"Maybe because I like seeing you unnerved." He tucked his hands into his pockets and strolled into the dining courtyard.

I pulled myself together and shook off the annoyance. He clearly wanted me to be flustered, and I wouldn't give him the satisfaction of knowing he'd thrown me off-balance. The fake truce was still in place. My heels clicked on the brick floor as I looked for my name card. Margo had assigned us seats, as if we were in grade school, or at a wedding. Mark and I sat with Emma and Nick on one side, while Allie, Charles, Charlotte, and Liam sat across from us. Margo, of course, was at the head of the table.

Emma unfolded her napkin and set it in her lap. "What's with the dinner?"

"All in good time." Margo beckoned the waitress. "Let's have some wine first."

The waitress, Auriane, was lithe and lovely. Very French. She probably smoked thin cigarettes with long filters while she cried silent, beautiful tears on the L. When she brought out a Pinot Noir, she let Margo have the first sniff and swig before serving the rest of us. She made to leave the bottle on the table, but Margo wisely ordered two more after glancing at Emma. As I sipped my wine, I took a moment to check out the other partnerships.

Liam and Charlotte seemed comfortable around each other, but I couldn't tell if it was a close friendship or something else going on there. If I had to guess, I'd have said platonic on Charlotte's side and quiet desperation on Liam's. The way he looked at her was anything but friendly. Allie and Charles were polite to each other, but I couldn't pick up any vibes from them, good, bad, or otherwise. At best, they were indifferent. Emma and Nick both looked like they'd rather be getting root canals than sharing a meal.

I ordered *magret de canard*, which Mark informed me was duck breast. I'd never had duck before, but I liked chicken, so it was a safe enough bet. Until it came to the table bloody. Apparently the French really liked their raw meat. Auriane informed me—with undisguised judgment—that it could not be well-done and could not be served with ketchup. I picked at my potatoes and ate around the semicooked edges of the duck.

"This food might be too hip for you," Mark whispered beside me.

"Shut it, you." I bumped his arm with my elbow. "I only ever looked at their wine and dessert menu online."

"To priorities." He raised his glass.

"To hitting up McDonald's after we leave here." I clinked my glass against his.

My phone buzzed in my clutch, and I pulled it out under the table.

EM: You're going home with him???
ME: We're sharing an Uber, nosy

Margo tapped her glass with her fork, and I put my phone away. *Here we go.*

I worried about what Emma would do. She'd been hit the hardest by the partnership. While we all had walls up because we'd been burned in the past, Emma's betrayal was directly related to work. Putting her in this position was the shittiest thing Margo had ever done, and truly, that was saying something.

"I brought the eight of you here tonight to talk about this first week." Margo's serene expression faltered when she glanced at Emma, but she quickly recovered. "I know this is still new for you girls, and you might not be a hundred percent sold on this idea yet, but you'll need to get along with the men if this is going to work. If you refuse to train them, you give me no choice. I will have to let you go."

I turned my head to Emma, whose lips had gone bone white as she pinched them together, a sure sign she was trying very hard to contain all her *fucks.* I reached over Nick for her hand, and she clutched mine like a child about to get her first tetanus shot.

"We'll train them." Charlotte looked around at the three of us, her eyes shining with fear. None of us wanted to lose our job. "I know it's been a long time since we worked with men, but we can do this."

"Don't speak for me." Emma's voice was barely above a whisper, as if she didn't trust herself to go any louder or she might start screaming and never stop.

"Emma, if you'll join me at the bar. We should have more of a private chat." Margo stood, giving me a pat on the shoulder as she left. My skin crawled under her touch, even as I leaned into it.

I stood, dropping my cloth napkin over the plate of food I'd hardly touched. "I'm going to the bathroom. Allie. Charlotte."

They both followed me to the ladies' room, which was nicer than my apartment. Travertine tiles covered the floor and walls. There were also walnut-framed mirrors, fluffy white hand towels, and baskets of leafy green plants spilling out of mosaic pots.

"I don't care if you're mad at me." Charlotte pulled on the ends of her dark hair. "I said what I had to say to keep my job. And I have a confession."

"You slept with Liam?" I asked.

"No!" Charlotte's face pinkened. "It's not like that, but we're friendly. He's a nice guy. But I also think he should be at H4H."

"Wow," I said, but I didn't have any bite. Mostly, I was sick of it all. Not just the men, but of H4H in general. "I thought we agreed they didn't belong."

"Maybe they don't belong in Egos. But Grifters is a different animal. So is Cheaters." Charlotte nodded to Allie. "My job is so much easier when I have someone who can help me run recon, and honestly, I'm surprised you don't feel the same way as me, Allie."

Allie held out her hands. "Don't drag me into this."

"Don't you think your job will be easier if you have a built-in partner?" Charlotte persisted. "You wouldn't need to schedule all your targets to show up at the same restaurant anymore."

Allie frowned at the floor. "It'd be easier, yeah."

My head swiveled between Charlotte and Allie. The tension in the room squeezed at the air in my lungs. If Charlotte and Allie were out of our pact, then I had no choice but to be out as well. I needed this job. But where would that leave Emma? She'd never agree to train a man to be a Heartbreaker. Not in a million years.

All of us had been brought on by Margo because we'd been broken in some way by the very archetypes we now targeted. It wasn't just a job or a paycheck. It had also been therapy or maybe even a religious experience that allowed us to exorcise our demons. Charlotte had inherited a small fortune from her parents' estate and lost it all when she married a grifter at the tender age of twenty. It had taken Allie six months before she told any of us her story. Her ex had cheated on her with her sister and given them both chlamydia.

I had no idea how Charlotte and Allie could fold so easily.

"I get why this is hard." Charlotte turned her pleading gaze to me. "You know I do. But Liam has become a friend, and he's a huge asset to me."

"It's fine if you feel that way." She was entitled to move on, to get over whatever kept her locked in this void, but I wasn't quite as ready to let go. Not yet. "But even after two years, I still see Aiden in every one of them."

"I still see Derek too," Allie said quietly. "I haven't been with a man since him, and I don't know if I'll ever get to a point where I can believe one enough to try."

"Do you think . . . ?" Charlotte cleared her throat. "Do you think maybe working with the men, getting to know them in this controlled environment, will help?"

"Maybe?" Allie said. "It's not like we have a choice."

I didn't want to give in quite yet. At least, I didn't want to say it out loud. It felt like too much of a betrayal of everything I'd signed up for, everything Margo had sold us on, which now turned out to be nothing but a fluffy fantasy, full of vague mission statements, pink hats, and empty promises. At the end of the day, she didn't give a shit about women, but she'd found a way to commodify feminism for a while.

Turned out, her principles stretched as far as her wallet.

Leaving the girls in the bathroom, I headed back toward our table, then stopped. Margo was chatting with the guys, but Emma was nowhere to be seen. Hazarding a guess, I went outside to find her.

Emma was leaning against the building, bent over with her head between her knees. I rubbed her back. "You don't have to be okay. You don't have to train Nick, you don't have to do anything at all."

Emma stood, and I wanted to wipe away every shadow in her eyes. "Margo fired me."

"What?" My heart stopped. She couldn't do this. Emma was the soul of our team. I didn't want to do my job without her. "No. I'm fixing this right now."

"B, don't." Emma grabbed my arm to keep me from marching inside and chewing Margo out for her colossal mistake. "She wanted to make an example of me, and it's fine. I'm ready to go. Don't put your job at risk."

"What do you mean, you're ready to go?" I couldn't imagine H4H without Emma. We'd been each other's rock for two years. We'd bounced ideas off each other and commiserated over the hardest assignments.

"Do you ever think Margo is messing with us?" Emma stared out into the street. "Sometimes I picture her as a bored millionaire who doesn't actually want to run a business. She just wants to provide some kind of fucked-up therapy for women, and introducing the men is an experiment. She's changing the pattern to see how we'll respond."

I had nothing to say to that, since I'd often had the same thoughts myself. H4H did well, if my commission checks were any proof. But Margo had also handpicked her Heartbreakers and placed us in the divisions where we'd not only do well, but take pleasure in the work. We got to play out our most vengeful fantasies, over and over, in real time. It wasn't Aiden on the receiving end, but they were all Aiden in a way. All the Egos I'd taken on had cut down and belittled the women in their lives so they could feel just a little bit bigger. But lately, the work we did at H4H had begun to feel so insignificant and petty. I still needed the paychecks, but I no longer needed the revenge.

"I'm thinking about therapy." Emma lit a cigarette. She took one puff, looked at it in disgust, and stomped it out. "Actual therapy, not whatever the fuck I did for Margo."

"I still go to therapy," I said. "Not as often as I used to, but I still go."

It had been an enormous eye-opener, though my therapist didn't approve of the walls I'd erected to protect myself. I'd studied gaslighting and still couldn't recognize it when it was happening to me. The way Aiden would use silence and short replies to punish me for his transgressions. I couldn't see it—even when I was crying and begging him to talk to me because I couldn't take the icy glares while I fumbled around and tried to figure out what I'd done wrong. Abuse wasn't always raised voices or raised fists. Sometimes it was quiet and insidious. It slid inside your head and twisted your thoughts so you didn't even know your own mind anymore. I'd needed months of therapy before I could admit that.

"I didn't know you were still going to therapy." Relief shone in Emma's eyes, as if she suddenly felt a little less alone. A little less ashamed. That had been tough for me too. I'd majored in psychology for three years, yet when I'd finally called a therapist, I was embarrassed.

"Once a month. Probably should go once a week, but it got expensive and our shitty insurance won't cover it. There's no shame in going to therapy. I wish it wasn't so stigmatized, so more people could get the help they need."

"It must help some. You look . . ." She rotated her wrist as if searching for the right word. "Softer. Less unhappy than you did two years ago."

"Isn't less unhappy just happy?"

"I don't know. Is it?" Emma tilted her head as she studied me. "Is it horrible that I don't even know the difference?"

I reached for her hand. "It's not horrible at all. I think we can all be happy; we don't have to settle for less unhappy. We just have some stuff to work through first."

"Thanks." She gave me a hug. "I'm going to call a therapist tomorrow and see about getting an appointment. Lord knows I should be doing something useful with all my blood money."

"Do you want me to come home with you?"

"I'm good. I have some things I need to put together on my own tonight, but we'll talk tomorrow. And don't worry about me. This is for the best."

Her Uber driver pulled up to the curb, and just like that, Emma was gone from H4H.

CHAPTER 15

>>>———————————————————>

"Oh God. It's so good," I moaned. I couldn't get enough.

"Fuck, yeah." Mark licked his finger, his eyes rolling into the back of his head. "I have never tasted anything so amazing in my life."

"We should've skipped Margo's dinner and done this instead."

His heated gaze dropped to my lips. "You've got a little something right here." He brushed his thumb over the corner of my mouth. "Mustard."

We sat in the corner booth of McDonald's with a pile of cheeseburgers and two large fries between us. Margo had announced that Emma couldn't come to terms with the new arrangements at H4H and had decided not to stay on. Which was how she let us know she'd fired her, without actually taking responsibility. As expected, Charlotte and Allie had promised to train the men and had given them inside information on their assignments, as well as passwords to their research folders. Margo didn't waste any time taking over Nick's training.

I'd wanted to leave right away. I couldn't stand to be in the same room with Margo after what she'd done, but Mark had muttered to me that I needed to stay and put on my game face. After the way I'd treated him the past week, I hadn't expected him to be helpful, but he was right. I had no doubt Margo would make a second example out of me if need be. She had too much riding on the men succeeding.

By the time we got out of there, we were starving. Turned out, just because Mark could pronounce the French dishes didn't mean he found them appealing. He'd deposited half his food into his napkin to avoid offending Margo.

"Looks like neither one of us is hip enough for the Gilded Swan." Mark bit into his cheeseburger, making more deeply orgasmic sounds as he chewed.

"I'm okay with not being hip." I took a sip of Coke. "That restaurant was so pretentious, if it was a person it would be Gwyneth Paltrow. Did you see the way the waitress looked at me when I asked for ketchup?"

"I did." His eyes lit with humor. "It was the highlight of my evening."

I threw a fry at him. "Yet here you are, slumming it with me in McDonald's."

He caught my hand and gave it an exaggerated kiss. A joke, but still, his lips felt nice pressed against my skin. "There's no place I'd rather be."

"Aww, such a charmer." I took my hand back before it could linger in his for too long and balled up the wrapper from my third cheeseburger. I debated going in for a fourth, but that was just asking for midnight heartburn and regrets. "We should go."

The Uber driver stopped at Mark's place first, and once he got out, he leaned down on the passenger door. "Want to come up for a cup of coffee?"

This guy. So much trouble. "Did you just give me a line?"

He shrugged. "Did it work?"

"No." I grabbed the door and slammed it shut in his face. I could've sworn I still heard his laughter as the driver turned the corner on my street.

At my building, I hesitated before getting out of the car. It would be so easy to go back to Mark's place and take him up on his offer of coffee. Maybe he'd been joking . . . or maybe not. If I spent the night with him, I'd probably regret it worse than if I'd eaten that fourth cheeseburger, but still. It was a hell of a lot more tempting than spending the night alone in my apartment with my murder cat. I shook my head and went inside.

When I got on the elevator, Mr. Turner, the grandfatherly old man who lived down the hall, gave me a friendly nod. "Tea with honey."

"I'm sorry, what?"

"You're looking a little a feverish," he said. "Tea with honey will clear that right up."

The elevator stopped at the tenth floor where his lady friend lived. It made me oddly happy to know that somewhere in my building, two eighty-year-olds were getting it on like a couple of teenagers. He got off the elevator, humming a jaunty tune as he headed down the hall to get some senior action.

Feverish, indeed.

I unlocked the door to my apartment. Winnie jumped on the couch and hissed, eyes glowing in the dark as if she'd come straight out of *Pet Sematary*. I loved my cat dearly, but I occasionally considered trading her in for a poltergeist.

As soon as I went to my bedroom and pulled out a new sweater for her, she rubbed against my leg. It was one of her prettiest, pink with a rosebud print, and it would look fantastic against her black fur. We had snuggle time while I changed her; then I got her some food and went back to my studio.

The painting I'd been working on had too much light where there should've been shadows. I'd meant to capture a woman sitting at a café with a man walking away from her, leaving his wedding band on the table. But somehow over the last week, the man wanted to sit down with the woman. He wanted to hold her hand while she cried and offer support when she needed it. It was warm and hopeful, and so far outside my usual repertoire that it wouldn't fit in with my current collection.

"What do you think, Winnie?" I tried to pet her, and she swiped at my hand. That was one way to answer, I supposed.

The painting was good. It didn't match the tone of my other work, but maybe it was time to move on from sad and empty and allow other feelings to breathe. Let a little more light in.

✕

I woke up to my phone hammering against my nightstand. Seven in the morning was too early to be bothered on a Saturday. I hadn't slept well. I'd woken up in the middle of the night cranky and sexually frustrated. Even masturbation hadn't taken the edge off. I ignored the buzzing and attempted to get back to my dream where Jason Momoa had Mark's face and three arms and he was bending me over a bale of hay, but my phone went off again. Only one person could be this relentlessly annoying at this time of day.

I picked it up without looking at the screen. "Hello, Mom."

"Were you sleeping? If you were, I can call back later." If she were really willing to call back later, she would've left a voice mail like a normal person, instead of dialing me over and over until I picked up. My mom excelled at pretending to be considerate while still managing to get what she wanted.

"I'm awake now." I rubbed a hand over my forehead and came away with a piece of shredded toilet paper. Sometimes I couldn't tell if Winnie's little "gifts" were signs of affection, or a warning. "Just tell me why you called."

"I had lunch with Eve Fillion the other day. You remember her, don't you?"

Like I could forget.

"What about Eve, Mom?" I couldn't keep the exasperation out of my voice.

My mom acted like my falling-out with my friends had been my fault. If I'd just stuck to psych, we'd still have things in common. It didn't surprise me that she felt that way, since all of her so-called friendships were also transactional in nature, but it stung. Not even my own mother could be bothered to stand by me. My friends had big, impressive careers in academia. They'd moved ahead in life, while I'd fallen so far behind I wasn't worth dragging along anymore.

"She mentioned Dr. Faber's retirement, and did you know Eve applied for his position? I was rather surprised. Of course, she's still working on her double doctorate in psych and anthropology, and they'd really prefer a candidate who is finished with their schooling, but—"

I sat straight up in bed. "No."

My mom huffed at the interruption. "What on earth are you saying no to?"

"Eve doesn't deserve that position." She shouldn't be rewarded for being a shitty friend. Karma had to pull through for me at least once in my life.

"I beg to differ. She's had some setbacks, sure. But she's been a highly adept adjunct, and her last peer-reviewed article is creating quite a buzz. Who knew that the correlation between social media usage and isolation in teenagers would be so successful?"

I knew. Because that was going to be the topic of my master's thesis if I'd stuck with psych, which Eve was well aware of. "Listen to me very carefully. If you love me at all, you will use whatever evil power you wield at Northwestern to make sure Eve doesn't get that job."

"What is this nonsense? I have no sway in the anthropology department."

"You have sway everywhere. You've never been modest a day in your life, so please don't start now." Eve could not get that position. "I know you think my friends ditching me is all my fault, but she used me to make connections she never would've made on her own." She had the personality of one of those oily rags mechanics kept tucked in their back pockets.

"We all use what we can to network, Brinkley. That's not a crime." Of course she couldn't take my side in that matter. Then she'd have to admit her own faults in the Being a Decent Human department. Using people was all part of the game.

"Maybe using someone isn't a big deal to you, but in the real world, we don't think of friends as juicy husks just waiting to be sucked dry. Oh, and that article she's getting buzz for? That was going to be my thesis if I'd completed my master's. She knew it too, because we'd discussed it at length several times."

"Come again?" Now I had her attention. It was perfectly fine for my friends to use me, then toss me away like yesterday's garbage when I fell on hard times, but taking an idea I had no intention of putting into action was abhorrent. My mother was nothing if not predictable.

"Guess I can't return to school now that my big idea was stolen by someone else." I might've dropped out for good, but I could still play the dirty politics of academia.

"We'll just see about that." As much as my mom pissed me off, I respected the way she chewed through the food chain like a boss-ass shark. "I have a lunch date the week after next with some of the committee members who will be deciding between applicants. I suppose it wouldn't hurt to let a few hints drop about Eve's lack of character."

We made plans to meet next weekend. Maybe I'd figure out a way to be civil to my mom. We could call a temporary ceasefire, at least until she blocked Eve from getting that job. Better if Mark got it and got out of my way. I didn't appreciate him invading my dreams, even if he did have Jason Momoa's body and a mysterious third arm that I was pretty sure was just a terrifyingly large dick.

Since I was already up, I called Emma. "How's day one of unemployment?"

"Glorious." Her voice reminded me of Winnie stretching under the window on a sunny day. "I was supposed to have dinner with that asshole pilot tonight, but instead I'll be watching *The Good Place* and drawing up my business plan."

"What plan? Tell me." I knew Emma wanted to start her own advertising agency, but I thought it was a lot like my gallery. A big-dream, someday kind of thing.

"I'm putting every cent of my H4H money into starting my own agency. I have experience from my advertising days, and I still have contacts from JBM. Getting out from under Margo's thumb has given me so much clarity. I don't need her, and I'm better than being someone else's little revenge puppet. No offense."

"None taken," I murmured.

I barely heard her as my thoughts had already gone running. Emma was starting her own business. She was actually doing what all of us had talked about for years. I was thrilled for her, but at the same time it felt like I was being left behind again. Because there was always a voice in my head that said I wasn't good enough, smart enough, fast enough to hustle in this city. I was a pretty face. Good for breaking hearts and egos and little else.

"And if you haven't opened your gallery by next year—which you might, in which case you can ignore me—I'd love to have you on board," Emma said.

"I'm sorry." I needed to pull my head out of my ass and be a friend. "You'd want to hire me? Why? I don't have any skills."

Emma laughed, and the careless freedom of it carried through the line. "Oh my God, B. You need to stop putting yourself down. Your mother already does enough of that for the both of you. Of course you have skills. You're a damn good artist. I'd love to have someone with even a fraction of your skills helping with preliminary sketches, and you have an eye for aesthetics that most advertising majors would kill for."

"Thanks." Everyone deserved an Emma in their life. She was good for my soul.

"What's up with you and Mark?" Emma asked.

"Nothing. Why are you asking me that?" I pulled my phone back and narrowed my eyes at it, like it was a can of snakes that would erupt at any moment. "Are you messing with me?"

"I think you like him," Emma sang.

"I tolerate him. There's a huge difference," I said.

"Oh, please." I could practically hear her eyes roll through the line. "You couldn't take your eyes off him when he showed up at the Gilded Swan in that suit."

"It was weird, like fun-house mirror weird. I wasn't used to it, that's all."

"You want Marky Mark to give you those good vibrations, and you know it."

"You're the worst, and I'm hanging up now."

I tossed my phone on my bed and frowned at my reflection in the closet mirror. One day away from H4H and Emma was already thriving. I hadn't heard her that excited about anything the entire time I'd known her. Maybe there was life outside the bubble I'd been living in after all.

CHAPTER 16

Emma sent me a video clip of the office space she'd put a down payment on as I put the finishing touches on my look for the evening. I sent her back a few confetti-cannon emojis. A second later, my phone buzzed. Probably Emma wanting to give me more details.

Without looking at the screen, I answered it using my breathy, phone-sex voice: "Brinkley's House of Blow Jobs. You fuck 'em, we'll suck 'em."

"Brinkley Marie. This is your mother."

Shit. I hung up and threw my phone across the room. Why was she calling? She'd already done her obligatory call this weekend. It started buzzing again, **MOM** clearly lit up on the screen. I let it go to voice mail. She wouldn't give up that easily though. On her fourth attempt, I finally answered.

"Mom, hey. Strangest thing. I was just on the line with the phone company, and they said I've been hacked and people I don't know and have never met are now answering my calls. Can you believe it?"

"Give me a break. Do you think I was born yesterday?" Her clipped tone, laced with her ever-present disappointment, had me seriously regretting not sending her to voice mail again. "I don't care about the pranks you play with your friends. I have important business to discuss."

She always had important business to discuss. "I'm not going back to school."

"You know my opinions on that matter, but that's not why I called. It turns out, the young man you tried to make me hide from in the bushes also applied for Dr. Faber's position. Is there something I should know about him? A reason why he wouldn't be a fit candidate?"

"No, Mom." Not that she'd take my word for it. She'd probably already run a background check on Mark the moment she found out his name. "We went on a date, but he was too into academics. You know that's a sore spot for me. He's also really career-focused and passionate about his work, and my taste runs more toward underemployed losers, so I had to cut him loose. But I'm sure he's better suited for someone who shares his thirst for knowledge and his dedication to teaching."

My mom's long-winded sigh rattled in my ear. "I had hoped when you couldn't find a suitable career, you'd at least find a suitable man, but I guess that's asking too much."

"You know me. Forever ruining the promising prospects in my life. It's almost like I'm doing it on purpose. I have to go now. I'm on my way to drink too much with friends at the local biker bar. I'll probably go home with a Hells Angel and have unprotected sex." I hung up and tossed my phone on my bed.

That was as close to an apology as Mark would ever get from me.

I went to the kitchen and downed a few aspirin, rubbing my temples. I'd spent an hour getting ready for tonight, and all I wanted to do was crawl under the covers and deal with my assignment tomorrow. But the knock at my apartment door had me scrambling. Earlier, Mark and I had agreed to meet at my place and share an Uber to the Stir-Up. He'd said it seemed only fair for him to know where I lived, in case he got drunk one night and needed somewhere to throw up. Bastard.

In a last-ditch effort to avoid his judgment, I shoveled my painting supplies into my studio, threw all my coffee cups into the dishwasher without rinsing them, and gathered up my clothes and shut them in my bedroom. There. Not as neat and sparse as his apartment, but passably clean.

I flung open the door and swiped at the bead of sweat that rolled down my ample cleavage thanks to my rush. "Almost ready."

He stood in my entryway, somehow taking up more space than his physical body allowed. He wore a flannel shirt with the sleeves rolled up, revealing a light dusting of dark hair on his strong forearms. He had on cowboy boots and a pair of tight jeans that left nothing to the imagination. My throat went dry at the bulge in his pants. There would be no need for him to stuff. The man was packing just fine on his own.

A warm tingling spread through my stomach at the sight of him in my doorway looking like a farmers-market wet dream. Unfortunately, I did *not* have the same effect on him. He threw back his head and laughed so hard he had to wipe the tears from his eyes. And knowing how ridiculous I looked, I couldn't help but crack a smile in return.

I'd gone full Dolly Parton circa 1985. I'd curled and teased my hair until it stood two feet high. Stiffly sprayed feathered waves stuck to my overblushed cheeks. My sparkly blue eye shadow matched my sequin-and-fringe vest and cowgirl boots. The falsies I'd tucked into my bra made my boobs so big, the vest could barely contain them. I'd be lucky if I got through the night without one of them popping out.

"You look great." He managed to get the last shaky word out before he lost it again. "I'm not sure why you go to all this trouble though. You're a beautiful woman, charming even, when you're not being a pain in the ass. Can't you get a guy's attention without the dramatics?"

I tucked away the words *beautiful* and *charming* to be examined at length later, when I was alone and feeling sorry for myself and questioning all of my life choices. "It's not just about getting attention. I have to make the guy believe I'd be his perfect match."

"You're certainly good at that." He cleared his throat. "I mean, you've been at this for two years, so you must know what you're doing."

"Margo trained me well." As much as I hated her sometimes— a lot of the time—she'd also plucked me off the street when I'd been at my lowest and given me a purpose. Something to channel all my helpless rage into. She'd honed me into a weapon and taught me how to take pleasure in the pain of others. "The trick is making them think of me as a reflection of how they view themselves. Their egos will tell them they deserve me. It's a blow to them when they figure out they don't."

"I'm aware of how it works." He pointed at himself. "Been there, done that."

"Right. Okay, let's move it along." I shooed him, but Winnie chose that moment to leap on the couch and hiss. She was not a fan of my look for the evening.

He slammed his back against the wall. If he'd been a cartoon, he would've Kool-Aid Manned right through it. Apprehension clouded his features as he took a careful sidestep toward the door. "What the hell is that thing?"

"This is Winnie." I reached out a hand to pet her, and she took a swipe at me with her claws. "We're thinking about couples counseling."

"Why is it wearing a sweater with bananas on it?"

"Because she's a fashionista. Aren't you, *bébé?*" I smooshed Winnie's head against my falsie. She growled and bit down on the fake nipple. Bless the extra layer of protection.

"Maybe she wouldn't try to eat you if you didn't dress her up like a doll." His voice dripped with disdain.

"Doubtful." Winnie let me love on her the most when I changed her sweaters, something most cats hated, while she growled and hissed whenever I tried to pet her. I appreciated her incongruity. "I know you don't like it when animals are dressed like people, but this is our thing. It keeps our love alive."

"How do you know—" He frowned. "Never mind. Cheat sheet."

He looked around my apartment, and I toed a lacy bra I'd missed under the couch. I never had company, so I generally didn't feel the need to waste time making my place look presentable. But most of the mess today was just paint supplies, which I tended to drag along with me while I paced for inspiration.

His gaze fell on the walls I'd covered in my art. Even if I didn't have the nerve to attempt to sell them yet, I still took a lot of pride in my pieces. Each of them reminded me of how far I'd come, and how far I still had to go. They pushed me to be better.

I had a few modernist florals from my Georgia O'Keeffe days. None of them looked like vaginas. But most of my more recent work had been inspired by scenes from Chicago, though not the fun and vibrant parts of the city. I'd always felt too separate from that hopeful world of first-date butterflies and career-win celebrations. I preferred to capture old ladies feeding birds in the park who still left room on the bench for their deceased husbands, women waiting for men who never showed at a coffee shop, little girls staring in wonder at the toys they'd never be able to afford in a display window. All the sad and empty places inside me I could only touch with oils and acrylics and brush.

"These are stunning." He gave me a funny look. "You're really an artist? That wasn't part of your act?"

None of my evening with him had been an act, but telling him that would've made me vulnerable in a way I hadn't been in a long time. Pretending it had all been bullshit kept a safe distance between us and that night. Though having him view my work already made me feel more stripped-down than when I'd writhed beneath his tongue.

"Aspiring artist." An important distinction. Real artists weren't afraid to put their work out there. I pushed past him, making it clear it was time to go. "It's not a big deal."

He caught my hand. "How much of that night was real?"

All of it. "It was just an act, Mark. Yes, I paint, but it doesn't mean anything."

He moved in closer, and the air left my lungs. The scent of rain and moonlight surrounded me as he leaned against me, his hard body pinning me to the wall. My legs became jelly, even as I tilted my hips toward him. I was already wet, and he'd barely touched me. I lifted my chin and met his gaze in challenge.

"How many of your other targets know you paint?" His breath whispered across my lips. "How many know you want to open your own gallery one day?"

"Just you." I trembled from the low rumble those words made in his throat.

And that's when Winnie gave him a scathing hiss and went for his legs. He let out a strangled yell as she dug in her claws, spitting and tearing at him as she tried to shred through his jeans. My protective little guard cat.

"Get it off, get it off!" He made a grab for Winnie, but she swiped at his hand. He ran in circles trying to dislodge her, but she held tight, growling as she bit his knee. She climbed higher, and he covered his crotch with his hands as he shook his leg.

"Hold still. I can't grab her with you flailing around like that." I shook with laughter as I plucked Winnie off his thigh and set her on the back of the couch. I'd have to give her a treat for saving me from myself.

Even if I was starting to find Mark not nearly as terrible as I'd assumed when he walked into the H4H conference room, he was still the enemy. My mark of a different sort. The other girls might've gotten on board thanks to Margo's scare tactics, but I'd never forgive her for hiring my former target.

With the moment now broken, I grabbed my purse and headed out of my apartment, with Mark behind me. He kept a wary eye on my cat as I shut the door. The weight of what we'd almost done hung between us, but neither of us mentioned it as we kept a safe distance from each other. We rode down the elevator in silence and left my building.

CHAPTER 17

The Stir-Up was just as tacky as the name suggested. Bales of hay around wooden crates served as chairs and tables. An Old West–looking bar, a huge space for line dancing, and the mechanical bull made up most of the ambience. The place was packed full of the glitter-and-fringe version of urban country folk, and even with his boots and Wranglers, Mark looked woefully under-cowboyed.

"I need you to stay out of my way tonight." That came out harsher than I'd intended, but that moment in my apartment had thrown off my equilibrium. One sexy stare-down that might or might not have been an almost kiss didn't change the fact that he was still my nemesis. "You're here to observe, so grab a seat at the bar and watch me work my magic."

"By magic, do you mean the double-Ds you're currently rocking?" He gestured to my chest. "Because from where I'm standing, they're the ones doing all the work tonight."

I flipped him off, even though it was true. I'd already gotten the look from more than one cowboy hoping to ride his horse over that mountain. But I intended to focus on just one guy. I glanced back at Mark. Okay, two guys. But only one I needed to coax into my web.

A man in a neon-green fringed shirt offered me a beer, and I took it, leaving him behind without saying another word. I kept an eye on Mark as I drank. I also kept an eye on how much I drank, since I didn't want a repeat performance of the night we found out about the men joining H4H. I had a hard enough time keeping my indecent thoughts in check when I was sober.

It wasn't long before the pretty brunette with store-bought lashes who'd been nursing her drink two stools down eyed the seat between her and Mark. He gave her a casual smile. Once again, I was struck by how good-looking he could be when he wasn't glaring at me. Any moment now they'd start chatting.

But he was supposed to be training this evening, and it was his job to pay attention to my performance. Sure, I'd snapped at him and told him to stay out of my way, but that wasn't code for him to hit on other women. He wasn't an official Heartbreaker yet. And even though I wasn't supposed to be talking to him right now, it annoyed me no end that he was about to flirt with another woman after he'd been pressed against me in my apartment less than an hour ago. Not that anything had happened, or would ever happen, but still. It was insulting. He needed to focus on his training and get his jollies on his own time.

I took a long drink from my beer, set it on an empty table, and made it to the bar right as she was about to sit next to him. She had that wide-eyed, enamored look on her face. God, I sincerely hoped that wasn't how I looked at him. I'd never get the upper hand.

I snagged the stool, cutting her off before she could make her move. A cute cowboy approached the woman and asked her to dance. She tried to bob her head around my massive pile of hair to catch Mark's eye, but eventually gave up and joined the cowboy on the dance floor.

He gave me a slow clap. "Well played. You got me. Now go away and let me drink in peace while you 'work your magic,' as you say."

He did not get to dismiss me that easily. I was technically his boss.

"I'm just ordering a drink." I snagged the bartender's attention, even though I'd discarded a nearly full one moments before. "But since you seem to have forgotten your place, you're supposed to be watching me." I took the beer out of his hand as he raised it to his lips. "How are you going to observe me when you've got your eyeballs glued to another woman's chest?"

"The only chest in this place I can't keep my eyes off is yours." He poked me in the falsie and took his beer back. "And that's only because it's so big, it's taking up my entire line of sight. It's a real shame you weren't on the *Titanic*. Those things could've kept the ship afloat."

I rolled my eyes. "Just stay on task."

"Sounds to me like you might be a little jealous." He gave me a cocky smirk.

"You wish." I pushed off from the bar and went to look for Jesse James.

I kept Mark in my sights as I skirted the perimeter of the dance floor. A cowboy with a flashy hat bejeweled in rhinestones asked me to boot, scoot, and boogie. He had a sweet smile and terrible taste in clothes, my usual brand of catnip, but I had to decline. One turn on the dance floor would expose the fact that I was not the country girl I wanted my target to think I was.

I was only halfheartedly looking for Jesse though, as I had become solely focused on what Mark was doing. So far, he'd kept to himself and his beer. He caught me staring and raised his drink with a look that could only be interpreted as *I see you checking me out.*

Two women drinking Coors approached him, and I was beginning to believe that line he'd fed me about how hard it was to meet people in the city was just that. A line. This was entirely too easy for him. Or maybe it was the Wranglers. They did an impressive job of highlighting his . . . attributes. I should've just let him wear khakis and a cable-knit sweater.

They giggled and touched his arm as they talked, and I couldn't blame them. The guy oozed adorable charm. He had a way of looking at you when you talked, like he was really listening. It's probably what had made him such a good teacher and anthropologist. He focused, studied, paid attention to the details.

I'd been slowly gravitating toward them, and when it looked like he was about to get two numbers for the price of one conversation, I tapped him on the arm.

"Jesus Christ. Really?" The exasperation in his tone had me biting back a smile.

"Oh my Lord, Ryan? Is that you?" I slung an arm over Mark's shoulders as if we were old buddies. "It *is* you. I'm so happy to see you got out." I glanced at the women he'd been talking to, who looked between us in confusion. "Can you believe they gave this cutie ten years for running a pit bull fighting ring?"

The woman on the left paled. I hadn't missed the way she constantly touched the dog charm on her Pandora bracelet. "Excuse me?"

"Don't believe a word this lunatic says." Mark glared at me. "She's a cat person."

"Look at this face." I gripped his chin in my hands hard enough to give him duck lips. "How could they send such a pretty man to prison for ten years? I mean, yeah, he gets hard watching dogs tear each other apart for sport, but it's a tragedy for all womankind to lose him for that long. Don't you think?"

"A real tragedy. Well, it was nice meeting you, but we have to go. Somewhere else." The women beat a hasty retreat. They grabbed one of their friends off the dance floor, and the three of them painted a target on Mark with their eyes.

Mark clenched his beer. "You do understand that I'm not out here trolling for women. They approached me. And I'm not wearing a fancy disguise like you, so I'd really appreciate it if you'd cut me some slack. I'm still waiting to hear back from Northwestern, and the last thing I need is for my face to show up on someone's Twitter feed as the dog fighter from the bar."

"Sorry." I didn't know what was wrong with me. I was supposed to be working, not throwing a tantrum over Mark getting a few numbers. Of course the guy was going to get approached. He was hot and alone, and had a bulge for days. I glanced up to find him gazing at me in a way I found completely unsettling. "What? Why are you looking at me like that?"

"You just said you were sorry to me."

I crossed my arms. "No, I didn't."

"You did." He grinned.

Ugh. Damn it. His smug expression would be the death of me. "Who cares? It was unconscious, so it doesn't count."

"I'm counting it."

I ignored him as I grabbed my beer off the bar. "I have to work. Go find something useful to do, like figure out where my target is hiding."

"I'd rather do something else." He stood and offered me his hand. "Dance with me, Dolly."

"You are out of your mind." I didn't dance. Not regular dancing when you could sort of fake your way through it, and definitely not line dancing, where every move had to be precise or you'd ruin the whole thing. "We're not supposed to be talking yet."

"You've been talking to me all night." He crooked a finger at me. "Is there a rule saying we can't have fun at work? Your target hasn't shown up yet. If he does, I'll act like I don't know you, but for now, I want to see your moves."

"Okay, fine." When he gave me that look, it was hard to resist him. "But you don't get to critique my dancing. I'm not good and have never pretended to be."

"That's because you haven't had the right partner." He took me out on the floor and spun me around, bringing me back against him and dipping me in time to the fast beat. "Your boobs are ridiculous, it's like trying to dance with a rubber raft."

"I thought men liked this look." I used the falsies more often than not. They had a way of drawing attention to me, which made my job easier.

"I like the real ones better." He turned me around and held my hips as he bumped up against my ass. Then he spun me out again and brought us chest to chest.

The music slowed to a softer love song, and I wrapped my arms around his neck. His hands glided down to the small of my back, and he pressed me closer, or as close as I could get with two gigantic water balloons between us. He moved with an easy grace I admired. I rested my head against his chest, fitting snugly under his chin, like we'd been made to mold together in the most perfect way.

"How's it going, Chicago?" A booming voice from the stage had us breaking apart. "I'm so glad y'all came out tonight. Give it up for our band, Lone Star Riders."

The man onstage gave an exaggerated wave to the crowd. I recognized his flat face and receding hairline from my Google and Facebook searches.

I'd finally found my target.

CHAPTER 18

I had no choice but to leave Mark on the dance floor and get to work. After my target made his grand entrance, he jumped off the stage and headed to the mechanical bull. I followed, keeping far enough back to assess the situation. He collected a twenty and thumbed a button on his headset, presumably to call one of his waitresses over to take a ride. That's when I took the opportunity to bump into him, spilling my drink down the front of his shirt.

"Oh my goodness." I made a big show of pressing my hands against his chest to wipe off the beer. He wasn't a big man, but he was soft. It was like kneading dough. "I'm just so gosh-darned clumsy. Forgive me." I gave him my best cow eyes, but he wasn't looking at my face. So I wrung my hands in a way that would press my cleavage together and got on with the show. "Tell me I can make it up to you."

"I wouldn't say no to a drink from a beauty like you," he

said to my chest. "Why don't you join me in the back, so I can change my shirt."

I resisted the urge to tell him my eyes were above my neck and offered him my arm. "A handsome man wants to have a drink with clumsy ol' me? Be still, my heart." I was laying it on thick, but insecure men always needed a little extra coddling.

"That's a mighty fine accent you have there." He led me through saloon-style doors to the employees-only area. "Texas?"

I squealed. "Born and raised. I'm new to this big city, but after I finish school, I'm heading right on back to my family's horse farm."

"Horses, huh? I'm a rider myself." He leered at my chest again. If I couldn't get him to look at my face just once, he wouldn't even notice if I left the bar with Mark. "I wonder if my dad ever shot a film there. He did a few westerns."

There it was. I wondered if the staff took a shot every time he mentioned his father. Probably not. They'd be dead from alcohol poisoning by the end of the night.

"Your daddy is an actor?" I let my voice go breathy with awe as I faux-swooned. "I bet you had all kinds of adventures growing up."

"Oh yeah." He led me into a small office with horseshoes and spurs hanging on the wall. A framed photo of him and his father hung next to the labor law posters and the bar's latest health inspection. He offered me a seat. "I've hung out with Brad a few times. You know, Pitt. He's a cool guy. Clooney is too, but he's slowed on the partying."

From my research, Jesse's father had had him when he

was sixty-five and died of a heart attack five years later. Jesse had never set foot in Hollywood. He sure did like to name-drop though. I might've felt sorry for him, if he weren't such a creep.

"That's so impressive." It took a lot of skill not to sound like I was watching grass grow. "I bet it's real nice having a lot of famous friends. But it must be hard sometimes too. My momma says it can be hard for my uncle Matt to be around all them fakers in Hollywood. That's why he comes to the ranch so much."

"You got an uncle in acting, pretty girl?" Jesse took off his shirt to change into a fresh one with a cactus design. His nipples were a strange copper color, which made them look like pennies resting on his sad, pale chest. He gave me a look that asked *like what you see?* and I nearly threw up in my mouth. "What's his last name? Maybe I know him."

"McConaughey."

He choked, a bit of spit flying off his lips. "Matthew Mc-Conaughey?"

"Yeah." I blinked up at Jesse. "Have you heard of him?"

Finally that prick looked at my face. "You have the same-color eyes."

"Momma says it's a family trait." Because no one else in the world had light-blue eyes. Good grief, this one was easy. "He's helping to pay for my schooling."

"Maybe I should be the one buying you a drink." He held out his hand to help me to my feet, glancing at my chest every other word. "How long are you in the city?"

"For the next year." I pouted. "But you're the first nice person I met here." I dipped my lashes. "The first handsome one I met here too."

"Aww, you're a sweet one. What's your name?"

Took him long enough to ask. "Anna."

One of these days the men of this city would form an Annas Anonymous and swap stories about the chameleon woman who wore a thousand masks and had crushed them all beneath the weight of their own egos. It would only take Jesse a quick Google search to figure out that Matthew McConaughey didn't have a niece named Anna, but I'd put money on him wanting to believe it so bad that he wouldn't risk the disappointing truth.

We exited the employee area and headed for the bar. There were two empty stools open next to Mark. Jesse put his hands on my waist to boost me up, and I giggled. Beside me, a muscle ticked in Mark's jaw. Jesse took the other open stool and only had to lift a finger before he had two Miller Lites plunked down in front of us. Of course he had shitty taste in beer.

"A guy was complaining about the twenty he paid for Misty to ride the bull, so I gave him his money back," the bartender said. By the way his mouth turned down, he wasn't a fan of Jesse's methods either, but he had to protect himself and account for the till.

"Shoot. Forgot to call her up." Jesse tapped his headset. "Misty. Bull. Now."

A blonde with large gray eyes wearing a similar headset put down her tray of drinks on the nearest table and shot death lasers at Jesse's back. She went to the back of the bar and climbed on the bull, her expression completely flat as she rode it. But that didn't stop a group of guys from crowding around to catcall as they held up their phones to record the video.

Jesse watched her for a minute with a satisfied smile. "You ever ride a bull, Anna?"

I'd rather skinny-dip with piranhas. "No, sir. I'd fear for my lady bits."

Mark snorted into his beer. Even though he was supposed to be the silent observer, I could feel him just dying to bait me.

"That's a real shame." Jesse was back to talking to my chest. "There's nothing I love more than seeing a pretty lady up on my bull."

"Oh, well." I laughed nervously. "I'm more of a horse girl."

"I can't imagine a horse and a mechanical bull are all that different." Mark rubbed his chin, his eyes lighting with humor. I wanted to punch him.

"Who invited you into this conversation?" I asked through clenched teeth.

"Your accent is slipping," Mark said, close enough to my ear so Jesse couldn't hear. His warm breath on my neck made my skin pebble.

"I think the gentleman has a point," Jesse said. "Come on, cowgirl. Why not show all these city slickers in here how it's done?"

"Fine." I took a long swig of beer. "How hard can it be?"

Jesse's wide, pallid face reminded me of a frog with a mouthful of flies. He tapped on his headset. "Bernie, cut Misty's ride. We got a very special customer who wants a go."

At least I'd spared poor Misty from her continued torture. She shot me a grateful look as she slid off the bull, and the cheers and catcalls followed her to the swinging doors into the employee area, where I imagined the waitresses went to scream.

The bull had an aggressive papier-mâché head, and its body was just a reedy cowhide rug screwed onto a machine that would twist and buck with the press of a button. I climbed on and gripped the cool metal handle that stuck up between my legs. As soon as I gave the thumbs-up, the ride started.

It wasn't so bad. Just a smooth up and down that probably looked like sex to the pervs who gathered around the pen screaming at me to ride it hard. Jesus. No wonder Jesse had to force waitresses on this thing, with the kind of crowd who frequented the bar. Suddenly the bull whipped to the side, and I had to grip my thighs to the cowhide to keep from falling off. Then it reared back, and gravity combined with the stretchy material of my glitter vest caused one of my enormous boobs to smack me under the chin.

I flung an arm over my chest before my vest lost all pretense of holding everything in, which triggered another wave of hoots and hollers from the crowd. Through a cut in the light, I caught sight of Mark's amused expression before the bull whipped to the side again. I gripped the metal handle with both hands, and my thighs dug into the cowhide so hard I went numb between my legs. Just as the bull whipped to the other side, one of my falsies gave up the fight and popped out over the top of my bra. As if in slow motion, it went flying and landed at Jesse's feet, nipple up. Since I'd invested in high-quality silicone, it looked like a real breast, and in the dark bar, he probably couldn't tell the difference. He went ash white, swayed, and passed out cold.

I flung myself off the still-bucking bull and narrowly avoided getting sideswiped in the head. The mat around the bull was squishy, which made for a painless fall, but a difficult time standing up.

Help me, I mouthed to Mark as I held my chest, where my actual boob was too small to accommodate the cup size.

He tried to push through the crowd, but a panic had broken out. Men screamed and pointed at my errant falsie. Someone called for an ambulance for Jesse. Another yelled that the woman whose boob had been cut off needed a doctor.

It was a complete disaster.

Mark finally made it to me and gripped my waist to lift me over the bullpen railing. I elbowed my way over to Jesse, who sat up, dazed. He glanced at my falsie lying there and scrambled back. As I picked it up and stuffed it back in my bra, his eyes widened with horror.

"Technical difficulty." I tried to give him a rueful grin, but he was having none of it. The damage had been done.

"Get out." His face scrunched with rage. Small men with big egos rarely knew how to take a joke. "I don't know who you really are, but I want you out of my bar now."

"Time to go." Mark took my arm, pulling me away from the crowd who were now pointing at me and laughing. "The jig is up."

"Not so fast." I yanked out of his grip. The waitresses here had paid good money to see Jesse's ego broken, and I intended to deliver the goods. Just not the way we'd originally planned. I ran up onstage, shoving the stunned singer out of the way midsong. I grabbed the microphone, sending out a loud screech of feedback. "Attention, everyone."

Security guards tried to get through the throng of people, but the dance floor had been packed and no one wanted to miss the show.

"The guy who owns this bar calls himself Jesse James," I said. "He's never been to Hollywood, he's never ridden a horse, and he has a really small penis."

One of the band members played the sad trombone, and the entire bar erupted in laughter. One of the security guards finally made it to the front of the dance floor. He grabbed me around the waist and hauled me off the stage, but not before I caught sight of the waitresses grinning and nudging each other near the bar.

"Throw her out on her ass!" Jesse yelled from the outskirts of the bull ring.

"Calm down, Little Dick," someone called, and the crowd broke out in more laughter.

I had one last glimpse of his red face and thin lips peeled back, before the security guard pushed me out onto the sidewalk. The night hadn't gone exactly according to plan, but I had a feeling I'd have satisfied customers. I tried to call Mark, but he didn't answer his phone. He must've gotten caught in the chaos. My legs hurt, and my boobs were annoying me, so rather than wait for him to make his way outside, I grabbed a taxi and headed home.

CHAPTER 19

When my phone alarm went off on Monday morning letting me know I needed to put on some pants and head to the office, I groaned. The insides of my thighs burned. I'd woken up on Sunday to find them covered in angry purple bruises. This was all Mark's fault. "Ride the bull," he'd said. "It'll be just like riding a horse," he'd said. My legs still throbbed so bad, I strapped a couple of ice packs to my legs before I threw on a dress, shuffled out of my apartment, and took an Uber to work.

Mark chuckled as I waddled into our glass cage. "Rough weekend?"

I reached up the skirt of my dress. He raised his eyebrows and then barked out a laugh as I pulled out the ice packs and slapped them down on his desk. "You're an asshole."

"Hey, now." He bumped his knee against mine. "Did you

forget about the dog fighting? Be happy the worst I did was suggest you ride the bull."

"Don't think for a second we're even." I sat at my desk and powered up my computer. "Our truce is over."

"No, it's not." He rolled his chair over to my desk. "You won't be able to stay mad at me. You like me too much."

I lifted my chin, refusing to look at him. "In your dreams."

"Speaking of, I had an interesting one last night. Do you want to hear about it?"

I typed, not really paying attention to the words I filled into my e-mail to Margo. I'd have to delete the whole thing and start over as soon as Mark went back to his side of the office. "Let me guess, you were the bull and I rode you oh so good?"

"Yes and no. I was definitely the bull, but everything was made of papier-mâché. And I do mean everything. It was horrifying, actually. I woke up in a cold sweat, clutching my junk, thinking my balls had been turned into plaster."

I cracked a smile. *Damn it.*

"Told you that you couldn't stay mad at me." He wheeled his chair back to his desk.

I deleted my e-mail and started over. Margo wouldn't be pleased with how things had gone down at the Stir-Up. She'd wanted me to use Mark, make it seem like I left the bar with him instead, but I had a feeling the waitresses liked my methods better than hers. I typed up a report on last night's events and hit send.

Margo fired back a reply almost immediately. She wanted to see both of us in her office, ASAP. "Shit," I breathed.

"What?" Mark swiveled his chair to face me. "What's wrong?"

I turned the screen toward him. He pressed his lips together, his frown deepening as he read. "Are we in trouble?"

"I don't know." With Margo, it really could go either way.

"I hope not. You were a star last night."

I snorted. "Yeah, right."

"No, really. I loved the way you handled things at the end. I stayed for another half hour to assess the damage, and Jesse's staff revolted. The girls refused to ride the bull, and everyone is calling him Little Dick now."

"That's something, I guess," I said, feeling lighter than I had all morning. Maybe people looked down their noses at me and what I did for a living, and I didn't always feel good about it myself, but I was proud of those waitresses for standing up to their tyrant of a boss. Proud of every woman who didn't simply plaster on a smile and take the shit handed to her.

Mark stood and offered me his hand. "Ready to face the music?"

I'd never admit this out loud, but I was beginning to like this bizarre dance between us. It wasn't his fault he'd been a target, or that Margo had offered him a position, or that I had strong feelings about men working at H4H. He had plenty of reasons to hate me, yet he didn't. I annoyed and frustrated him, but he never crossed the line or treated me like shit.

Maybe it was time to give Mark a break.

He nudged me with his elbow. "I will never forget the sight of your boob flying through the air and landing at Jesse's feet. This job doesn't have many dull moments, does it?"

Then again, maybe not.

I knocked on Margo's door, and when she told us to come in, I entered her office with Mark behind me. Steaming gold-filigree cups awaited us. The tea was a good sign, but we still took our seats with our heads bowed and hands in our laps.

"Your commission for Saturday night." Margo pushed a check toward me.

I opened it, and blinked at the amount. Eight hundred fifty dollars. A hundred more than I was supposed to be paid after Margo's cut. "Is this a mistake?"

"No mistake." Margo sat back with her fingers laced on her desk. "The bartender and dishwashers all pitched in to give you a tip. Seems you went above and beyond what they'd been expecting, and they want you to know how appreciative they are."

"That was really nice. Am I going to be able to thank them?"

"I'm afraid not." Margo reached into her desk and rifled through some papers. "They need to stay anonymous and didn't even want to risk the trip for the debriefing. But that's only part of why I called you both down here."

Mark and I glanced at each other.

"I want to commend the two of you for working so well together." Margo looked up from her desk drawer and smiled. "You both went way off the rails, but this job sometimes calls for quick thinking. As long as you make the client happy, that's all that matters."

Mark tapped the side of my foot with his.

"You have a new assignment, Brinkley, not due to launch until the Saturday after next at an accounting convention. That will be Markus's last night of training. Afterward, he'll be taking on his own assignments."

I sucked in a sharp breath. I'd known it would come to this eventually, but that looming deadline threw a dark cloud over the room. In just two short weeks Mark would be out there, breaking the heart of an unsuspecting woman who'd never see him coming. Maybe she'd be the type of person who stepped on cats' tails on purpose and stole Halloween candy from little kids. Or maybe she'd be someone who was misunderstood because she had to exert dominance in a male-heavy field in order to be taken seriously. We'd never know, because it wasn't going to be Mark's job to ask anyone, not even himself, if she deserved it.

Interestingly enough, Mark didn't look thrilled by this news either. I would've thought he'd want to start earning his own money.

"I'm not sure what you want me to say." Did she expect me to buy him a cake? Emma had refused to betray her principles and was in a better place now than when she'd worked here—so why couldn't I make the same leap? Why was I so afraid of leaving this life behind?

"Trust me, it's for the best." Margo put her hand over mine, and the chill in her grip sank into my bones. This wasn't right. This hadn't ever been right. "Remember that I'm always looking out for you. Once Markus gets his first assignment, you'll be able to have a look at it. You'll see he's doing important work as well. Not all women are good women."

Margo was proof enough of that. It wasn't even about the men becoming Heartbreakers anymore; it was about all of us. What we'd all been willing to do for money.

"I was hoping to pop down to Starbucks for some coffee

before I have to get back to UoC and prep for my next class," Mark said. "If we're all set here, would you join me, Brinkley?"

"Sure." I was surprisingly steady as I rose to my feet, but I had some serious thinking to do about my role in this company and how much further I wanted to go.

"I'm probably going to be hearing from Northwestern soon," Mark said as soon as we left Margo's office. "So I'm not sure if I'll even make it to the point of taking on my own assignments, in case you're still mad about that."

"It's just a job, right?" I kept my voice light, but there was an edge to it.

He rubbed the back of his neck while we waited for the elevator to crawl up to the twenty-fourth floor. "It's just that we've come a long way these last few weeks. I like you. I like spending time with you, and I don't want anything to mess that up."

I gave him a considering look. "I guess you're okay too."

The elevator stopped on our floor, and we stepped inside. As soon as the door shut, he turned to me. "Is there a camera in here?"

"I don't think so."

"Good. There's something I've been dying to do all week." He backed me against the rail and took my mouth with his.

Holy hell. My lips parted on a breathy sigh. His tongue stroked mine like a familiar lover. No one kissed like this man. I combed my fingers through his thick hair, then gripped the back of his head to drag him closer. A deep moan rumbled in his chest. He lifted me clean off the ground and settled between my legs. Heat gathered around me as I rubbed my hips against his hard length. I could come right here, just like this.

He broke our kiss to run his tongue down the column of my neck. "I want you so fucking bad. We've got twenty more floors to go. Let me make you feel good before we hit the bottom."

"Yes." I wanted to feel good. "Touch me. Please. God. Do it now."

He grinned against my neck and pushed my dress up to my waist. Nudging my legs open wider, he thumbed my thong aside and rubbed me straight up my center. My hips moved by instinct, desperate for that friction that would bring the release I needed. "I want to taste you again. I want to feel your entire body shake while you come on my tongue."

"N-not here." I could barely think around his fingers working me, but the elevator would be stopping soon. "We shouldn't be doing this."

His fingers stilled. "Do you want me to stop?"

"No." I didn't care if the elevator doors opened and every barista in Starbucks got a free show. "Keep going. Please."

"Twelve floors." He pumped two fingers inside me while he rolled circles over my clit with his thumb. "I've been dreaming of the noises you make every night, and I need to know what you sound like when I'm making you lose your mind."

I bit my lip, but a strangled cry came out of me as I worked my hips against his fingers.

"Eight more floors. Stop fighting it." Mark nipped the soft skin between my neck and shoulder. "Come for me, Brinkley."

The sound of my name on his lips was my undoing. I cried out as the orgasm barreled through me, lighting the tips of my nerve endings. My toes tingled as heat turned to a warm glow that spread through me, relaxing all my muscles until I wasn't sure if I could stand anymore. My breath came out in short gasps.

"I love the feel of you pulsing around me." He eased his fingers out of me, and I shuddered with the aftershocks.

My first non-self-induced orgasm in two years, and I had to have it in a time crunch.

"That was . . . um . . . nice?" How did one go about thanking her coworker for elevator finger-banging? Did Hallmark make cards for such occasions?

He chuckled as he set me down. I yanked my dress back down and tried to pull myself together. The elevator dinged on the ground floor, and I wobbled on my feet.

As I exited the elevator, he grabbed my hand, pulling me back against his chest. "This isn't over between us."

"It is for this morning," I said.

I hadn't decided how to compartmentalize this new development yet. I pushed out of his embrace, flipped my hair over my shoulder, and walked ahead of him into Starbucks.

CHAPTER 20

Mark and I worked three more jobs together, where I trained and he took notes. Only one more week to go before the accounting convention—his last night of tagging along with me. After that, he'd be on his own. Breaking hearts. The thought nauseated me.

Nothing else had happened between us since the elevator. At the end of each night, I made excuses about needing to paint or go home to take care of Winnie. I didn't know why I was hesitating. I found him interesting and attractive, and I hadn't had sex in years. But the same fear that kept me from taking the leap on my gallery kept me from trying with Mark.

Saturday rolled around, which meant I had an obligation to meet with my mom. Eventually I'd learn to start bringing a flask to these lunch dates. Or earplugs. I wasn't in the mood to hear about how I'd never be satisfied unless I had a career in academia, I'd never find a man if I kept slouching, I'd never live to see retirement if I kept eating junk. But I'd promised myself I'd make an effort to avoid a fight, so I entered the psychology hall of Northwestern with my back straight and carrying an apple. If I could keep at least two of my mom's three favorite lectures at bay, I might stand a chance.

She sat in her office with Dr. Faber, and the two of them looked up as I entered.

"Mom." I set the apple on her desk. "Dr. Faber. Nice to see you."

He shook my hand with both of his. "Your mother has been telling me you might be going back to school to finish your master's."

So much for getting through the day without a fight. Maybe it was the lack of sleep, or maybe it was my growing frustration with Margo and H4H, but either way I'd had enough of being pushed into something I'd stated—over and over—I didn't want to do. "Mom has been sniffing glue in her office between classes."

"Brinkley!" My mother gave Dr. Faber an apologetic smile. "Forgive my darling daughter. She's been under a lot of stress since her boyfriend left her for another woman and her dream of being an artist hasn't taken off."

Vicious. But she hadn't clawed her way to the top of a male-dominated profession by being sweet. A year ago, a comment like that would've destroyed me. A month ago, it still would've stung. Now, I considered it an invitation for open warfare.

I picked up the apple I'd brought and took a bite, letting the sugar soothe the poison coating my tongue. "And Mom's been under a lot of stress since the last good lay she got was from the turkey baster that injected half my DNA into her fallopian tubes."

"I . . . ah." Dr. Faber pulled at the collar of his shirt. "I've clearly come at a bad time. It looks like you two have some things to sort out. It was good seeing you, Brinkley."

As soon as he left, my mom whirled on me. "Good going. Now we'll be the topic of gossip at his retirement party."

"Who cares?" I turned on my heel as we did our usual pre-lunch ritual of fighting, me walking away and her hurling the last word at my back.

"Maybe you don't care because you seem determined to throw away your entire future to be an administrative assistant at an insurance agency, of all things, but I'm trying to help you. Especially since you told me Eve took your thesis idea. If you'd let me, I could find another way for you to get back into school and pick up where you left off."

"I don't want your help." I shoved open the doors and stepped into the courtyard. Fall had come to the Northwestern campus, painting the trees and bushes in vibrant reds, oranges, and golds. "I'm doing just fine on my own."

"If you were really doing fine on your own, you'd have a career, not a job. You'd be spending your evenings with someone other than that horrid beast you dress like a—" She stopped mid-rant and put on a polite mask for a man walking through the courtyard. "Dr. Park."

"Dr. Saunders." He nodded, and continued on his way.

I took advantage of the distraction to head toward her car. By the time she caught up to me, she'd cooled off some. The drive to the café was still tense and uncomfortable, but at least she'd stopped talking.

Café Eight catered to the college crowd who wanted lighter fare than the on-campus selections offered. It specialized in vegan wraps and beet salads, but there was also a delicious white chicken chili for us meat-eaters, so I didn't mind coming here. We'd arrived early enough that we were the only people in the restaurant. We ordered our food and sat down at one of the round tables next to the chalkboard wall.

I took some chalk from a cup on the table and doodled two stick figures facing off with frowns and knives. "Look, it's us."

She did not find me amusing. "One would think, as an artist, you would've moved beyond stick figures." My mom excelled at the stiff upper lip. She must've been British in another life.

"I can do much better." I sketched a rushed replica of one of my favorite Georgia O'Keeffes. "See?"

She sighed and wiped it away with her napkin. "Must you be so crude?"

"It was a flower, you perv."

She didn't rise to the bait though. Her face had gone pale, her eyes bugging out, as she stared past me. Curious, I turned around, but I only saw an older man I didn't recognize. He didn't look like a Northwestern professor. He was missing the requisite tweed jacket with leather elbow patches.

I waved a hand in front of my mom's face. "Are you having a stroke?"

"Quiet." She clamped down on my wrist. "We need to leave here now. I'll go anywhere you want, even that atrocious hamburger place you like, if you move quickly."

"Really?" Unwilling to miss an opportunity to see my unflappable mom come unglued, I sat back with a grin. "Tell me about the guy. Here I thought you were married to behavioral science, like a psychology nun, but you surprise me."

I glanced around and examined the man who had successfully shut up my mom. Maybe I could learn a few tricks from him. He was tall, at least six foot four. His curly gray hair had a few sandy wisps hanging on for dear life, and he had a wide, friendly mouth and blue eyes. Paul Newman meets that old guy from the diabetes commercials.

"Should we go say hi?" I asked.

"Don't you dare do this to me today," Mom hissed. "We're leaving."

I was prepared to linger there for another five minutes heckling my mom, since I rarely got the pleasure, but another woman entered the restaurant—and, oh shit, I knew that woman. The last time I'd seen her, she'd been in Margo's office, complimenting me on what a good job I'd done breaking her jerk-off coworker. Mark.

"You're right, we should go." I stood, practically dragging my mom, who still clutched my wrist, out of her chair. If Selena opened her mouth to even hint about what I did for Margo, I'd never hear the end of it. My mom would hound me into the grave, and then perform a séance to awaken my spirit so she could hound me in the afterlife.

Mom's eyes narrowed as she halted. "Why do you want to leave?"

"Why do you?" Instead of making a quick escape, which we both clearly wanted to do, we got into another argument. Because this was how we functioned.

A couple more people walked into the restaurant, and one of them tapped Selena on the shoulder. University professors, judging by the sea of tweed. Her eyes locked on mine and widened. I had a feeling she didn't want to be approached by me any more than I wanted her to come over here. We had no reason to know each other, and we both wanted to keep it that way. She whispered to a guy with wire-rim glasses, and she and her party left.

But while I'd wasted time on another pointless fight with my mom, the man she'd been trying to avoid joined us. "Carolyn, it's been a long time." The man was talking to my mom, but he looked at me with a flicker of recognition. Strange. I'd never seen him in my life.

"Not long enough," my mom snapped.

I gaped at her. Usually she reserved that tone for me.

"I'm sorry." The man's expression fell. "I thought it would be okay to say hello."

"Well, it's not." Mom turned up her nose, and it was, honest to God, the first time I'd ever seen myself in her. The shock of it all made me light-headed. The bite in her tone caused a million questions to explode in my head. "We're leaving now. I'd say it was good to see you, Richard, but then we'd both know I was lying."

Mom spun on her heel and marched away. Damn, who knew she could mic-drop like that? If she wasn't . . . her, I would've been impressed with the exit. Not wanting to hang around the awkward scene a second longer, I turned to go.

I needed to get answers.

Trying to get answers from my mom proved to be futile. She refused to speak on the way back to campus. As soon as she parked, I tried one last time. "About that man in the café. Did he do something to you? If you want to drag him through the mud, I'm here for it."

"For God's sake, Brinkley. Not every man did something."

Sometimes I didn't know why I bothered. I closed my eyes and counted to ten before responding. My therapist would be proud. "Obviously that man did something terrible, since you tend to save your crotchety attitude for me."

"I didn't give you this much grief when you made me hide in the bushes from that nice interview candidate, so why can't you give me the same respect when I tell you I don't want to talk about Richard Vaden?" She got out of the car and slung her purse over her shoulder. "Thank you for lunch. I'll call you later."

Without another word, she left me standing in the parking lot alone. Which meant I had to do all my digging alone. Fortunately, being a professional Heartbreaker had its perks. Margo paid top dollar to subscribe to a website that allowed us to go through anyone's personal history, things that wouldn't normally pop up on a Google search. It was for our safety—but today, I'd use it for more nefarious purposes. I wandered over to a nearby bench and opened my browser.

Richard Vaden didn't have a criminal record. He'd previously been a professor at Northwestern, which explained how he knew my mom. He'd worked in the anthropology department under Dr. Faber, but had quit to take a position at the Field Museum, where he was now a curator. Nothing else of interest about him came up. Who even knew what my mom's deal was with him? She'd once managed to make enemies with the ducks at Diversey Harbor because they wouldn't strut for their bread crumbs.

I sat back and closed my eyes. I got so little time off, and this was how I chose to spend it? Stalking old guys online? Fully disgusted with myself, I shut down my browser and put my head in my hands. I couldn't believe I'd run into Selena. If she hadn't been with her colleagues, she could've very well exposed me to my mom. I was so tired of sneaking around and hiding what I did for a living. One of these days a former client—or worse, a former target—would recognize me in public, and I'd have no disguise to hide behind.

Maybe my mom was right, inadvertently, about how I was wasting my life. I didn't want to be a Heartbreaker forever, and ever since Margo had hired the men, I wasn't sure I even wanted to be a Heartbreaker for the rest of the year. Emma had finally made the break. She was putting all of her grand plans into action. What was stopping me from doing the same? How long would I keep holding back from making my dream a reality?

It wouldn't hurt to take one more look at the place I'd already begun to think of as my gallery. Just to see how it felt. Maybe it would finally be time for me to take a leap of my own.

I took an Uber over to River North. As soon as the driver dropped me off, I spotted a woman in her midforties locking up the place. She turned to face me, smiling with more gums than teeth. Her glasses magnified her eyes so much, they appeared as large as her lenses.

I sucked in a breath, and a prickling sensation blew through me on the Chicago wind, like fate intervening. I had enough money for a down payment. I had a collection of my own work I could sell until I was able to invite in other artists. I didn't have any excuses left.

"Hi." I approached the woman. "I'm sorry to bother you, but do you own this building?"

"I do." She dusted off her hands. "Name is Bridget. I was just doing some last-minute cleanup before a showing tonight. Are you interested?"

"I am." I peeked into the windows, and the space took my breath away all over again. The honey oak floors. The exposed brick wall. The Other Chicago Bean coffee shop right next door. I loved everything about this place. "Is there any chance you could give me a quick tour?"

"Sure thing. I'm ready to get this off my hands." Bridget unlocked the door, and the scent of fresh paint and hope filled my senses. I could feel it. This was mine.

"I'll take it," I said, then immediately clamped a hand over my mouth. I was so in love with the place, I'd forgotten to play it cool. But how cool could one play it when her dream stared her in the face? I'd already been haunting the outside of this building for weeks.

It was now or never.

Bridget eyed me with apprehension. "I'm asking for six hundred thousand, with ten percent down. Will you be able to secure funding?"

I didn't even have it in me to barter for a lower price. I'd have to shuffle my setup budget around, but the inside was nearly turnkey, perfect for what I needed. "I have the down payment now. Do you need me to forward you my bank statements?"

I did so, and once she'd confirmed I had the necessary cash, Bridget and I shook hands. She told me she still had to show the building tonight as a courtesy, but since I'd come in at full price and had the 10 percent, it was pretty much a done deal. She took my number, and we arranged to meet the next day to sign the paperwork.

I'd secured my gallery. By myself. Without help from anyone. I'd been living alone for the past two years, but for the first time, I felt like I was really *standing* on my own.

As soon as Bridget left, I hugged the front door, rubbing my cheek against the hard metal and chipped paint. The outside needed a little love. It would all be a lot of work, months before I could open, but it was mine. Every penny I'd saved, every shitty meet-cute, every day I'd dreamed had all been worth it. Even my horrendous breakup with Aiden had been worth it. If I hadn't crawled where I did then, I wouldn't have walked where I was now.

Ava poked her head out of her studio and came across the

street with a bottle of champagne. "I've been saving this for when you finally got the guts to do the thing." She popped the cork, and beautiful bubbles spilled onto the concrete. "Welcome to the neighborhood. It's about fucking time." I took a swig, and the fizz matched the feeling in my head.

I felt bold and powerful in a way I hadn't . . . maybe ever. If I could secure my gallery, I could do anything. Maybe I could even make the move I'd been wanting to since that afternoon in the elevator. Before I could talk myself out of it, I said good-bye to Ava and took an Uber over to Mark's building. I rushed up the stairs without waiting for the elevator and knocked on his door. No one answered, but I could hear the low hum of the television.

I knocked again. "I know you're in there. Something really huge happened for me today."

Insecurity set in. Maybe he didn't want me like I thought. Still, I gave it one last try. "I'm not wearing underwear and I hope you'll do that thing you did in the elevator with your fingers."

The door flung open—nothing got a guy moving faster than the promise of sex—but it wasn't Mark on the other side. A woman in her late thirties with big brown eyes stared at me with a shocked expression.

I glanced down to where she worried the wedding band on her left hand.

Beside her stood a girl who couldn't be more than twelve. She had Mark's storm-cloud eyes, which were currently aimed at me with curiosity. "Mom, what does she mean by that thing with his fingers in the elevator?"

Oh. My. God.

He had a wife. And a kid. They probably went to church and played board games and ate ice cream together straight out of the container, never knowing their adoring husband/ father had a side piece just a few blocks away. I had to get out of there.

I stumbled back. As Mark appeared in the doorway, I turned and ran.

CHAPTER 21

'd been so stupid to think Mark might be different. I'd given him a chance. I didn't give anyone a chance. His sparse apartment made sense now. He'd probably bought the place but hadn't moved in all the way. Until his family could join him, it was just his sterile little fuck pad.

"No, you don't. Not again." At the end of the hallway, Mark caught me around the waist and pulled me against him. "I don't know why you're running, but I think you owe me an explanation this time."

"Get off me, you bastard." I flung my body around and beat my fists against his chest. "You have a wife and a kid, you lying sack of dicks."

"Hold on. Slow down. What wife?" He whipped his head back toward his apartment. "Do you think . . . ?" He choked, then started laughing. "Holy shit. You do. Wow. That is some serious Oedipus shit right there."

I put my hands on my hips to keep from hitting him again. "I fail to see how this is so funny. You just got caught cheating, and your kid now knows you finger-banged me in an elevator, so good luck with the sex talk."

His eyes sparked with amusement, and I wanted to light him on fire. "I'm adding that one to the highlight reel. Though it's my sister you traumatized with an early education, not my kid."

"Oh, please." I clenched my fists. Did he really think I'd buy that bullshit? "I saw the wedding ring and the kid with your eyes. The woman who answered the door is thirty-eight at most, and you're what? Thirty-two? Did she have you when she was six?"

"Ouch." He laid a hand over his heart. "I'm only thirty, but I'll try not to take it personally since my mom will be pleased. She's actually forty-six. And since you inquired so nicely, my sister and I both got our eyes from our grandfather."

"Your mom is forty-six?"

He nodded.

"And your sister is . . . twelve?"

He nodded again.

"And that makes me a giant asshole?"

He grinned.

Jesus. I'd been terrified of boys at sixteen. I was still having distant and safe crushes on boy bands. In secret, so my friends wouldn't make fun of me. But still.

"Let me put it this way," he said. "If that was my wife in there, why isn't she out here confronting both of us right now?"

An excellent point. I sniffed and patted down his chest where I'd punched him. "I'm sorry I called you a lying sack of dicks."

"You're apologizing? On purpose?" He put a hand on my forehead. "Are you feeling all right? Or is the ground going to be cold tomorrow since hell has frozen over?"

"Stop it." I batted his hand away, but I couldn't prevent my smile. "I'm capable of admitting when I'm wrong, and in this case, I was really wrong."

"Grossly wrong." He shuddered. "Don't be surprised if I have nightmares worse than the one where I had papier-mâché balls."

I pulled at a loose thread on my sweater. I wanted to tell him about my gallery, but now that I'd made things sufficiently awkward, it would be a good time to leave. "I should let you get back to your family."

"Nah, they're just here to feed me and annoy me about the depressing lack of color in my apartment. They love nothing more than judging my bachelor life."

"I like them already."

"You would."

His mom—not wife—stepped out of the apartment and approached me. She smelled like clean cotton and oregano. "You must be Brinkley."

She knew my name? This could not be any more uncomfortable. I'd just come by here for a quickie, not family hour. "I'm so sorry for that awful faux pas at the door. I didn't know Mark had company."

"No worries." She waved it away. "I'm a nurse. I've heard it all. I'm just glad we get to meet properly. I've heard so much about you."

"Really?" I raised my eyebrows at Mark.

"She hasn't heard *that* much about you," he grumbled.

"I'll bet." I smirked.

"You should stay for dinner." His mom glanced back at the door. "I have to check on the pasta, but please. I made too much food as it is."

She hurried back inside, and Mark turned to me with a devious grin on his face.

No. No, thank you. While I seemed to lack the shame gene everyone else possessed, I'd dealt with mothers before. Not even my own seemed to care all that much for me. "I'm not staying."

"Hell yeah, you are." He slung an arm over my shoulders and pulled me against his side. "It's going to be hilarious for me and torture for you. Trust me, there is nothing I would love more than to watch you endure that—unless you're scared?"

"Excuse me?" I pushed off of him, meeting his challenging stare with one of my own. "I don't know who you think I am, but I can handle dinner with your family."

He crossed his arms over his chest. "Prove it."

Ugh. He could be so infuriating. If I walked away now, he'd have the upper hand. Again. I could not abide that. "Fine. I'll stay."

I had difficult encounters all the time. It was what I did

for a living. All I had to do was adjust my posture and change the cadence of my voice—I didn't have to really be here at all when I could easily act the part of someone else. Mark eyed me as I straightened my back and tilted my head to get into character.

"Knock it off." He squeezed my arms. "This isn't an assignment. If you think you can handle a meal with my family, you come as yourself."

"I'm not sure who I'm supposed to be." God, that sounded so sad. It was the truth though. Most people my age had started careers and families and 401(k)s, while I was moonlighting as *Jersey Shore* castoffs, low-rent Dolly Partons, and a dozen other cheap personas.

"You're a woman who loves to paint. Who dreams of something bigger, not just for her own art, but for artists all over the city." He rubbed his thumb over my bottom lip, and my whole body shivered in response. "And who drives me absolutely nuts."

I shooed his hand away to regain my balance. "That's nice, but spoiler alert: I'm actually a mess."

"I like your mess. Sometimes I think you could never be into me. Then you do something totally insane, and I think I might actually have a shot."

"Wow." I glared at him. "With lines like that, how do you manage to stay single?"

He let out a low chuckle, and tucked a lock of hair behind my ear. "By all means, keep twisting yourself into knots, trying to hate me. It's amusing."

"You're the worst." I couldn't stop myself from grinning though.

Groaning, he laid a hand over his chest. "That smile kills me. Why did you come over anyway? Not that I'm complaining."

I didn't want to get in the way of his family time, but I couldn't hold it in any longer. My heart sped up with each passing second, like the news was ready to burst out of me. "I wanted to celebrate. I made a deal on a space for my gallery."

"Are you serious?" His face lit up. "That's amazing."

"You should see it." My voice took on a dreamy quality, as if I were describing a lover or a delicious piece of chocolate. Mark laughed as he opened his front door and gestured for me to go ahead of him. "It's got gorgeous wood floors and incredible light and an exposed brick wall. I love exposed brick. It's a bit small, but a great starting point. I'm already itching to get it cleaned up. I'm meeting the owner—whoa."

It took me a few moments of dumbstruck blinking to finally absorb the sight of his apartment. Where it had once looked like a portal to the afterlife, he now had splashes of color everywhere. Warm gray and turquoise pillows adorned the white couches; a dark-walnut bookcase held a collection of novels with vibrant covers and candles in the same shade of turquoise as his throw pillows. Propped against the wall were three different kinds of metal detectors, and he had several framed prints of places I assumed he wanted to explore one day, including Pompeii and Chichén Itzá, plus one Georgia O'Keeffe.

"Interesting choice in art." I nodded at the reproduced painting of an iris.

He came up behind me. "What can I say? I'm a man who loves looking at a beautiful—"

"Markus Michael, don't you dare finish that sentence," his mom said.

"What?" He widened his eyes in innocence. "I was going to say 'flower.' What did you think I was going to say?"

"Never mind." His mom's cheeks turned red. "Dinner is almost ready. You should offer your guest a glass of wine. It's the polite thing to do."

"Yes, Mom." The exasperation in his tone made me want to laugh because it was so similar to my own when I spoke to my mom. "Red or white?" he asked me.

"White, please." I took a seat on the couch, where his sister sat on the other end with a book, picking at her black nail polish. I didn't do well with kids. But considering I'd already shared more with this one than I had with people I considered friends, I could make conversation. "What are you reading?"

She looked at me with Mark's big, cloudy eyes. "*Throwaway Girls*." She glanced at the cover. "It's by Andrea Contos."

"Cool, what's it about?"

"Murder."

Hearing that word out of the mouth of a child wasn't at all terrifying. At a complete loss, I tried to lighten the mood. "One of my favorite pastimes."

"You're funny." She didn't even crack a smile as she returned to her book.

That had gone well.

Mark returned, handing me a glass of wine as he settled into the chair. "I see you've met Kelsey. Don't mind her black clothes, gloomy expression, and penchant for books about murder. She's going through an emo phase right now."

His sister didn't even glance up at her name.

"I don't think she likes me," I whispered.

"If she bothered to acknowledge you while reading, then she likes you. I can't ever get her to talk to me when she's buried in a book."

"That's because you're annoying," Kelsey said.

"She speaks." Mark clutched his chest in relief. "It's a miracle."

Kelsey rolled her eyes, but the ghost of a smile quirked her lips.

"Dinner's on," Mark's mom called from the kitchen. She fidgeted in front of the table, waiting for the rest of us to sit first. "It's not anything fancy, just spaghetti."

"It smells wonderful, Ms. Cavanaugh." I took a seat to Mark's left, with his mom and Kelsey across from us. "Mark is lucky to have someone cook for him."

"Please, call me Rachel. And if we didn't come into the city, his fridge would have nothing but beer and ketchup packets." She gave her son a brilliant smile, so like his own.

"True." Mark grabbed the steaming bowl of pasta and meat sauce from the center and offered it to me before taking any for himself. Such manners when Mom was watching.

Kelsey pulled a couple of tortillas out of a foil wrapping and set them on her plate.

"You're not having spaghetti?" I asked.

"No, I am." She took the bowl and proceeded to dump a forkful of pasta onto a tortilla. "But it's Saturday. Saturday is Burrito Day."

"Ah, well. Can't mess with tradition."

She gazed at me with a solemn expression. "Burrito Day is nothing to joke about."

"I can see that." I took a long swallow of wine. This was why I didn't do well with kids. They intimidated the hell out of me. "Do you come to the city often?" I asked Rachel.

She nodded. "Not every Saturday, but we try for a few times a month."

"She comes under the guise of serving me a home-cooked meal, but really it's so she can sneak color into my apartment when she thinks I'm not paying attention." He gave me a wink.

"Honestly, Markus." Rachel shot a stern look at him. "You can't bring a girl home to an all-white apartment. She's going to think you'll murder her."

I choked on my wine and glanced at Mark, who was smirking into his pasta with a knowing grin. Kelsey opened her book again and proceeded to ignore us as she ate her spaghetti burritos. Conversation flowed easily enough, becoming tense for only a moment when Mark asked Rachel if she'd heard from him. I had no idea who this mysterious "him" was, but from the way she shook her head and glanced at her daughter, I didn't want to ask.

"So, Mark tells me you're an artist," Rachel said.

"Aspiring, but I'm hoping to be one day. I just secured space for a gallery."

"If you paint, you're an artist." Mark set down his wine and gave me one of his weirdly intense looks. "Don't sell yourself short or act like what you do is just a hobby."

Huh. That was exactly what I'd been doing. Maybe part of it was my mom's nagging filtering through my own thoughts, but a bigger part of it, I knew, was a form of self-preservation. If I called myself "aspiring," I never had to own the label. And if I never had to own it, I never had to let it really hurt me if I failed.

"She's an incredible artist," Mark said. "Her paintings have so much depth. It's not just images on a canvas. Looking at them makes me sad, but in a good way. Like a necessary sadness, the kind you have to feel in order to appreciate all the other emotions."

Now he'd rendered me speechless. No one had ever talked about my art that way. It was exactly what I'd been hoping to accomplish every time I sat down to paint. It was what I'd felt every time I bled my soul onto a canvas. I'd thought I was the only one who noticed.

"That's lovely." Rachel smiled at me.

"Can we go now?" Kelsey turned her big, stormy eyes on her mom. "I have book club at eight, remember?"

Rachel glanced at her phone and jumped up. "Right. Sorry. Time must've gotten away from me. It was so nice to meet you, Brinkley."

Kelsey picked up her book and managed to keep reading

while she put on her coat and shoes. That took a serious amount of skill. At the door, Mark pushed a check into his mom's hand, which she tried to push back, but he put it in her coat pocket.

She gave him a kiss on the cheek. "Put that spaghetti away. It should be cooled by now."

"I will." The exasperation in his voice was back. "I'm not a caveman."

"I know, honey. You'd just live like one if it wasn't for me." With a final wave, she put her arm around a still-reading Kelsey and guided her out the door.

I picked up my purse by the door. "I should go too."

"Stay."

I stared at the clouds in his eyes. I could see every which way he'd press me down and lift me up and bend me over in his dark gaze. Hadn't I come here for this exact reason? I could take this chance. I'd just put a down payment on my gallery. I'd proven to myself that my past would no longer hold me back from living in the now.

My phone buzzed in my purse, and I pulled it out. I had five missed calls and two messages. "Can you give me a second?"

He nodded and went back to his kitchen to put the pasta away.

With my heart in my throat, I pressed play on my voice mail. *"Hey, Brinkley. It's Bridget. I'm at my building with another couple, and they just came in above your offer. They really want to close the deal tonight. Call me back if you can go to six-fifty."*

I could go to six-fifty, she knew I could. She'd seen my bank statements. My hands shook as I skipped to the next message, left an hour after the first. *"Hi, it's Bridget again. I'm so sorry, but you haven't called me back and I can't hold out any longer. I've signed the deal with the other couple, so I'm afraid I won't be accepting your offer."*

The one night I hadn't kept my phone attached to me like an extension of my arm.

With a handful of missed calls, I'd lost my gallery.

CHAPTER 22

Nothing put a damper on your sex drive like losing something you'd finally gotten the courage to reach for. Mark had given me a long, lingering hug before I left his place the night before. Not a sexy hug, a comforting one with superior back-rubbing.

Once I got home, I'd texted Ava and let her know I wouldn't be moving into the neighborhood after all. She'd asked me if I wanted her to egg the place, which I regretfully declined. I should've made Bridget sign paperwork with me before she left. Now all I wanted to do was bury myself under the covers and brood for a day. Then I'd get up and keep working for Margo, because that was my life always.

At noon, someone knocked on my door, and I threw a shoe at it in response.

"Open up," Mark said. "I brought coffee. We're going out."

Not a chance in hell. "Go away."

I gathered up my cozy blanket and magazine, preparing to take them into my bedroom. Mark would get the hint and leave eventually.

"I also brought a coconut pecan muffin from Milk and Honey Café."

I paused. That was just mean. "Leave it at the door."

"Nope. If you want this muffin, you have to answer." I could hear the bag rattling through my paper-thin walls. "Oh no, what's that, tiny muffin? You say it's dark in this bag and you're getting cold?"

Oh my God. I'd brought this nonsense on myself by going to his apartment yesterday to . . . what? Throw myself at him? Did I really think I could do a casual hookup with a guy I was training to be a Heartbreaker? At least losing my gallery had cured me of that temporary fit of delusion. Glass half-full and all.

I dropped my magazine, threw my blanket on the back of my couch, and flung open the door, snatching the bag out of his hand.

He shook his head as he studied me. "You look awful."

"Stop. If you keep saying things like that, I might swoon so hard I'll pass out and choke on this muffin." I took a feral bite, spewing crumbs as I tore through the fluffy pecan top.

"Tragic." He flicked a crumb off his cable-knit sweater. "Luckily, you can stay your messy self for what I have planned for today, since we'll be getting dirty anyway."

"Sorry. Not in the mood this morning."

"Come on." He took my hand. "Let's go."

I looked down at my oversize sweatshirt with Bob Ross

painting happy trees and my ice cream sandwich leggings. "I'm not leaving my apartment like this."

"It won't matter. There won't be people where we're going."

Curiosity more than anything else had me grabbing my purse and locking the door behind me. I followed him to the elevator, and when we stepped out onto Michigan Avenue, he gestured to the most beat-up van I'd ever seen in my life. It was mud brown with rusted sides and a door that creaked and looked about one roll of duct tape away from falling off.

"What is that?" I asked.

"I borrowed it from a cousin. It's not fancy, but it runs." Mark gave it an affectionate pat, then looked down at his hand in disgust before wiping it on his jeans.

"You know how to drive?"

"You don't?"

I'd never learned. I'd grown up in the city, and when I was old enough for a license, my mom didn't want me zipping around in the Chicago traffic. By the time I got a place of my own, the storage and upkeep of a car in the city cost way more than taking an Uber or the L.

I peeked my head into the van and glanced at the back. One of Mark's metal detectors rested on an old flannel blanket peppered with wood chips. "Where are we going?"

"It's a surprise." He started the engine, which belched a dark cloud of smoke before settling into a steady rumble. "Buckle up."

He drove us to a public forest with a small lake outside the city. I didn't spend much time in nature. It was full of weird noises. Every time something buzzed past my ear, I jumped.

The crisp scent of the earth and fall leaves surrounded us. Away from the bitter wind of the city, I could appreciate how lovely fall could be. At least, I would've, if I weren't still throwing a personal tantrum over losing my gallery.

Mark walked along the lake with his metal detector and motioned for me to join him. "I know you're not into metal detecting, but I thought it might help take your mind off things."

When his machine started beeping, he pulled out a small shovel with a pointed tip and crouched down to begin digging. He looked like he was having the time of his life, but I couldn't understand why. He was just tossing around dirt.

"You've been here before?" His enthusiasm got the better of me. I wandered over to see what he'd picked out of the ground.

"I usually come out here on weekends after I hit the gym. It's quiet, and this smaller lake gets its water from a stream connecting to Lake Michigan, so all kinds of interesting things could wash up on the beach." When he pulled out a piece of flat metal with no real shape, he tossed it aside. "Part of a corroded beer can. They can't all be winners."

"Have you found anything good here?"

"Found this last week." He reached into his pocket and pulled out two pennies and what looked like a lump of mud.

"That's very . . . impressive?" I didn't want to hurt his feelings, but I had no idea what I was supposed to say. I tended to find more than that in the lint trap of my dryer. "It's nice to have a few extra pennies, I guess."

"These are Indian Head pennies from 1907 and 1908 and a silver button from somewhere between 1850 and 1910."

"That's marginally cooler, I suppose. How much is that all worth?"

"At least five dollars." He grinned like he'd discovered a Van Gogh in an old truck he'd bought at an estate sale. "I haven't had a find this good in a while. Do you want to try it?"

"Oh. No." I held my hands up, backing away a step. "I'm sure it lets you live out your Indiana Jones fantasies, but it's not really my thing."

"If you find any jewelry, I'll let you keep it."

Well. Since he put it that way.

He showed me how to sweep the ground, what beeps to ignore because they merely indicated iron in the soil, and how to clear away the dirt around an object. I picked through bottle tops, scrap metal, and a few rusty bobby pins.

I wiped my arm across my brow. "I get why you're so thrilled with a couple of pennies."

"Yeah?" His face lit up, as if he'd been waiting for me to understand this very fundamental part of his psyche.

"After hauling up all this junk, I'd be thrilled with the bare minimum too."

He laughed. "You're not wrong. But isn't it kind of fun?"

I surveyed where we'd been digging in the dirt like little kids. The anticipation of working the spade into the earth. Hope that it wouldn't be another bottle cap. Frustration when it turned out to be, in fact, another bottle cap. "It's okay."

"You once said the same thing about me, so I'll take it." His expression softened. "Did it at least get your mind off the gallery?"

"A little." More than a little. I hadn't thought about my gallery since I'd started tracking those little beeps on the metal detector. I rubbed my hands on my leggings, but mud had caked into my nails and the grooves of my palms. "Thank you for getting me out of my funk, and for dinner last night. Your mom is great."

His face lit up. "She's the best. Kelsey's dad recently took off, and it's been tough. He emptied Mom's bank account in the process, but she'll land on her feet. She always does."

"I can't believe she had you so young."

He tucked his hands in his pockets. "My father was eighteen and a drug addict. He had no business messing with a sixteen-year-old."

"I'm so sorry." I couldn't imagine how hard it must've been for him and how many challenges he'd had to overcome to get where he was now. "I didn't have a father growing up either. My mom picked out my better half at a sperm bank, and I always thought I was missing something, but maybe there are times when it's better not knowing."

"Maybe." He rubbed his jaw. "Though I think knowing is what pushed me so hard in school. All of my classmates had bright futures on these distant horizons. They didn't know what it would look like, but they knew it would be sunny. While I had demons chasing me. All those things I never wanted to be kept me running forward."

"Is that why you're so determined to be the distinguished professor?"

His lips thinned as he stared out at the lake, but he didn't deny it. "I like teaching. I just don't think about climbing the ranks of academia the same way you do about painting."

"What about this?" I swayed my hips as I gave the metal detector a sassy sweep across the earth. "Don't you still want to be Indiana Jones?"

"My grandfather would be disappointed I gave up that dream." A faint smile touched his lips. "I'd gotten into trouble in middle school, poor grades, drugs. He took me out to the river behind his house, handed me a metal detector, and taught me how to understand people by the objects they leave behind."

"He sounds like a wonderful man."

"He was. He would've liked you too. He had a thing for pretty girls with smart mouths." He gazed out over the water. "That afternoon changed everything for me. It made me want to study people and understand them, and it gave me something to care about, when up until that point I hadn't cared about much, especially myself."

"So why not follow that passion?" I nudged him.

He shook his head. "It's a hobby. The total on my finds in the last month might come up to ten dollars. Can't make a living doing that."

"What about teaching in a middle school? You could start a metal detecting club with kids who are looking for something. Like you were. It doesn't have to be all prestige."

He shook his head. "You don't get it."

"Try me."

"My father OD'd before I was born, and before my grandfather intervened, I was headed down the same path." His voice became detached, as if he were talking about someone else, a stranger, or an anonymous story on the news, not his own life. "My grandfather pushed hard for me to go to college. That was always the pinnacle of success for him. No one else in my family had gone, and he wanted me to be the first. He wanted me to be someone people could respect."

"And people don't respect middle school teachers?"

"Not like university professors. My grandfather thought it was impressive just to learn from them, but if I became one of them . . ." He shook his head, as if he had to mentally trudge out of a deep and murky lake. As if he could no longer separate himself from the person he talked about. "I wanted to make him proud, but I also know I'll always have something inside of me that's trying to self-destruct. And the higher the standard I hold myself to—the more I have to lose—the less likely I'll be to risk falling back into those self-destructive patterns and disappointing him."

"What if dedicating your life to climbing a slippery ladder you don't even enjoy is how you're self-destructing?"

His expression went blank. He put his emotions on lockdown, but a storm raged in his cloudy eyes. He shook his head and walked to the edge of the water.

I'd pushed him too far, and I wasn't sorry about it. The more he opened up to me, the more I realized just how wrong he was for academic life. He wasn't built for ass-kissing and backstabbing. He was worth so much more.

And I was too. I was worth more than what I'd been doing for the last few years.

I joined him on the damp sand and sat down next to him, trying not to think about how warm and solid he felt beside me as I rubbed my arms against the chilly lake air. "I know what it's like. Trying to be the exact opposite of your parents." I picked up a rock and tossed it into the water. "My mom wanted me to go into academics. I wasn't lying that first night when I said I'd been raised in the library. She always pushed me to take an interest in behavioral science, and I ended up disappointing her."

I shrugged it off, but my entire life had been a roller coaster of trying and failing to live up to her standards. If I came home with an A, she'd ask me why it wasn't an A+. When a paper I wrote in high school received state-level recognition, it was a shame it hadn't gone national. Even when I went into psych, she was disappointed that I was third in our year, though that had been infinitely more tolerable to her than my changing my major to art.

"I doubt you've disappointed her." He leaned back on his hands. "She must be proud of your gallery plans."

"I didn't even tell her I'd made the offer. Although now I'm glad I didn't. She hates my paintings—or at least, hates the idea of them. She's never actually seen them."

"She's never been to your apartment?" He gave me an incredulous look.

"No. We only see each other for weekly lunches, and even then we meet at her office." She did that on purpose. She seemed to hope I'd skip over to the admissions building one day and reenroll. "That's just the way things are between us. . . . Are you familiar with Harlow's monkey experiment?"

At least all those psych classes had been good for something. They'd helped me see how screwed up my relationship with my mom was. They'd also explained why I constantly sought validation from people like Aiden, Eliza, and Eve.

The problems I had with my mom hit home the hardest when I learned about Harry Harlow in one of my social cognition classes. He'd set up two surrogate monkey mothers, one made of wire mesh that was cold and uncomfortable to the touch but provided food and other basic physiological needs. The other was a terry-cloth towel mother who aesthetically gave love and comfort, but no food. He found that baby monkeys would cling to the terry-cloth mom, even though she didn't supply nourishment.

"Are you saying you were raised by the wire-mesh monkey?" he asked.

"Essentially." I pulled my knees up to my chest. "We used to tolerate each other, but when I dropped out, we started a fight that hasn't really ended."

"If you don't mind me asking, why did you drop out?" His hand brushed mine, sending little tingles up my arm. "Weren't you pretty close to having your master's?"

"I had an ugly breakup that kind of sent me spiraling." It was strange, mentioning that time in my life to someone who hadn't known me when I'd gone through the worst of it. Margo liked to remind me, and often, that I was damaged, but Mark didn't see me that way. And I didn't see myself that way either. Not anymore.

"Tell me about it."

"Why do you want to know?" My shoulders hunched instinctively.

I really didn't want to rehash all my shitty Aiden memories. Like the time he'd made me drive myself to the hospital when I was having a stress-induced panic attack, because he had to study for midterms. Or that time he didn't talk to me for a week because I bought him regular M&M's instead of the peanut ones.

Not only did I feel foolish for giving Aiden so much of my time, but there would be no turning back once I shared that ugly side of me. Not many people stuck by me once they got a look at my baggage. Not even my own mother.

"I want to know the parts of you I haven't seen yet. And I don't mean that in a naked kind of way. Well, mostly not." Mark grinned at me, and I got a glimpse of the wild boy just under the surface of all that college professor polish.

"Cute." I rolled my eyes. "Aiden, my ex, wasn't very nice."

Mark's expression darkened. "What do you mean?"

"He was smart, top of the class in psych." Last I'd heard, he'd opened his own practice and was doing quite well, despite that black magic spell I'd paid to have put on him during a moment of weakness. "But he also had an ego. He was the type of guy who had to make himself feel more important by stepping on other people, and I was his favorite target."

Mark shook his head. "You eventually broke it off with him though?"

Here's where all my ugly lived. "Only after he cheated. I let it go on for three years before that, just taking the insults. About me or my mannerisms, the way I wore my hair, the way I dressed, my art, my grades, the way I chewed my food. Nothing was off-limits. Every day, for three years, he'd strip away little pieces of my self-worth—and still I wanted him to love me. I begged for it."

"That's not your fault. None of that was. Him cutting you down, it's only because he was a small and insecure man. He knew he didn't deserve you."

He laid his hand on top of mine and squeezed it. It felt nice.

Maybe, just for a little while, I could leave everything that had happened between us behind in the city. I could take the comfort offered and just let it be without overthinking it.

"Anyway, that's why I dropped out of school," I said. "My relationship wrecked me, but the longer I stayed away, the more I realized I didn't want that life. I'd only been trying to win approval from my mom. . . . Then Margo approached me at the restaurant where I'd just given my apartment key to Aiden. I didn't start working for her right away. A few other things happened in the process." Like all of my friends ditching me because watching me fall apart made them uncomfortable.

"Did you ever have reservations about working for Margo?"

Yes. But I'd bought Margo's bullshit about what H4H was supposed to represent. It made me feel good to take control of my interactions with men, even if they were staged, even if they hurt real people. For all the Aiden purging I thought I'd done, he had still managed to exert control over my life. I didn't owe him a damned thing, but I couldn't begin to explain why I'd insisted on a payback he'd never see or feel.

"I used to think I was helping women and helping myself by bringing down other people's Aidens. But it's not about him anymore." It hadn't been for a while, if I was being honest with myself. "I stayed to save for my gallery, but I lost that, so now I don't know what's next for me. I guess I'm stuck at H4H."

"Why are you stuck? You had a setback on your gallery, it happens. It's not like you'd really invested anything. You can find another building."

I pulled my hand out from under his. The quiet, comforting moment between us was over. How dare he wave off losing my gallery like it wasn't a big deal? It wasn't just the rejection on top of more rejection, or feeling that I never got anything right, or trying to find another place in a neighborhood that wasn't exactly brimming with storefronts in my price range. It was bigger than all of that. For a moment, I'd believed I could be more than a Heartbreaker.

But who cared about my problems, right? My gallery was just a silly little pipe dream, so it didn't really matter where I opened it. I was never going to have an impressive university career, and in his eyes, everything else was insignificant. That's the way it was with all academics. I didn't know why I'd thought for a second that he'd understand.

"It's so easy for you to blow off my loss when you don't take any risks." I jumped to my feet and paced in front of the lake. He'd touched a nerve, and much like my personal mascot, Winnie, I spit and hissed when I got backed into a corner. "You don't know what it feels like when you put your heart on the line and fail, because you don't put anything on the line. You take the safe and dependable route so you can feel like you've accomplished something without having to feel anything at all."

He stood and strode over to me. "You tried one serious relationship and haven't dated since it ended. You've had one job since you left college that makes you feel like shit. You made an offer on one gallery, and when you lost it, you're ready to just throw in the towel. So, remind me again, what risks do you take?"

"At least I tried. Which is more than I can say for you." I turned and made my way to the passenger door of the van and crossed my arms, making it more than obvious it was time to go.

"You're a trier, all right. That's why you run every time things get hard."

This was why I didn't open myself up. Things had been perfectly fine before I pulled out all my broken toys and asked if he wanted to play. "Fuck you, Mark."

He rested his arm above his head on the van. "If you want to say fuck you and run again because you're uncomfortable with the truth, because things aren't always easy, fine, but I'm done chasing after you. Whatever this thing is between us, it's over."

I lifted my chin. "Can't end what never began."

A spark of hurt leaped into his eyes, and I turned my head. I didn't want to deal with any of this. All I wanted was to bury my head under my covers, like I'd planned to do before he showed up with his pity muffin.

Better to walk away now and save myself a whole lot of heartache down the road.

CHAPTER 23

On Friday morning, I decided to stay home to prep for my weekend assignment. It was supposed to be Mark's last night of training with me. I didn't know if he would be there, but I'd rather have chewed off my own arm than text him to ask. We hadn't talked since our fight at the lake, and he hadn't shown up for the minor assignment I worked on Wednesday night. If he was going into the office, it was on the days I was working from home.

I spent most of the week replaying the fight in my mind, but I wasn't going to cave and call him. I wasn't that person anymore. The only reasonable course of action was to let it eat away at me instead.

His assessment of me had been so wrong. Maybe I didn't take a lot of risks, but it was hard to justify continually putting myself out there when I always ended up on the losing side. Case in point: letting him in had been a risk, and that had turned out to be a huge mistake. And if the last few days had felt a little colder and a little emptier, well, that wasn't because of the absence of Mark. That was just my life.

Unable to concentrate, I dumped all my notes on the accountant assignment on my couch and went straight into my studio. What I really needed to do was paint. Something new into which I could channel all my conflicting emotions. A blank canvas had always allowed me to say the things I'd never been able to put into words.

Leaving the café scene on the easel, I put a blank canvas on the floor and mixed together stormy grays and twilight blues with cracks of electric yellow. The scene came to me so clearly—a lone house with chipped paint on a barren field. The front yard held a single tree, leafless, with crooked limbs reaching toward a violent sky.

I worked for four hours straight. Paint streaked my face and clumped in my hair, and my hand ached from how tight I'd been clutching my brush. The result didn't satisfy me though. I still had a million conflicting feelings about my fight with Mark, all of them ramming against each other. I wanted to both call him and block his number, apologize and make him grovel, fight until it was all out of my system and give him the silent treatment while I stewed in my resentment.

Most of all, I wanted him to understand that I *had* invested in my gallery. Maybe not in money, but in hope, and between the two, hope was a lot harder to come by. The fact that he couldn't see that meant he'd never really seen me.

My phone buzzed, and I pushed my hair out of my face,

dragging a streak of midnight-blue paint across my forehead. It was an e-mail from the background check company I used for higher-profile targets. Whenever I did a basic search on someone, the company would then dig up even more personal information, such as dating history, photos uploaded to the cloud, and large monetary transactions. I'd get an alert about a week later, the main reason why some of my bigger assignments took more time to execute.

This alert was for the esteemed curator Dr. Richard Vaden. I'd almost forgotten I'd looked him up. Curiosity more than anything made me open the e-mail, and I nearly dropped my phone when I read what it contained. Nearly ten years ago, he had sent a wire transfer for $200,000 to Dr. Carolyn Saunders.

I closed my e-mail and immediately called my mom. It went to voice mail. "Call me as soon as you get this message. I have some questions about Richard Vaden."

Fifteen minutes later, I called back. This time she sent me straight to voice mail. She was avoiding me. Forget about texting. The only thing I could do to get hold of her was show up unannounced. She hated that, which only made me want to do it more.

In the courtyard, I ran into Dr. Faber. I wanted to confront my mom before she left her office for the day, but it would have been rude not to stop and say hello. "Almost time," I said. "Are you ready to leave all this behind?"

"I think so. I'd like to travel." His wrinkled eyes took on a distant look. "I'd also like to find a nice girlfriend. My career hasn't given me a lot of time to do that, but I think now is a good time to find someone to build a life with."

Sure. Seventy seemed about the right age to settle down and start a family. I gave him a pat on the arm. "She'll be a lucky lady. Have you heard any news on your replacement?"

"As a matter of fact, it was just decided this afternoon." He rubbed his chin. "Can't remember the name. They'll be getting a call though."

I didn't push him for more information. Mark would find out soon enough, and I wasn't sure which outcome to keep my fingers crossed for. I didn't want him to continue at H4H, but even if he left, it wouldn't solve my growing issues with working for Margo. On the other hand, while I was still pissed at him, he deserved better than this academic life. He was worth so much more than the weight of his past.

I headed down the psychology hall to my mom's office. Outside the door of another professor, a student was camped out like he was waiting for a discount TV on Black Friday, a paper clutched in his hands. I recognized the bloodshot eyes and nervous tic. I didn't miss the days of arguing for a higher grade one bit. Despite my mom's best efforts, I'd never been cut out for school. The struggle to maintain my GPA, the pressure during exams, the politics of impressing my professors—it had all started to feel like a game I could never win.

Without knocking, I flung open the door to my mother's office. A young student who couldn't have been more than nineteen jumped to her feet, spilling the contents of her backpack on the floor. Her bottom lip trembled.

"I'm so sorry." I got down on my knees and helped her scoop up her stuff. "I didn't know she had office hours right now."

"I don't." At the frost in my mom's tone, the girl let out a squeak. She shoveled the rest of her books and papers into her backpack and hustled out of the room.

"What did you do to her?" I asked.

"She was trying to hand in a paper late. I don't have time to grade outside my schedule just because she wanted to party at a frat house instead of buckling down to do her assignment over the weekend." My mom had a reputation for being ruthless, but it was always a little terrifying to see it in action.

"If you want your students to like you, maybe you should loosen the reins a little, give them some room to breathe. Who knows? They might even end up liking the subject too."

Her nostrils flared as she stacked a group of papers into neat little piles. "Do I come to your office and tell you how to file things?"

Point taken. "I didn't come here to argue."

"Really? Because I can't recall the last time you came here for another reason."

I closed my eyes. *Breathe. Count to ten. Don't rise to the bait.* "I came because you didn't answer my calls."

"I'm a very busy woman. Midterms are coming up, and I have to rewrite the exam because someone leaked the latest one online. I have papers to grade. Important functions to attend. I didn't know my adult daughter needed so much coddling."

She knew where and how to cut the deepest. "I'm not here because I want you to pat me on the head and tell me I'm pretty. I want to talk about Richard Vaden. Specifically, why he paid you two hundred thousand dollars."

My mom's angular face paled. "How did you find out about that?"

"It doesn't matter how I found out. I want an explanation."

"Absolutely not." She ground her teeth so hard, I was surprised she didn't wear them down to stumps. "That subject is off-limits." She put on her reading glasses and opened the textbook next to her computer. "If you'll excuse me, I only have a few days to write this exam for approval and I don't have time to indulge your nosiness."

Her refusal to answer any questions before I could even ask them put me on edge. What was she hiding? It must've been bad if she thought I would judge her, considering how she viewed me.

"Fine. If you don't want to discuss this, I guess I'll head over to the Field Museum. Maybe Richard Vaden would be open for a little chat."

She slammed her book shut. "You want to drag up my painful history and force me to relive it? Fine. Let's. But I will only speak of this once. I don't want to answer any questions, and you will not bring this up again. Understood?"

I nodded and sat down, resting my chin in my hands.

"I had a fling with Richard when I was an undergrad student and he was a teacher's assistant, before he became a professor. We didn't end on good terms. He's the reason I opted for a sperm donor when I decided it was time to have a child. You know my father couldn't stand scandal, so he paid Richard a large sum of money to leave Northwestern and keep our affair quiet. I never knew about it, but after my father died, Richard's guilty conscience got to him and he gave the money back."

So, Richard had been her Aiden. Still didn't explain the caginess. "That's it? I had to twist your arm for that?"

"It could've been bad for my career." She sniffed. "People would've questioned whether I'd gotten my position fairly, or if I had to sleep my way to the top. Fortunately, no one found out. Richard went on to marry shortly afterward and eventually took over as curator of anthropology at the Field Museum."

Her definition of scandal and mine clearly differed. She needed to read TMZ if she really wanted to see some doozies. "No offense, but I've seen more drama on the Home Shopping Network. He was a TA. Big deal. At least it was a fellow student and not one of your professors. Now, that would've been salacious."

"Yes. Well. Like I said, we didn't end on good terms, but I'd rather not discuss it any further." She grabbed a stack of papers. "Can I get back to work? Or do you have more irrelevant nonsense to pester me about when I'm busy?"

I rolled my eyes and stood. "Good luck with your exam writing. I hope it's tough enough to fail half your class."

"That's not what I—"

I shut her door, cutting off the rest of her sentence. Stopping by her office had been a total bust. Of course she didn't have any deep dark secrets I'd find in a worn leather journal after her passing. This was my mom. The woman whose biggest risks included buying an off-brand jigsaw puzzle and drinking from a public water fountain.

As soon as I stepped into the courtyard, my phone buzzed.

MARK: Meet me on the corner of May and Carroll. I have something for you.

I hadn't heard from him in five days, and that was the text he sent me? Not fully trusting it, I screenshot his text and sent it to Emma. Location of his murder warehouse?

EM: He has something for you? 50 bucks says it's his dick.

I sent her back the middle finger emoji. Clearly I was on my own here. No big deal. Regardless of what he thought, I could take risks. I wasn't going to end up like my mom.

I pulled up the Uber app and let them know I needed a ride to May and Carroll.

CHAPTER 24

I got out on a busy street next to a cute little photography studio and a gothic gift shop that specialized in the macabre. Mark strolled up to me with his hands in his pockets, acting all cool and casual. The exact opposite of what brewed inside me. My breath caught in my throat as he raised his gaze to meet mine. A thousand unsaid things swirled in his eyes. I hated how much I'd missed seeing that pouty lip turned down in a frown, the arch of his brow that always seemed to be challenging me. I simultaneously wanted to kiss him and shove him away, but I did neither. Because I was exactly the kind of coward he believed me to be.

"Where's the big surprise?" I tore my gaze away from him, faking nonchalance as I glanced at the gift shop. "I've been to Tilly's House of Horrors. It's a sweet little place, but I'm all stocked up on shrunken heads at the moment."

"I didn't ask you to come down here for the gift shop." He

turned to the empty space tucked against Tilly's, its ridged metal exterior giving it a warehouse feel. He punched in a code on a box hanging from the door and took out a key. "I wanted you to see this."

Sheetrock covered the interior walls, making it appear half-finished, but a fresh coat of paint would clean it up. It had concrete floors with a few stains, which could be sanded down or painted, and I couldn't get enough of the exposed ductwork. Its massive windows let in lots of light, and the air smelled like homemade bread and something herbal. It might've been a bakery run by potheads before it was abandoned. A few days of open windows would air the place out.

I didn't dare wonder if this space was for sale. It was empty, but I'd already had my heart broken this week. I needed time to lick my wounds. Like months. Maybe a year.

Feigning disinterest, I crossed my arms. "Is this where you take all the girls foolish enough to believe you're a mild-mannered professor?"

"Funny." Mark stood behind me, close enough for me to be tempted to lean into the warmth of his body. "I think it can be your gallery."

"No." The word flew out of my mouth by instinct as I spun around. "You're not serious."

His grin was so large, it took up half his face. "I did a little poking around, and this space is up for sale by the owner. I thought it suited you."

"It's nice." It was better than nice, but I'd learned to keep my cards close. "How much?"

"Five hundred thousand. They want twenty percent down."

"Oh." That's why I didn't get my hopes up. Wanting was a dangerous thing. "I don't have enough. That's okay though."

"It's been on the market for three months. I'm sure the owner could work out something with you, maybe go to ten percent down?"

"I'm not interested." Even though I'd mentally started choosing which of my paintings I'd bring in and where I'd put them. I couldn't shut that part of my brain off. "But I bet you knew that already. I'm not a risk-taker, remember?"

"About that." Mark rubbed the back of his neck. "I said some things I didn't mean on Sunday, or rather, I meant them, but I'm sorry they hurt. This is my way of apologizing."

His sort-of-not-really apology put my back up. "By pushing a gallery on me after I told you I didn't want to try again anytime soon? I'm not sure if you're trying to annoy me, or if it really is that effortless for you."

"What are you afraid of?" he asked quietly.

"Everything." I threw my hands in the air. "I'm afraid of failing and having no one to blame but myself. I'm afraid of falling in love with this place and having it snatched away. I'm afraid of feeling too much and not being able to turn it off when I need to be safe."

He cupped my face and tilted it upward so I'd meet his eyes. "There's a lot going on inside there. Want to know what I'm afraid of?"

"Not being named one of Chicago's Forty under Forty by the time you're thirty-one?"

He huffed out a breath, not appreciating my sarcasm. "I'm afraid of waking up one day and realizing that no matter how far I run from my past, it will always define me. Trying to overcome it is still giving it control."

I knew this was his way of trying to delicately push me to escape my past as well, but I didn't want to give him that satisfaction. "So what are you going to do about it?"

"I don't know." He dropped his hands to his sides. "Maybe I am self-destructing through overachieving, but this is who I am. I'm not sure how to be any other way."

I recognized the conflict warring inside him, similar in nature, though not in execution, to my own. The opposite side of the same coin. Instead of hiding in cold comfort, he threw himself into the fire. But it wasn't on me to point that out to him. We weren't together. We weren't really friends either. We were just . . . nothing. Absolutely nothing.

"I think you already know what you want." I walked away and pretended to examine the caulking on the windows. "And believe it or not, a job title isn't what makes people impressive."

"I know that," he said in a tone that suggested he knew no such thing. "And I think you already know what you want too. Are you going to take a chance on this place?"

The neighborhood didn't have the posh gallery row of River North. West Loop was for the foodies, but it had some up-and-coming galleries and shops. Places for people to browse after a meal. Unlike the near-turnkey condition of the building I'd lost, this space was in rough shape, which just made me like it more. I'd be able to make it my own. It made sense to have a gallery here, especially since I wanted to have mixed media and didn't want to step on my neighbors' toes. It made so much sense that I knew the universe wouldn't let me have this one.

I worried my bottom lip between my teeth. "I don't think it'll work."

"Bullshit." If I'd thought he was going to let it go, I was sadly mistaken. Mark had zero interest in playing the Humor Brinkley game.

"Excuse you, but it is *not* bullshit. I just lost my other place and need some time. Why can't you respect that?"

"Just like you needed time after your breakup. How long ago was that again?" He held up a hand as soon as he felt my claws come out, cutting me off before I could utter a word. "If you walk away, this place will be gone before you work up the courage to go for it, and you know it. It's perfect for what you want to do—so yeah, I call bullshit. Tell me I'm wrong."

I wanted to. I wanted to tell him off so badly I could feel the words burning in my throat, just waiting to be unleashed. But I couldn't. I hated how right he was about this place. Someone would buy it before I could get over myself. I had an opportunity staring me in the face, and I was too afraid to go for it. Why? At what point would I stop feeding my fear of failure?

I couldn't believe what I was about to do, but it was past time to make my dream a reality. Gritting my teeth, I kicked at a loose board. "Let me talk to the owner."

Mark didn't make a smartass remark or rub my face in it, much to my surprise. He just called up the owner. Fifteen minutes later the three of us were sitting in steel chairs around a mosaic table at the Hot Tin Roof bar. Freddie was a petite woman with leathery skin and a hawklike face. When her beady eyes blinked at me, I felt very much like an exposed mouse in an open field.

She had originally bought the place to start a small brewery. That explained the scent of yeast and hops that still hung in the air. When she got picked up by a national chain a few months ago, the limited space could no longer accommodate her needs.

"I don't mind renting it out," Freddie said. "But I had hoped to sell."

"I'm not looking to rent." I knew how that game worked. If my gallery ended up being a success, she'd jack up the rates or force me to buy at a higher price. "I can do ten percent, but I don't have enough for twenty." I could've gone to fifteen if I was willing to drain my savings, but I still needed to fix the place up. There was no point in buying if I couldn't do anything with it. "I was hoping we could work out a deal?"

"What about a land contract?" Mark asked. "The limited space is going to make it hard for you to sell to any other business in the city. Although, since it's been on the market for so long, I'm sure you already understand that."

"I don't know." Freddie rolled a bottle of Two Hearted Ale between her hands. "Land contracts are risky. If your business falls apart—no offense, it happens all the time—then I'm the one left holding the bag."

"Not necessarily. I have another job, and this won't be a full-time venture for me for at least another year." Mark's belief in me was nice, but it wouldn't pay my rent. "I'll be able to make payments, even if my business isn't doing well."

Freddie tapped the edge of the table. "How long are you proposing for this contract? I'm not willing to go longer than five years before you buy outright. I'm moving my operation to Michigan, and I'm counting on this sale to pay the mortgage on my new building."

We spent the next half hour hammering out the details. When we'd come to an agreement, Mark called a lawyer friend of his to draw up a contract. We signed papers promising the place to me, but we couldn't close for a few weeks, at which point I'd get the key. Thanks to the contract though, it couldn't be taken back. I was now the owner of my own gallery.

When Freddie made her exit, Mark and I crossed the street to stand outside my building—my building! For all the saving and hoping and disappointments, it was finally happening. I peered through the dusty windows at the potential that waited beyond. The place needed so much work. I'd paint everything a brilliant white, so the colorful art would pop. I had to buy a counter for a register, lacquered red, since I'd heard somewhere that red increased sales. Items to stage vignettes in the windows, glass-covered podiums for metalwork, discreet price tags. It would be a lot, but I could do it. I could make this space mine.

I wrapped my arms around Mark and screamed into his chest: "I did it! I really just did that!" Then, remembering myself, I released my grip on him and took a full step back with a short cough. "Anyway. Yay me."

He laughed. "What are you doing with the rest of the day?"

"I'm in the middle of a painting, and Winnie needs a sweater change."

Mark mimed gagging. "Animals in clothes."

"What is your issue with that? Winnie loves it." I pulled out my phone and showed him a picture of my Christmas card from last year: the two of us in matching reindeer sweaters. Winnie had a paw up, claws out, aimed for my face. But otherwise, adorable.

He shook his head. "It's just wrong. Nature gave them fur for a reason."

I had a lot of hills I was willing to die on, but my cat's sweater collection wasn't one of them. We'd just have to agree to disagree. "Thanks for bringing me out here. Really." I couldn't hide my grin as I peeked in the windows. "I wish I'd gotten some pictures while we were inside."

"You still can . . . if you want." He pulled out the key to my building with a glint in his eye that didn't belong to a stuffy college professor.

My toes curled as he unlocked the door and pushed it open.

CHAPTER 25

He put his hand on my lower back as we walked into the building. From the moment he touched me, heat pooled in my core. It became a roaring inferno that threatened to consume me. All my limbs went loose as my stomach tightened with need.

It couldn't just be me. He had to feel this too.

I made quick work of taking pictures with my phone to send to Emma later. When I finished, I turned to Mark. The intensity of his stare drew me closer. I wrapped my arms around his neck. "What should we do now that we've got this place all to ourselves?"

His fingers traced the curve of my spine. "Whatever you want."

I pushed up on my toes. Maybe it was the triumph of finally owning my own space, or maybe it was the way his fingers skimmed my back, but I was tired of being cautious with

Mark. I trembled as my lips brushed his ear, and I whispered, "I want you to fuck me so good I forget how to breathe."

He groaned and claimed my mouth with his as he walked me back until we hit the wall. His tongue stroked mine with such perfect rhythm, I had no doubt what he'd do with other body parts. The thick strands of his hair wound around my fingers as I pulled him closer. He lifted me up, pinning me against the Sheetrock. As I tugged my sweater over my head, I gripped him with my thighs. He slowly pulled the straps down on my bra, then pinched and rolled my nipples before lifting one of them into his mouth and sucking gently. My hips rocked forward, but he held me still, teasing me with his lips. I yanked his cable-knit sweater, tugging him toward me with urgency.

"I need more." The throbbing between my legs had turned to an ache.

He put his hand between us, rubbing his thumb over my jeans, against my clit, in a slow circle. "Is this what you need?"

"Yes." I shuddered, gripping his hand as he pulled it away.

He smirked and set me on my feet. He undressed me the rest of the way and flipped me around. I pressed my hands against the wall as he spread my legs. I should've felt insecure being wholly naked while he was still fully dressed, but the moment his finger swept over the dampness at my center, I forgot how to think. He grabbed my hips and brought me against his length. I turned around to reach for the button on his pants, but he stopped me.

"Not so fast." He anchored my hands above my head as he leaned down and gave me another searing kiss. His lips trailed the curve of my neck. "We're not going to rush this." The vibration of his voice against my skin nearly undid me. "Not when I've had weeks to fantasize about all the ways I'm going to make you scream my name."

I couldn't do much more than whimper.

"No cheeky reply?" His fingers skimmed my waist, my hips, between my legs, and I broke out in goose bumps. "That's a first."

Cocky bastard. But if he wanted to play, I could play. "What's the point? I don't need to talk a big game because I'm going to ride you so good, *you'll* be the one screaming *my* name."

"There's my smartass girl." He thrust against me as he kissed me deeply.

I ran my hands down his chest and up under his sweater. "Get rid of this."

"So bossy." He grinned and tugged the sweater over his head, tossing it to the ground.

My mouth watered as I took in the hard planes of muscle, the ridges in his abs. I ran a finger down the trail of hair under his belly button and hooked it into his pants. He placed his hands on either side of my hips. His arms flexed, and I pictured him stripped down while I traced the lines of his muscles on a blank canvas. All that time he spent in the gym really, really paid off. I kissed his bicep, his shoulder, his collarbone, and licked my way across his chest. He was warm and solid and mine.

He brushed back my hair and kissed my collarbone. Cupping my breasts, he took one of my nipples in his mouth and scraped his teeth over it. I let out a noise that sounded a lot like that time I'd shut Winnie's tail in the bathroom door.

"That's a new one." He chuckled against my chest, then kissed his way down my stomach. "I've been dying to taste you again since that first night, but this time you're going to let me finish the job."

"Who's the bossy one now?" I gave him a playful smile, and he nudged my legs open, dragging his thumb down and back up, using light pressure and my own wetness to bring me closer to the edge. When he gave me a long, slow lick, I flattened my palms against the Sheetrock. He did it again, and the moan I'd been trying to hold back escaped. I gripped his head as he licked and sucked me. My hips began to move against his mouth, and his tongue matched my rhythm.

He pushed my legs farther apart and swirled his tongue over the tight bud at my center. "I could lick you every day for the rest of my life."

My body quivered as I let out another moan.

He kissed the inside of my thigh.

My legs shook, until everything clenched and loosened in that bright fire. It spread through every one of my nerves. I screamed out his name as I dug my nails into his head. His tongue stroked me harder, working me through the last of my tremors.

His fingers replaced his tongue as he built me toward another peak. "It's incredible to watch you give up control and let go."

"We're not done yet." I thought I'd been wrung out, but the way he touched me had me wanting more. I needed to feel him inside me.

He hoisted me around his waist. As soon as my back hit the wall, his gaze drank me in as if he wanted to memorize every one of my dips and curves. I trailed a finger down his chest, down between us where our bodies met, and his pupils flared. A thrill raced up my spine.

I pressed a light kiss to his jaw. "Are you going to stand there watching me? Or are you going to put on a condom and show me what you can really do?"

I touched my toes to the ground, and this time he didn't stop me when I unbuttoned his pants. As I pushed them down with his briefs, his erection sprang free. He was so hard and sleek. I took his tip in my mouth, rolling my tongue around his head.

"Holy fuck." His eyes clouded as his fingers plunged into my hair.

I gave his shaft a long stroke with my mouth, then released him.

Without taking his eyes off me, he took a condom out of his wallet, unwrapped it, and rolled it on. He gripped my ass as he held me up. The delicious weight of his body against mine pressed my back against the wall. The head of his cock nudged my entrance, but he didn't go any farther. He held himself, circling the tip.

I tilted my hips. "What are you waiting for?"

"Are you sure you want to do this?" He kissed me. "Because if you say no, I'll back off right now. No questions asked."

I tilted my head and nipped his bottom lip. "Shut up and fuck me."

His moan vibrated against my mouth and traveled down my spine as he slid into me. My body stretched to accommodate his size, and heat poured through me. He paused for a few seconds, allowing me to get used to the feel of him, then he thrust.

"Oh, God." He felt so good I was ready to burst out of my skin.

He continued to move inside me, each long stroke bringing me higher and higher. He kissed me as he rolled his hips.

My breath came out in short gasps. I clenched around him, and he groaned, thrusting harder.

The way he moved hit the exact spot that threatened to ruin me. Sweat slicked our skin as he pumped faster, sending us both climbing toward the edge. "I'm close."

"Not yet." I slapped a hand on his chest. My body wanted more, harder, faster. I worked my hips until my vision clouded and my legs trembled, but my orgasm hovered just out of reach. He palmed my breasts, pinching and stroking my nipples.

His neck strained as he fought his own orgasm. "Come for me. I can't hold out when you ride me like that."

Each stroke brought me higher. "You. Feel. So. Fucking. Good."

He put his hand between us, and with one slick motion of his fingers, I cried out as I pulsed around him. My orgasm rolled over me in waves, threatening to knock me out or drag me under. He yelled out my name as he pulled me against him and pumped into me with his own release. This one took my breath, leaving me loose and warm, my finger-tips tingling.

He held me against him, both of us slicked with sweat and worn out. I didn't want to move or think or do anything other than hold on to him.

"That was . . ." The best sex of my life.

He took my hand and kissed it. "Same."

Gingerly, I unwrapped my legs from his waist and got dressed. I was always awkward after sex, and this was no exception. Especially because I now needed to make my graceful exit. "This was great. And fun. And great. But I should probably go now."

"Not a fucking chance." He pulled me against his bare chest. "You don't get to blow my mind and then run."

He gave me a long, lingering kiss that threatened to turn me into a puddle. My legs were still weak, and my body was completely sated. I traced patterns over his broad shoulders with my fingertip as I breathed in his scent.

I was such a goner.

CHAPTER 26

The next morning, I went over my notes for the night's assignment. Mark's last as a trainee. After tonight, he'd be taking on clients of his own. I still didn't know how to feel about that. I'd done a decent job of shutting down all my human feelings to do what I needed to for H4H, so maybe I'd be able to do the same regarding Mark's position. Or maybe it would gnaw at me until it destroyed me completely. It really could go either way.

The sex had been incredible. I shivered just thinking about the way his body had moved against mine—but what if it was only a one-time thing? After tonight's assignment, we could theoretically go our separate ways. The thought settled like a boulder in my gut. I didn't want us to be one and done. But I couldn't ignore that he'd be a Heartbreaker, and I didn't know how to reconcile wanting him and hating that part of him at the same time.

I let out a frustrated sigh. Nothing between Mark and me could ever be easy. I rummaged through my purse for my phone. Even though I'd signed paperwork promising the mini-warehouse in West Loop to me, I was still going to be jumpy until I had keys in hand.

I only had one text, from Emma: Was I right about his surprise? Does that mean I get 50 bucks?

I tossed my phone back in my purse.

I pulled out my folder on the accountant and threw myself into work. My client, Greta Timmer, had a CPA and five years' seniority at Bells and Stern. She'd been working toward a partnership, but her boss made her dress up like the Statue of Liberty and dance in the street to attract end-of-year filers.

Bells and Stern was a large midwestern accounting firm that franchised its name out to individual offices, and the company held its yearly convention at the Chicago JW Marriott. It had started last night and was set to run through Sunday. Mark would pose as an accountant, and I'd already gotten him a lanyard and ID badge with all the appropriate information. I'd be playing a mermaid. Sadly, not the oddest role I'd taken on.

The client had promised to throw in a bonus if the target lost his cool in front of the CEO, so we needed to make it splashy. Since I wouldn't be asking for permission to record, I'd be tiptoeing on some fine legal lines, but my client had no interest in a lawsuit. She just wanted complete and total annihilation of his career.

George Ritsema, my target, had also turned his other female accountant into little more than a secretary. And as a bonus, he left "helpful" dieting articles on their desks before they went to lunch. He was a real peach.

I had the perfect plan for him, though. By the end of the night, he'd be taking himself down. Turned out, he had a mermaid fetish. His Facebook was practically dedicated to them. Aside from his annual MILF (Mermaids I'd Like to Fuck) List, he took vacation days every year to attend the Coney Island Mermaid Parade, he'd briefly dated an instructor at AquaMermaid, and he had a tattoo of a mermaid on his incredibly hairy upper thigh. He also had a GoFundMe set up to back his summer expedition, where he claimed he'd find photographic proof of real mermaids. So far, his fund had managed to collect two dollars.

All the big names at Bells and Stern Accounting would be at the JW. I had no idea what they did at these things. Probably listened to boring lectures, sipped tepid water, and compared allergies. At least they had an open bar. But when the program boasted a live mermaid tank, I didn't have to guess who'd booked the entertainment.

Margo had worked whatever magic she possessed on the owner of Tealights and Mermaids, and I had spent Thursday evening getting outfitted for my tail. To my relief, I didn't have to do any swimming. I'd sit on one of the foam rocks under the guise of being in training.

A literal siren singing his destruction.

✕

As the accountants filed into the domed conference room at the JW, Annette—the only mermaid actually hired for this event—began to splash around. I sat on a foam rock just outside the tank, flipping my tail, while she did a series of complicated spins and turns in the water. If I hadn't been working, I might've enjoyed the show.

Mark entered the room, wearing a suit. A warm flicker of lust sent tingles straight up my center. As much as I enjoyed his Hot Professor attire, nothing compared to the sight of that man in a suit. Broad shoulders, tapered waist, strong forearms just begging to be flashed beneath rolled-up sleeves. I pressed a hand to my stomach to steady myself.

He gave me a wink, but I couldn't react. For our setup, I could only have eyes for George. The plan was for Mark to chat George up, buy him a drink, and pretend to share some of his interests that didn't include mermaids. It wasn't easy. George practically had a one-track mind. He wasted no time making a beeline for the tank, with Mark behind him.

"Now, how did I get lucky enough to get two for the price of one?" George asked.

At first I thought he was wearing a dark shirt under his short-sleeved polo, but no. He had an obscene amount of body hair. Sweater arms, scarf neck—even his pale hands were covered in that fuzzy outer layer. He probably shed worse than Winnie.

I gave George a flirty smile as I flipped my tail. "I'm only here to observe for training. Think of me as part of the set design."

"I don't think anyone could mistake you for part of the

set." His leering gaze dropped to my purple seashells. "What are you doing after the show?"

Damn. That hadn't taken long. I'd seriously underestimated this guy's hard-on for mermaids. Though I supposed I could credit my red wig and green tail, since Ariel had made the top of George's MILF List for the last two years. "We're finished in an hour, but I might be persuaded to stay, if a handsome man bought me a drink."

"For you, dollface? I'll buy you all the drinks you want." He ran a finger down my bare arm, as if he had the right to touch me just because I wore this costume. It took everything in me not to physically recoil. From the clenching of Mark's fists, I gathered he wasn't thrilled either.

I gave George my best pout. Even though he grossed me out, I had a job to do. "Aren't you part of this convention?"

"The workshops are done for the day. It's party time now." The look he gave me suggested it would be a party in his pants if he had his way. I didn't always enjoy the work I did for H4H—not all the targets were this awful—but I couldn't dredge up any sympathy for George. He'd already managed to show me exactly why I shouldn't.

"Meet me at the bar?" I batted my lashes. "They let me keep the seashells."

His eyes glazed over, and I thought he'd pass out right there, but no such luck.

Mark wore a bored expression as he tapped George on the shoulder. "I was hoping to meet some of your employees. I hear the ladies are pretty hot."

"Not my type, but have at it." George pointed toward the other side of the room.

"If you introduce me, maybe I can keep them distracted while you do other things." Mark tilted his head toward me. "Since the dinner and video presentation are set to run for at least two hours. That's time you can skip out on."

"Good point, my man." George finally tore his gaze away from my boobs, and I felt like I could breathe again. "You don't have a Statue of Liberty fetish by any chance, do you?"

As they finally walked away, giving me a much-needed break from George's slimy stare, Annette rested her elbows on the edge of the tank. "That guy is such a creep."

"You know him?" I asked.

"Oh yeah. He tried to hire me for a 'bachelor party.'" She air-quoted those last two words. "But when my guys started to set up the tank, they realized there was no party. They got me out of there before I even got my tail on. If I'd known he was going to be here, I never would've agreed to do this venue."

"I'm so sorry." Now I was going to really enjoy George's impending downfall. "Don't worry about me though. I assume Margo filled you in on why I'm here?"

"Why do you think I'm not packing up my tank until the dinner is over?" She smirked and flipped back into the water.

The next hour dragged. I kept my eye on Mark, and he played his part well: laughing at George's jokes, plying him with tequila shots to loosen his tongue, making small talk with the other accountants, keeping his eyes off me as if I didn't interest him at all. Finally I got his signal—a yank on his earlobe—and immediately hopped over to the curtained area to change into a tight skirt with a flare at the knee and one of Mark's collared shirts, left unbuttoned and tied above my belly button, revealing the seashells I'd kept on as a distraction.

The convention had its own bar set up with drink tokens, and George was cheap enough to "buy" me a drink from there. But it was Mark's job to steer him toward where I waited in the hotel's lounge.

As soon as George appeared, I ducked my head, hoping to appear coy. In reality, I was putting on my game face for a guy whose very presence made the air feel oilier. Everything about him disgusted me, and not just because he looked like an unwatered Chia Pet. I decided I'd be sticking it to him not just for Greta, the woman who was paying me, but also for Annette.

He took a seat, blocking me into the booth. I had hoped he'd sit across from me like a normal person, but I should've known better. I was dealing with a classic creep. As he called the waitress over, I reached up to the shelf above our booth and adjusted a small frog statue containing a hidden camera. He ordered us both a Sex on the Beach. Of course that was his drink of choice. I tried not to shudder when the waitress set it in front of me. I didn't even get a tiny umbrella out of the deal.

"I can't believe you skipped that big presentation." I giggled and touched his arm.

George waved it off. "My buddy Jim is covering for me. If the bosses ask what I thought of it, he'll be able to fill me in."

His buddy Jim, aka Mark, wouldn't be able to tell him a thing about the video presentation, since he'd removed the disk and hooked up the screen to live-stream this little corner of the JW lounge instead. By the time they figured out how to shut it off, the damage would be done.

"Wow." I twirled a lock from the wig around my finger. "That's a good friend."

"I just met him tonight."

"No way." I gave myself a mental high-five on nailing the beachy Valley girl vibes. "I thought you all worked together."

"We're all part of the Bells and Stern corporation, but we have individual offices all over the Midwest. Mine is on the corner of Lakewood and Nelson."

"Oh. Em. Gee." My squeal was too high-pitched to be real, but he didn't notice. He was too busy checking out my shells. "Is that the one with the dancing Statue of Liberty?"

"Yeah." He gave me a smug grin. "That was all my idea. The bosses don't like it, think it's tacky, but I call the shots in my office."

"Ooh. I love a man who takes control." I put my hand on his knee. He grabbed it under the table and tried to drag it up higher. The move caught me off guard, and I pretended to have a coughing fit, just to get him to release me. I needed to wrap this up. After I swallowed half my drink, I gave him a tentative smile. "I'm so sorry. What were you saying?"

He opened his mouth, probably to say something terrible, but I cut him off.

"Oh, that's right." I bounced in my seat, and the motion of the seashells temporarily preoccupied him. "You said the bosses don't like the dancing Statue of Liberty. But how do you keep her on your payroll without them knowing?"

"I make a senior accountant do it." He rubbed the fabric where my skirt fanned, as if it were a tail. It made my skin crawl. "She hates it, but she likes being employed. Did you know I have a thing for mermaids?"

"You don't say?" I inched away from him, but there was only so much space between me and the wall. "No wonder you talked me up when you could have any girl in that room."

"Those women don't interest me." He tugged on my skirt. "Do they let you keep the tail too? The seashells are nice." He bit his lip. "But the tail really gets me going."

"Gets you going how?" Why did I insist on asking questions I didn't want the answers to? "Like, you think it's pretty?"

"Like, I want to stroke it while you stick a finger in my ass."

Nope. I was so fucking out of here.

He leaned forward, eyes closed, with his tongue already hanging out. I slid down off the booth's leatherette seat, and my palm hit a stuffed mushroom someone had dropped on the floor. This was too far above my pay grade. As I crawled through the food debris that wouldn't get swept up until the end of the night, he ducked his head under the table.

"What are you doing?" He reached for me, and I scrambled past his hairy hand.

I cleared the booth and got to my feet, putting a considerable distance between us. "I need to go. Whatever you were expecting, it's so not happening."

"Are you kidding me?" His face twisted with rage. "I

thought you were going to show me a good time. Isn't that why you flirted with me and asked me to buy you a drink?"

"A drink doesn't entitle you to a finger in the asshole!" I yelled, and didn't give a damn who overheard.

I stormed back toward the conference center. It was time to get Mark and go. The sound of hurried footsteps behind me had me picking up my pace.

I'd made it to the doorway when a security guard stopped me. "This room is reserved for a private event. Do you have a badge, miss?"

"No, she doesn't." George held up his lanyard. "Don't let her go any farther. She's been stalking me all night, and I'm afraid she's only here to stir up trouble."

He disappeared down the hall, and I pulled out my phone to text Mark.

ME: I'm stuck outside the conference. Ready to go.

MARK: Give me fifteen. Grab the camera. Ditch the costume.

Fifteen minutes was about fourteen minutes longer than I wanted to wait, but I went back to the bar and grabbed the ceramic frog off the ledge above the booth. Then I slipped into the bathroom, pulled off the wig, used a paper towel to rub the glitter off my face, changed into the sweater and leggings I'd stashed in my oversize purse, and called an Uber.

By the time I was back at the entrance of the conference center, Mark was waiting for me. He took my arm. "We've gotta move."

"I've been ready. You're the one who said I should change."

"Where the hell did that bitch go?" George's booming voice sent a wave of fear skittering through my chest. "WHERE DID SHE GO?"

"That's why I wanted you to change," Mark said.

He picked up his pace, and I had to jog to keep up. Once we hit the sidewalk, he grabbed a cab, not bothering to wait for the Uber.

CHAPTER 27

M y place was in its usual state of chaos. Art supplies had been left on my couch, on the end tables, and on the bookshelf. A paint-splattered T-shirt hung over the back of one of my dining room chairs, and shredded pieces of toilet paper were scattered around the living room. I had to give Mark credit; his jaw barely ticked as he took it all in.

Winnie jumped on the couch and hissed. "Is your cat ever going to stop hating me?"

"Not as long as you make fun of her sweaters. She's sensitive."

The adrenaline from our getaway started to ease up. I collapsed on my couch, my limbs looser than after he'd fucked me against a wall yesterday.

Mark went into my kitchen; a series of pops from the microwave soon followed. "You want to watch a movie?"

Not what I had in mind, but okay.

He brought out the bowl of popcorn, pushing aside tubes of acrylic paint and settling beside me on the couch. We probably looked like an ad for Redbox. "I thought we could watch the highlight reel together. It really does deserve the popcorn."

"You recorded it?"

"I didn't want you to miss the good part." He unlocked his phone, which was already open to the video, and pressed play.

The lights dimmed in the conference room for the presentation. Every major player from the Bells and Stern accounting firm was present. A confused hum spread through the crowd when George and I appeared on the screen, but as he continued to run his mouth, that hum turned to an angry buzz. Mark had angled his phone to record *the* Bells and Stern, and wow, the ice in their expressions could've frozen lava.

"Best movie night ever." I tossed a kernel into my mouth.

"It gets better," Mark whispered in my ear.

It gave me great pleasure to see Annette perched on the edge of her tank with a shit-eating grin on her face. Technically her time was up when the presentation started, but she'd hung around to watch the real show.

The moment I had my coughing fit, someone from the crowd yelled, "Run, girl, run," and nervous laughter followed.

Mark had filmed various reactions, ranging from amusement to anger to disgust. George's casual dismissal of his employee's feelings and the threat to eliminate her job if she didn't dress up and dance in the street had more than one person swearing out loud. When he asked to stroke my tail while I fingered his ass, the entire room erupted. Two men stood and called for the people in the back to shut off the screen. Several attendees had taken out their phones to record or laughed and nudged their coworkers.

I grabbed Mark's wrist for the climax, as his video showed George reentering the room. Every single person fell silent and turned their head toward him. He froze, not entirely understanding the shitstorm he'd walked into, but knowing something had gone very wrong. Then one guy started chanting, "Finger in the ass. Finger in the ass." Within seconds, half the room picked up the chant. George's face turned red, then contorted with rage as he looked up at the screen and saw me plucking the camera off the ledge.

The best part, the cinematic poetry of Mark's film, came when he'd turned his phone to the woman who had hired us, the one who'd been forced to put on a ridiculous costume and dance in the street, even though she'd fought for years to prove her professionalism in a male-dominated field. The look of pure, unfiltered joy on Greta's face made it all worth it. I wanted to wrap her in a fur coat, hand her a glass of wine, and put a tiara on her head like the goddamn queen she deserved to be.

Mark shut off his phone and set it on the coffee table. "Thoughts?"

"George is so getting fired." I grinned.

"Fuck yeah, he is. I hope Greta gets his job."

"If she doesn't, we riot. If you send this to her, you know she's going to watch it every day. It truly is the feel-good movie of the year."

"I hope they take cuts for a training video on sexual harassment."

I turned my head, taking in his profile as we sat close enough to share the same air. My palm tingled as I took in his light scruff, wanting to feel that rough texture against my skin. He only let a little stubble grow on the weekends, when he didn't have to put on his Professor Cavanaugh mask. Not many people got to see this side of him, unpolished and a little rough. I trailed a finger along the line of his jaw, feeling the prickles everywhere. He raised an eyebrow. Taking the popcorn bowl, I placed it on the coffee table. I ran my hands up his chest and circled the back of his neck. He cupped my face, kissing me deeply, and nearly knocking the wind out of me. This. This was what I needed.

I straddled him and unknotted his tie, letting the cool silk glide beneath my fingers. Licking his throat, I undid the first button on his shirt. I pushed off his jacket, letting it crumple on the couch beside us, then put his hands behind his head, where he laced his fingers.

"Don't move them," I said.

With each button, I kissed his chest, until I'd reached the trail of hair on his stomach. I lowered myself to the floor between his legs and swirled my tongue around his belly button. He sucked in a sharp breath. Working my way back up, I licked and nipped his skin, then took off his shirt. I held on to his shoulders as I pushed up and caught his bottom lip with my teeth. His arms twitched, but he didn't reach for me. That was the nice thing about academics. They knew how to listen to directions.

I explored his body all over again, and every hard muscle and ridge felt new. His skin heated as I dipped my fingers into the waist of his pants. I dropped to my knees, undid the button, then pulled his zipper down slowly.

"Let me touch you." His voice was a plea I ignored.

Over his briefs, I put my lips against his erection and let out a warm breath of air. He got even harder. I smiled as I lowered his briefs, then took his cock in my mouth. He buried his fingers in my hair.

I sat back on my heels. "What did I say about the touching?"

He groaned and put his hands behind his head again.

I leaned forward and licked him from the base of his shaft up to the head. The throbbing between my legs grew more intense as I sucked him.

"Fuck. I'm going to come."

Not yet. Not without me. I released him and leaned forward, running my hands up his chest. "You can touch me now."

He didn't hesitate. Kicking his pants and briefs off, he pulled me into his lap. He lifted my sweater over my head and made quick work of stripping me bare. He kissed my neck as he rolled my nipples. I ground against his hard length, wanting more, needing to be closer. Winnie spit at us both and went running for my bedroom. At least she wouldn't attack.

I adjusted my position, and my knee fell on an uncapped tube of teal acrylic paint. It splattered against the wall. Not really caring about the mess, I ground my slick and aching core against him. His hand hit the cushion next to him, landing on a tube of yellow acrylic. A splatter hit my thigh. Laughing, he scooped the paint off my leg and rubbed it down my chest.

"So that's how you want to play." I grabbed a tube of magenta sitting on the back of the couch and squeezed it out over his head, then kissed him as I rubbed it into his scalp.

"That's it, you're in for it now." He pushed me onto the couch and squeezed some green onto my stomach. The cold paint made me arch my back, and his eyes darkened. "Mmm. I should probably do that again."

"Don't even think about it." I pressed myself against him, rubbing the green and yellow together until his chest and abs were covered.

He reached for a tube of salmon, but I beat him to the tube of plum and squeezed it out on his shoulder. It splattered as I wrapped my arms around him and pulled him down so I could be on top again. I drew a flower on his chest with my finger, and he laughed. In return, he drew a stick figure lying on top of another stick figure on my stomach.

I tilted my head as I looked down. "Your line work is a little raw, but your technique shows promise."

"I'll need to work on that." He gripped my hips, rolling against me.

I reached down to grab a condom from the back pocket of his pants. He took it from me, pushed me onto my back, then flipped me onto my stomach. Sliding his hand down my back, he cupped me from underneath. I clenched with anticipation as he bent over and placed kisses down my spine before he lifted me and licked my center.

"Oh God." I braced myself against the couch.

My legs began to tremble as he continued to stroke my clit with his tongue. He let go of me right before I fell over the edge, flipped me back over, then lifted one of my legs and wrapped it around his waist.

"Hold on." With a sweep of his arms, we both sat up, with me straddling him. He rolled on the condom and teased me with his head. My entire frame shook with anticipation. I ached to get him closer. Unable to stand it any longer, I guided him into me.

I took him all the way to the base in one swift motion and let out a satisfied moan. This was what I needed, to be surrounded by his rain and moonlight scent as our bodies collided. As I moved against him, he thrust his hips upward, matching my rhythm, stroke for stroke. I clung to him as he picked up speed, just the way I wanted it.

"So good," I said. "It's so good with you."

He circled his hips, and I bit my lip to keep from crying out. The heat inside me began to build, and as I trembled from my toes all the way up, I buried my face in his shoulder.

"Look at me." He caressed my cheek as his cock continued to do delicious things to my body.

Release barreled through me, and I couldn't stop it, couldn't take my eyes off him as he shuddered beneath me. We came hard and fast at the same time, and when he looked at me like I was the most precious thing in the world, it was too much, too consuming. Feelings I couldn't grasp and didn't dare name rose up inside me. I couldn't stop the tears from falling.

"I don't know why I'm crying." I hugged him against me as I tried to get a grip on my emotions, but they were too intense.

"It's okay." He rubbed a thumb against my jaw and wiped away my tears. "I feel it too."

Neither of us said the word, but it hung between us anyway.

I got up to go to the bathroom. When I came back out, he'd put his pants back on, but hadn't buttoned them, so they hung loose on his hips. He paced my living room with his phone against his ear. He motioned for me to come over. As I approached him, he hung up and pulled me into a hug.

"I was just checking my voice mail." His grin was so huge, it could've split the world. "I got the job. I'm the new anthropology professor at Northwestern University."

"Congrats." I meant to sound cheery, but it came out a little flat. I was happy for him and happy he'd be leaving H4H, of course, but the more time I spent with him, the less I believed he was built for that life. If that was what he wanted, though, who was I to tell him it wasn't right?

In bed, he snuggled me against him, stroking my back, but I barely noticed because my mind was too busy trying to sort out all my overlapping thoughts. We shared something incredible. When I was with him, I didn't see who I'd been; I saw who I could be. But I didn't know how much further we could go, if he became immersed in the academic world. I had firsthand experience of what it did to otherwise decent people. Which would make things painfully complicated. Especially because I couldn't deny the truth any longer.

I was in love with Mark.

CHAPTER 28

Two Fridays later, I'd signed all the necessary paperwork and closed on my gallery. The space wouldn't fully be mine for another five years, but this was a critical step. I had keys. I had free rein. Now all I needed was the time to get it ready. I'd have to do it in little chunks, an hour here, two hours there.

Mark had been a rock through the process. He had my contract looked over to make sure I didn't get scammed on the terms, and he stayed with me in the building for three hours after I got my keys while I sketched preliminary ideas for the setup. He must've been bored out of his mind, though he did make a helpful suggestion about shelving when I didn't think he'd been paying attention to my rambling.

At night, we'd gotten into the habit of both staying at my place or his, easily falling into a couple's routine. While I hadn't brought up the l-word—or even let myself examine those feelings too closely—it hung there, this unsaid thing, between us. He said he felt it too—but felt what? The after-orgasm high? Sated satisfaction? Post-sex hunger pangs? He never did elaborate. And this felt too new, too delicate, for me to ruin everything by asking.

And now tonight, we'd be attending Dr. Faber's retirement party together. Mark and I had been invited separately, and the crossover between his new life and my old one made me mildly uncomfortable. Okay, more than mildly. He'd only just started, and already he had put in more than fifty hours this week and was becoming overly concerned about building connections with people who'd sooner slit his throat than offer him a genuine welcome.

Even though Margo was still upset over losing Mark to Northwestern, and she hadn't yet found anyone to replace Emma, surprisingly she'd let me push off tonight's assignment so I could attend. I had considered saying screw the party, just to avoid the eggshells I'd surely be walking on come Monday, but Margo assured me that pushing my assignment back by one night wouldn't make or break it. A pity, really. There would be a lot of people at the party I used to call friends, and I wasn't looking forward to playing old politics.

At Mark's knock, I opened the door. He stood before me in a black suit with a soft gray shirt and pewter tie. I couldn't get enough of him in a suit. He knew it was a weakness of mine. I ran a finger down the lapel of his jacket. "I was hoping you'd show up in leather with a neck tattoo, since my mom is going to be there, but this is okay too."

"Glad you approve." He handed me a single rose. Like this was a real date, not a networking opportunity for him and a personal obligation for me. "You look stunning."

"What? This old thing?" I swept a hand down the slinky emerald gown with a low dip in front and an open back. "I just wear this around the house on laundry days." I turned to put the rose in a cup of water by the sink, since I didn't own a vase, and had the pleasure of hearing his sharp intake of breath.

"Let's skip the party." He came up behind me and rubbed his hands down my bare back, teasing the sides of my breasts with his fingers.

Tempting, but . . . "Dr. Faber is an old family friend. Our only family friend, actually. It would reflect badly on my mom if I didn't show up, and then I'd have to deal with her hissy fits for the next eternity because she holds grudges until the end of time. Maybe we can sneak away to the rooftop. You can bend me over the balcony and fuck me under the stars."

"Save that thought." His eyes darkened as his gaze skimmed my body. "It would probably be poor form if I showed up to a work function with a raging hard-on."

"They'll just think you're really excited about your new job."

He laughed and took my hand. "Let's go, sassy pants."

Nightingale Grove was an upscale club for the fifty-plus crowd who generally had a divorce or two behind them and money to burn into retirement. It had white walls with black trim and moldings. Potted orange and lemon trees spaced around the perimeter gave the air a citrusy scent. Round black tables with white-and-chrome stools had been placed around the open floor, giving people plenty of spots to enjoy a private conversation. A jazz band was set up at the back of the room, and a few people were on the dance floor, while most mingled near the bar. The academic crowd cleaned up nice. I didn't see a single stitch of tweed.

I spotted my mom and steeled myself for her inevitable questioning. "Incoming. Prepare yourself," I whispered to Mark.

"Brinkley." My mom gave me a stiff nod. "I'm glad to see you arrived with a proper date for once. We met before you were hired," she said to Mark. "I'm Dr. Saunders, head of the psychology department."

"Nice to see you again." Mark shook my mom's hand as he looked over her head. "I should go say hi to a few people, but thank you for birthing such a lovely daughter."

Jesus. He sucked in social situations.

"Yes. Well." My mom shifted her stance. "Thirty-six hours of labor. I should've known right then and there she'd be a handful."

Mark didn't respond, focused on the other side of the room. I tried to tilt my head to see what had caught his attention, but he put a hand on my back and steered me in the opposite direction.

"'Thank you for birthing a lovely daughter?'" I laughed as I poked him in the side. "The look on my mom's face when you said that was priceless."

"I panicked." He grabbed us both glasses of wine off a passing tray and led me over to a table behind a lemon tree on the opposite side of the club. "After everything you've told me about her, I was expecting her to fillet my balls."

"She'd serve them with a nice rosemary sauce, so at least they'd have a tasty end." I glanced over my shoulder. "Who did you see on the other side of the room?"

"No one. Why?" He wouldn't meet my eyes.

"It just seemed like you were in a hurry to get away, and now you've got us sequestered in this hidden corner. What's going on? You can't be having issues with coworkers already; you just started." Although, this was academia. I wouldn't have been surprised if some of the more eager adjuncts had already started a sabotage campaign.

"Listen. There's something I need to tell you." He set his wine aside and took both my hands. "I've been wanting to tell you, but it's tricky and I don't want you to—"

"Brinkley! Is that you?" A shrill voice made me cringe. "It *is* you! What are you doing at an academic function?"

"Hello, Eliza." I'd hoped she wasn't important enough to score an invitation to this event, but it seemed like the whole of Northwestern's faculty and grad students were in attendance. "You know Dr. Faber is a friend of my mother's. I came for him."

My old college roommate looked exactly the same: honey-colored hair, apple cheeks that always seemed to be a light shade of pink, little upturned nose, and a top-heavy lip that gave her a slight lisp. Pretty, in an apple pie kind of way. She was the one who had introduced me to Aiden, defended him after he cheated on me, and ditched me after I dropped out. I suspected that she and Aiden had hooked up behind my back, but I could never prove it.

"Wait until everyone knows you're here. They're going to flip."

Great. More people I didn't want to see.

I gave her an apologetic smile. "I'm actually in the middle of—"

"It's fine," Mark said. "I'll catch up with you later."

I threw him a pleading look to rescue me, but his mind was clearly elsewhere, and Eliza was already dragging me toward a group I hadn't seen outside of my Instagram feed in years. No Aiden—he'd fallen out of their circle since he'd graduated and moved into private practice—but I still didn't want to play nice with those who had hurt me just as badly.

Eve stood with her husband, Quincey, who was an adjunct in psychology. It must've killed them that an outsider had gotten Dr. Faber's spot, and it gave me some satisfaction knowing I'd had a hand in that. However tiny that hand might've been.

They'd just started dating the last time I saw them in person, but social media made it nearly impossible to cut people out of your life completely. There was always the unfollow option, but that felt like admitting defeat. So instead I'd scrolled through pictures of her wedding day and tried to ignore the pang in my chest at not even getting a pity invite.

At least I hadn't liked any of those pictures. I had to keep some dignity.

"Brinkley, it's so good to see you." Eve gave me a limp hug—her signature embrace. Quincey followed up with a dead-fish handshake. I had to imagine their lovemaking looked a lot like spaghetti boiling in a pot. "I'm surprised to see you here."

Why was everyone so surprised to see me here? While I

didn't make it a point to attend most functions, it's not like they were unaware of my mom's relationship with Dr. Faber. Eve had been a psychology and anthropology double major, and she'd always been the one who pushed hardest for me to use my family connection to help boost her grade.

"Just because I chose not to finish my master's doesn't mean I fell off the face of the earth." Where was that waiter with the drink tray when I needed him? "I'm here to support an old friend. One of the few people who didn't ditch me when my education ended."

Eliza let out an uncomfortable giggle. "You make it sound like we ghosted you. We just got busy. You have no idea how much time we had to dedicate to our theses."

"I'm aware of how time-consuming a thesis can be." All of my hurt and frustration with my former so-called friends bubbled to the surface.

"I don't know why you're taking this personally." Eve frowned as she snuggled closer to Quincey. Or as close as two wet noodles could snuggle. "All our free time went to trading papers for critique and networking with future colleagues."

"Honestly," Eliza chirped, "forming connections with others in our graduate classes had to come first. It took a lot of emotional energy to maintain a friendship with someone we had nothing in common with anymore."

"You mean associating with me was no longer a rung you could step on for your ladder of success. My friendship was worth maintaining when I was a rising star in academics, the daughter of Dr. Saunders, close family friend of Dr. Faber, but the moment I became just an administrative assistant at an insurance company, suddenly I required too much emotional energy." *Finally* the waiter came around with drinks. I took two, downed the first in one gulp and set the glass back on the tray, then took a third. "I know you want to tell yourselves that you're good people, that you would never use someone to further your own careers, but the fact is, you're all a bunch of two-faced assholes. I hope you enjoy the taste of flesh as you swallow your own tails."

I turned on my heel and stormed away. Now would be a good time to hit that unfollow on Instagram and get on with my life. I didn't need the remnants of my past reminding me of all the ways I'd failed. I had something good now, with people who genuinely cared about me. The rest was just background noise.

I made my way over to the bar. Those three glasses of wine weren't enough.

Dr. Faber stood in a circle of his admirers, but as soon as I caught his eye, he waved me over. "Brinkley, so nice of you to come and see me off."

"I wouldn't miss it." I'd never hear the end of it from my mom if I did, but he'd also been kind to me growing up. He'd always sneaked me butterscotch candies and quarters.

"I saw you did some catching up with your old cohorts." That was one way of putting it. "You all used to be thick as thieves. Reminded me of your mother when she took my classes."

"I didn't know you taught psychology." I gave him a gentle

smile as I eyed the bar for an opening. Those academics could drink. The line was ten people deep. I'd have to find my old friend, the waiter with the wine tray.

"Oh no, dear. This was back when she was a double doctoral candidate in anthropology and psychology. She never could decide which she liked better."

"Wait. What?" No way. "Mom studied anthropology? And dropped it?" After all the shit she'd given me about wasted time in wasted classes when I switched my major senior year. She had some serious nerve. "When was this?"

"Right before she completed her doctorate." He rubbed the patch of hair on his chin. "It was quite a shock to all of us, but she ended up where she needed to be. I'm surprised she hasn't told you this before."

"I'm not." I gave him a pat on the arm. "I'm really happy for you, and we'll have to get together for dinner soon. If you'll excuse me, I have something I need to attend to."

He chuckled. "Try not to give your mother too much grief. She's under a lot of pressure."

We'd see about that. I wouldn't ruin the retirement party with an all-out fight, but I'd certainly let her know that I knew. Of all the things she liked to pick at, changing my major was her forever favorite. And I was about to mark it off her list for good.

I searched the lower level but didn't see her with her usual band of ass-kissers. Mark stood near the dance floor, talking to Eve. Seeing them together unnerved me. I considered stopping to say something, but their conversation looked intense. She was probably just sucking up.

My mom had disappeared, but she couldn't have gone home already. This was too good of a networking opportunity. Maybe she'd gone to get some air. I climbed the spiral staircase up to the second floor, which had a balcony that got much more use in the summer.

Out on the terrace, next to the Nightingale Grove's signature potted orange trees, my mom faced Richard Vaden with her hands on her hips and a pinched expression on her face. That breakup must've been really ugly if she still had so much hatred for him after all these years. I wondered if I'd look at Aiden like that if I ran into him thirty years from now.

I turned away to give them some privacy, but my mom's clipped tone stopped me short. "I don't care if Brinkley is your daughter. It's too little, too late."

The world tipped as everything I knew to be true was pulled out from under me.

CHAPTER 29

I must've made a noise, which seemed impossible, since I wasn't actually breathing. Both of them turned to me with matching looks of horror on their faces. If I hadn't been rooted to the spot in shock, I would've run. Instead, I stood there with my dropped jaw flapping in the wind.

I had a father.

I didn't know what to do with that information, how to act, how to feel. My fingers had gone numb, as if my brain was using so much energy trying to process this information, it had forgotten to tell my heart to keep pumping blood.

"Brinkley. Darling." My mom took a step toward me, and I stumbled backward. "I don't know what you just overheard, but I can explain."

The earnest pleading in her expression snapped something in me. My entire life had been a lie. How had I missed the signs? Why hadn't I pushed her harder when she fed me that bullshit story about him being a TA while she was an under-grad? She'd been so cagey and weird about the whole thing. Way more than a simple breakup warranted.

"How are you going to explain this, Mom?" I exploded in a bright flash of claws and teeth. She flinched as I advanced on her with my fists balled. "How are you going to work around the fact that you told me you picked my father out from the local sperm bank?"

Richard cleared his throat. "I'm going to give you two a moment."

"Don't bother. I'm leaving." I burned him with a searing glare, but even through my rage-haze I examined him, look-ing for the similarities, hungry to see something of myself in him that would explain my entire existence.

"You should talk to your mother," he said.

"Are you really telling me what to do? Wow. Now I know where I get my gall."

"I'm . . ." Indecision clouded his expression. "I don't know what to do here. I'd like a chance to talk with you, if you want, but I don't think this is my place."

"No, it's not," my mom said. "You made your choice twenty-seven years ago. You don't get to come back just because you're old, your life is a sad, pathetic mess, and you want a second chance now that the hard part is over."

"I didn't mean for any of this to happen this way. I'm ter-ribly sorry for the trouble this might cause both of you." He walked away, pausing for only a moment beside me. My fa-ther. I couldn't wrap my head around it.

Whatever he saw on my face had him making a quicker

exit, and I turned back to my mom. I was pretty sure I'd let out an honest-to-God snarl. She moved closer to the balcony railing, and her pale lips trembled.

There was a time not so long ago, like fifteen minutes ago, when I would've given anything to see my mom lose her shit. To just once have her trade places with me and know what it felt like to be under constant scrutiny and never measure up. It didn't make me feel happy or superior the way I'd always imagined. I just felt tired.

"Tell me everything," I said without much heat. "Now. I deserve the truth."

"Richard was a professor in the anthropology department when I was studying for my doctorate." She chewed on her bottom lip.

"So he wasn't a TA after all. Fascinating." Huh. Turned out I still had some anger left. "I gave you a chance to explain this to me weeks ago. Why didn't you tell me the truth? I would've been upset, but I would've found a way to deal with it."

"I didn't want you to look at me the way you're looking at me now."

"You prefer me groveling for your affection, is that it?"

"I'd prefer if you respected me." She let out a sigh. "But I've probably lost any chance of that for good."

"I don't even know who you are. You lied about everything, even the stuff that shouldn't have mattered. Like how you weren't always just a psychology student." Her head snapped up, and I nodded. "Yeah, I learned that little tidbit down at the bar." My palms hurt from pressing my nails into them so tightly. "Thanks for making me feel like a complete loser when I changed my major as an undergrad though. Really puts that time into perspective."

"I tried to push you in the right direction because you changed your major to something utterly useless." It amazed me how quickly she could flip the switch and bring back that haughty attitude as if all of her lies hadn't just blown up in her face. "And now look at you, an administrative assistant for an insurance company. Bravo."

"Are you really going to lecture me? Right now, of all times?" I'd never had a stronger urge to tell her what I really did for a living than at this moment. Not because I wanted to come clean, but because I wanted it to eat away at her at night. I wanted her to lie awake and contemplate all the ways she'd failed as a parent.

"Now isn't the time. You're right." Her back stiffened on those last two words, like it physically pained her to admit I was right about something.

"I want the full story." Every gory detail. Maybe I'd rehash it every year at Christmas, just to make the season a little more merry and bright for one of us.

"Are you sure you want to hear this?" She wrung her hands. "It's not a very pretty story."

"Might as well get on with it."

"I had an affair with Richard while he was a professor and I was his student. That's bad enough on its own, but it gets a little more complicated from here."

As much as I didn't want to feel any kind of pity or empathy for my mom, I knew how dependent grad students were on the approval of their professors. The power differential in that scenario made my blood run cold. "That makes him a predatory piece of shit, but I already have an abysmal opinion of him."

She sucked in a deep breath, as if she wanted to get the words out in one rush without having to pause. "He was married, and I knew he was married when I got involved with him."

Whoa. Even though a part of me had known that confession was coming, I leaned a hand against the rough brick building. After everything I'd gone through with Aiden and his cheating, that hit me nearly as hard as finding out I'd had a secret father this whole time. He'd been married when I was conceived, but to hear it out loud like that was a shock to my system. My mom, who judged and turned her nose up at all of my decisions, had willingly and knowingly had an affair with a married man. Even in my worst and most self-destructive moments—and I was far from angelic—I'd never crawled into that particular swamp.

"How could you do that?" I couldn't imagine what it would be like to take a man into my bed, knowing full well he'd made promises to another. "What were you thinking?"

"I thought I was in love." She rolled her eyes, and I saw the sharp and jaded edges she'd turned on me because he wasn't around anymore. A picture of who I could've become if I'd held on to the bitterness from my breakup with Aiden.

"Is that why he quit?" His background check had stated that he'd left Northwestern right around the time my mom would've been three months pregnant. "Because you told him about me?"

"No." She closed her eyes for a beat. "This is where I'm going to look even worse, and before I say anything, I need you to remember that I was only twenty-seven."

How could it get any worse? This was about as low as anyone could go.

"I'm twenty-seven." And according to her, I'd been a disappointment ever since I came out of the womb not potty-trained.

"Right. Well. I called his wife and told her I was pregnant. Before I told him."

"What happened next?" I struggled to keep my voice calm and even. This was beginning to make all of my mistakes look like a brochure for Good Life Choices.

"Nothing good." She bit out the words. "Richard had to leave his position at Northwestern if he wanted to save his marriage, so he broke things off with me. Not long after, his wife revealed she was pregnant, but she lost the baby and they divorced."

I pressed my fingers to my temples just to keep my brain from leaking out on the concrete. Who was this woman before me? I couldn't reconcile the mother I'd always known with this version she described. For all her faults, she'd always been poised and put-together. She'd been aggressive and pushy, a terrible parent, but not necessarily a terrible person. The whole time, I thought she'd been holding me to the moral standard she held herself to. More like she'd been trying to atone vicariously through me.

"I was selfish." It wasn't often I saw genuine regret in my mom's eyes, and it was always a little jarring. "I have so many regrets from that time. When Richard came to me after his divorce and said he wanted to be a part of your life, I told him no."

I didn't know how to feel about that. On one hand, Richard was clearly awful. Knowing that half my DNA came from an adulterer who'd used his power position to prey on his student probably would've messed with my already precarious psyche. However, it didn't excuse the fact that I had a father, flesh and blood, not Sperm Donor #345, and she'd never told me. I had no doubt her reasons for keeping me in the dark had nothing to do with me and what I needed. It had been about her and her reputation. It always had been.

"Did it ever occur to you that I might've wanted to know?" Not that Richard and I would be braiding each other's hair anytime soon, but it would've been nice to know. Maybe we could've had a relationship. Maybe I wouldn't have felt so alone growing up in the library with only books to keep me company.

"I couldn't afford the scandal." There it was. I knew it was only a matter of time before the real reason for her lies came out. "Richard moved on to the Field Museum, but I was still at Northwestern. If anyone found out the truth, my career would've been over before it began."

I wouldn't feel sorry for her. Maybe if she'd been honest with me from the outset, I would've felt bad that she'd been taken advantage of by a man who held all her cards, but she'd made it impossible for me to dredge up any sympathy for her situation. She'd had an affair because she thought she was in love. She'd kept it a secret because she thought it would ruin her career. Everything came down to her selfish choices, and she didn't give a damn about anyone else. Least of all the life her little tryst had produced.

"I'm glad your precious career didn't suffer." She took a step forward, but I held up a hand. "Don't come any closer. I can't even look at you right now."

I whirled around and left her on the second-floor balcony. Tears stung the corners of my eyes, but I willed them not to fall. Growing up, I'd bent over backward trying to please her, to be the daughter she'd always wanted, to do something worthy enough.

It had nearly broken me.

The patterns in my life played in my mind. The way I always sought affection from people who didn't want me, because I'd been raised to believe love had to be earned—it could never be given freely. I'd given my mom so much, put the career I wanted on hold for years, because I'd been subconsciously waiting for her approval. This time I wouldn't give her my tears.

She didn't deserve them.

CHAPTER 30

I found Mark standing by the bar with Dr. Faber. I made a beeline for him, not wanting to spend another second at this party. If he needed to network, he could do it alone, the way he had been all night. He must've seen something in my expression, because he immediately ditched Dr. Faber and ran over to me.

He searched my eyes. "What happened? Did you run into Eve?"

"What? No." What did Eve have to do with anything? "I just confronted my mom and a man named Richard Vaden, otherwise known as my father."

"I thought you didn't have a father?" He gave me the same look he had when I'd gotten my hand stuck in a pickle jar because I refused to drop the pickle. "Or was the sperm bank thing one of your weird jokes?"

If only. "I didn't know until about half an hour ago. I overheard my mom talking to him on the second-floor balcony. He used to be an anthropology professor at Northwestern. He knows Dr. Faber, that's why he's here."

"I'm so sorry." He pulled me against his chest, running soothing hands down my bare back. "Are you okay?"

"I'm pissed. Pissed she lied. Pissed she had an affair with a married man and she didn't tell me because her reputation was more important. Pissed at him for screwing one of his grad students while his wife was pregnant. What kind of a man even does that? What does that say about me? Nature versus nurture, right? Well, I ended up empty in both departments."

"It doesn't say anything about you." He tilted my face up and kissed me gently.

There was no way he could believe that. Not with his own history and the way he let it run his life, even now. "Like it doesn't say anything about you?"

"Can we not get into that right now?" At the anguish in his expression, a lead weight dropped into my stomach. "Let's just—"

"What a cozy couple you two make." Eve's voice dripped with poison. "I had no idea you were seeing each other. It's a little shocking."

"Is it really *that* shocking to find me amongst the great minds of the city?" Okay, so I was a dropout turned professional heartbreaker who wanted to put ketchup on fancy French food, but that didn't make me less than any of these people. There was more to life than pretending to be the smartest person in the room.

"I'm just surprised, after what he did to you to get Dr. Faber's job. And I'm sorry your breakup with Aiden drove you to such an extreme." Her lips puffed with sympathy.

"What are you talking about?" I turned to Mark, hoping he'd brush her off or tell her to get lost. But his face had paled, and a light sheen of sweat touched his forehead.

"I'm sorry you lost the job, but this isn't the right way to vent, Eve." Mark put a protective arm around my shoulders. "Don't say something you'll regret."

A warning bell went off in my head. I shook him off. "What's going on here?"

"I promise, the minute we leave, I'll explain everything." The remorse in his tone, the offer to explain, all sounded eerily similar to the way my mom had reacted on the balcony. What secrets could he possibly have with Eve?

Everything went cold and numb. I turned my back on him as I faced Eve, catching a glimmer of triumph in her eyes. "What did Mark do to get this job?"

"Well, to start, he—"

"Stop. This isn't going to make her mom force me out, and it's not getting you closer to the position. You're just making unnecessary enemies." He cut a scathing look in her direction, worse than the one he'd given me on his first day at H4H. But underneath his anger, his eyes were a bit wild with something that worried me more: fear.

He took my arm. "Forget about Eve for a second. This is about us. Can we go somewhere and talk?"

Everything went light and woozy as I struggled to make sense of their interaction. What could Mark have done to me to win this job? I had no ties to Northwestern anymore . . . except my mom. My heart stopped. I'd encouraged my mom to talk him up to the committee. Had he gotten involved with me on a personal level because he knew my mom had sway? I needed to get out of here and clear my head. Too much had been thrown at me at once, and I didn't know what was real anymore.

"Both of you can go to hell." I turned and marched toward the front door, pulling up the Uber app on my phone.

"Brinkley. Wait." Mark caught up to me outside the club. He moved to touch me, but dropped his hand when I backed away. "Don't leave before hearing me out. Please."

The urge to run was so strong, but this was Mark. The guy who knew all my messiness and wanted me anyway. Unless he was just a really good actor. "You have five minutes."

The chilly wind on my back froze me down to my toes, and I tried to control my shivering. Mark draped his jacket over my shoulders. I wanted to shrug it to the ground and kick it, but I also didn't want to catch pneumonia.

Mark rubbed his hands over his face. "Eve and I have been friendly for a few years. We met at a lecture given at the Field Museum by Richard Vaden. Which is . . ."

Three million people in Chicago. Three. Million. And all my paths led to the same people. Hell was probably one of those moving sidewalks that never went anywhere.

Mark cleared his throat. "Anyway, I never thought we were competing when we both started teaching, since we were adjuncts at different schools. We shared lecture tips, critiqued grant proposals, shared the upswings and setbacks."

"I don't care." If he told me they'd hooked up, I'd scream.

"We never dated, if that's what you're thinking."

"I wasn't." I wanted to choke him for being able to read me so easily.

"She really wanted this position. I guess friends and career aspirations don't mix. Especially in academics."

"They mix just fine if you're not an asshole." I didn't care if he and Eve had been besties who sang campfire songs together. I wanted to know the truth about the present.

He bowed his head. "Maybe. I was never good at playing politics though. I'd hoped to go full-time at UoC, but they didn't have any spots open. They barely had spots for adjuncts."

"So you applied for Dr. Faber's position. I know this already." My patience was wearing thin. He was two minutes into the five I'd given him, and he hadn't told me anything new.

"I want to teach more than anything." He lifted his gaze to mine, and the pain in his eyes likely matched my own. "I thought I needed to be a professor, teaching at the collegiate level. I have my doctorate in anthropology, but I'm young. I needed a groundbreaking article to stand out as an applicant to Northwestern."

"And Selena stole all your research for said article and published it herself, knocking you out of the running at UoC, so you applied to Northwestern. Great. Now that we're all caught up, I want to know what I have to do with you securing that job."

"Selena really did steal my research to jump ahead of me at UoC, but I'm not talking about that one. The article I'm referring to, the one I wrote to get the job at Northwestern, is a little different. Talking with Margo that first time gave me the idea."

"What idea?" I knew. Right then, I knew, but I wanted to hear him say it anyway.

"I thought it would be an interesting subject, diving into the psychology of what would make someone want to work at a place like H4H. I trained as a Heartbreaker so I could have insider information that would allow me to write an article with enough buzz to give me an edge in the interview. They gave me the job because the article is going to be published in *Cultural Anthropology* next quarter."

None of it had been real. I'd been an experiment. A Skinner lab rat.

Even when I left academia, I couldn't really leave. It was Eliza and Eve all over again, cozying up to me to get a one-up in their careers. But they'd never gone this far. They'd used me while I was a resource, then shut me out, made me feel worthless when I was no longer useful. But it didn't compare to the job Mark had done on me. They'd just wanted better grades. Mark had gone for the long con and snagged a tenure opportunity.

"Are you proud of yourself? Do you sleep better at night knowing you won?"

"I had no intention of hurting you. The article was meant to generate buzz, but only in the anthropology community. It wasn't ever supposed to go outside that."

I crossed my arms and leaned back to examine him, to see who he really was beneath the Hot Professor exterior, and I didn't like it one bit. "So you thought it was okay because only the anthropology community would know you used me?"

"No." He shook his head. "I never used you. Yes, I wrote an article about H4H, but I kept it all anonymous and mostly focused on Margo. I asked Eve to critique it, the way we've critiqued dozens of papers for each other. I didn't think she would connect the dots. And I really didn't think she'd rub it in your face, hoping you'd tell your mom and use her influence to run me out so she could take my place."

"Then you don't know Eve at all." I didn't want to hear his excuses. "You put all of us at Heartbreak for Hire at risk."

H4H was a strictly undercover, cash operation, and he'd exposed us all. For a job he thought he needed, but never really wanted. Maybe I deserved this for two years of heartbreaking. Karma had finally come to collect. Silly of me to think I still had a deficit.

"I didn't name any of you or the business," he said. "I was careful."

Not careful enough. Eve knew. It wouldn't take long for her to spread it around. Everyone who'd known me at Northwestern would have a good laugh at my expense. What little dignity I'd managed to scrape up after Aiden would blow away like ash between my fingers.

"I hate you." My voice was barely above a whisper.

"I'm so sorry. You have no idea how sorry I am." His eyes pleaded with me. Begged. I couldn't stand it. "I wanted to tell you every night we were together, but it was so good with us, I was afraid you'd push me away."

A horrifying thought dawned on me. "Did you know who I was that first night? Was it a setup? Is that why you brought me back to your apartment?"

"No." He reached for me, and I recoiled. "I had no idea H4H even existed until I found that card with all my information on it and called Margo. I swear."

"You want my trust?" I let out a humorless laugh. "I gave it to you already. You threw it in the dirt to advance your career. Congratulations, you've officially topped my mom tonight."

"Please." He folded his hands together, actually begging now, but nothing could thaw the hard exterior I'd built around me. "You used me as part of your job too, and I forgave you. We moved past it. Can't we find a way past this too?"

"That's not even close to the same thing." For him to throw that in my face now to deflect his betrayal infuriated me. Would he always bring up how we'd met whenever he wanted the upper hand in an argument? I wouldn't live that way, just waiting for him to mention it. "I didn't know you at all. You've been sleeping with me for weeks."

"You're right. I'm sorry." He rubbed his hands over his face. "What can I do to fix this?"

"Don't let them publish the article," I said. "That's the least you can do."

His face fell. "I can't take it back. My career is literally hanging on it now. I promised them the paper before I fell in love with you."

I'd been waiting to hear those words. For him to confirm that his feelings matched my own. This should've been a romantic moment, the start of something new and deeper between us. He should've said those words by candlelight or while he was buried inside of me.

Not here. Not like this.

"You love me?"

He nodded, his expression bleak, as my Uber pulled up next to us.

"I didn't think it was possible to give fewer fucks than when I found out my mom had been lying to me about my father. Yet here we are."

I got in the car and slammed the door in his face.

CHAPTER 31

ME: Meet me at my place ASAP. Bring emergency liquor.

EM: on my way

I made it back to my apartment without breaking down.
A major feat. I took stock of my evening. I'd left Dr. Faber's
retirement party down one Mark, but up one father who
was a Grade A creep, but down one mother who hadn't been
all that great to begin with. At least I still had Winnie and
vodka. Fuck everything else.

Mark's last words had been that he loved me. What a
joke. He'd thrown us away for a job he still couldn't admit
he wasn't suited for because he needed to prove himself to
a ghost more than he needed me. At least he'd finally nailed
the backstabbing antics of a true academic. I just wished I'd
known I'd be the first casualty.

It probably made me a hypocrite to be so pissed—more than

a few of my previous targets would say I was past due for a spin on the misery-go-round—but I didn't know how to stop the hurt. If he'd been honest with me sooner, maybe I could've forgiven him for writing that research article to secure the position, if that really was his dream. What I couldn't forgive were the lies he continued to tell me after we got involved. I'd shared personal things with him, things I'd never talked about with anyone else, and the whole time he'd been making me think I could trust him so he could dissect me for career kudos.

I leaned against my door after I shut it behind me. Winnie rubbed against my legs, purring. God, I must've been in rough shape if she hadn't tried to chew on my ankles the moment I got home. I picked her up and nuzzled her soft black fur against my cheek. The dark and empty place inside me throbbed like a fresh bruise, though it had always been there, waiting, knowing it would only be a matter of time before it could envelop me once more.

My phone buzzed in my clutch. Five missed calls from my mom, ten missed calls from Mark, and one missed call from a number I didn't recognize. I also had two texts from Mark.

MARK: Please believe me when I say I've been trying to find a way to tell you that wouldn't result in you walking away from me. I never wanted to hurt you. I know I probably fucked this up forever, and I can't begin to tell you how sorry I am. I wish I could go back and be honest from the start. If you'll just talk to me . . . I'll do anything to earn your forgiveness.

MARK: I meant it when I said I love you.

I powered down my phone and went into my studio, where I grabbed my most recent work off the easel. The one full of light and love and all the things I'd just begun to allow myself to feel again. I went out to my balcony and threw it into the alley behind my building. Leaving the slider open, I let the cold wash over me.

After putting a fresh canvas up on my easel, I grabbed a brush and smashed it into the black and gray and midnight blue. I attacked the blank white space with a fury. All the roiling clouds clashing inside me became an angry collision of paint. I didn't think or consider, I just felt and let it flow through every brushstroke. Within an hour, I'd created a storm of emotion filled with shadows and pain and the sensation of falling down a long dark well with no bottom. Not my usual street scene, but it was raw and furious and better than anything I'd put on a canvas in months. My style of art thrived in dark corners.

Hearing a knock, I abandoned my latest work and threw open my front door. Emma stood before me with two bottles of Absolut and cranberry juice.

"I came as soon as I could." She pressed a bottle into my hand. "What did he do? I'm not above hiring a hit man, as long as they take Visa."

I twisted the cap off the bottle and took a swig. The bitter vodka burned my throat and warmed my stomach. "I don't even know where to begin."

"Go change. I'll mix us drinks, and you can tell me everything." Emma shooed me toward my bedroom. "Not that you don't look pretty."

I probably looked like I'd been run over by a truck while wearing a nice dress, but I appreciated the sentiment. My cozy flannel pajama pants lay in the heap next to my dresser that I referred to as my clean-clothes pile. I pulled them on with my threadbare Mr. Peanut T-shirt and went back out to the living room, where Emma had two mixed drinks waiting.

I curled up on the opposite end of the couch and tucked a throw pillow under my chin. "I should probably start with my mom and Richard Vaden."

I told Emma everything that had happened from the time I'd confronted my old friends, to when I walked in on my mom's revelation, to Mark coming clean about why he'd taken the job at H4H. She let me purge every ugly detail without interruption, though she snarled with indignation under her breath.

When I'd finished, I sagged into the couch, feeling sucked dry. Emma poured me another drink, then wrapped her arms around me. I buried my face in her silky hair as she stroked my back. She didn't say a word. She didn't need to. Having someone who loved me unconditionally, who didn't want to mold me or use me, was enough.

It made the hurt bearable.

Another knock sounded at my door. Mark's voice filtered through from the other side. "I know you don't want to see me right now, but please let me fix this. Tell me what to do, and I'll do it. We're too good together for this to be the end."

"Want me to deal with him?" Emma asked.

"No. He'll get tired of standing out there and leave eventually."

"I'll sleep on your doorstep if that's what it takes."

I stood and flung open the door. He looked about as bad as I felt. I had a twinge of weakness, an urge to invite him in and push aside his lies and go on as we had been before tonight, but I knew how that would play out. Being with him wasn't worth sacrificing myself. "If you love me, you'll turn around, go home, and never call me again."

"Is that what you really want?"

I nodded.

"I know I'm doing this all wrong." His shoulders slumped. "But if this is the only way I can show you I'm serious, okay. I'll go. I won't call you again."

I shut the door in his face.

My heart cracked with each step he took away from me, until it broke completely.

Emma spent Saturday night with me. After our sixth vodka cranberry, we walked to CVS and bought a cake and a $6.99 body wash gift set. We both woke up with hot-pink lipstick on our eyelids.

My hangover was brutal. Worse than the night we got drunk on Lemon Drops and split a bag of Sour Patch Kids on the Navy Pier Ferris wheel. Wine and vodka really didn't mix. After vomiting up cranberry-flavored bile, I curled up on the couch and prayed for death. Emma had to leave early—she took client meetings on Sundays because all the other firms in the city were closed and it gave her an edge—but she made a coffee and Motrin run for me first.

I should've spent Sunday working on my gallery, but movement was out of the question. At least my hangover distracted me from all my other issues. It hurt too much to think, so I watched true crime documentaries on Netflix as I slipped in and out of fitful sleep.

Sometime around noon, there was a knock at my door. Mark had sent me irises with a card that read: *This is me not calling you.* They went straight over the balcony after my painting.

Come Monday morning, I began to feel like myself again. The bitter and jaded version of myself I'd been before Mark. My true form. I only looked at the empty desk that used to be occupied by him five times in the first hour. Tomorrow it might only be four times. Then three. Then I wouldn't have the urge to look over there at all.

I'd be okay.

I spent most of the morning attempting to throw myself into my newest assignment, but my old methods of self-soothing when I'd been hurt didn't do it for me anymore. Normally I'd relish taking down the kind of target I'd been assigned: a hotel manager who fired women for not being pretty enough to work the front desk, and who'd been caught more than once sabotaging them so he'd have a legitimate excuse to let them go. But it just felt like another week, with another round of men who showed their asses.

I used to think I was evening the odds, but if I became just as terrible as them, all I'd managed to accomplish was doubling the awfulness in the world. Ultimately, I wasn't doing anything to empower people or create beauty or spread kindness. And the men I took down wouldn't stop being terrible just because they'd been served their own medicine. It was akin to standing on the corner and shouting angry words into the wind.

Margo called my extension. "Can I see you in my office?"

"Sure." I pushed off from my desk. She probably wanted to mother-hen me or give me more ideas on how to handle the hotel manager. She could give me all the ideas she wanted. I didn't care anymore. I needed more from life than other people's misery.

My heels clicked on the marble floor, and I knocked once before entering. Margo sat with her hands folded on her desk. She wore a grim expression. No tea in sight. This was no comfort meeting.

"Have a seat, Brinkley."

I sat on the edge of the poufy chair. My spine straightened, as if my body knew to go on the defense. "What's going on?"

"You've been distracted today. I thought you'd be more focused now that your former target is no longer employed here, but that doesn't seem to be the case." Her sharp nails clicked on the polished mahogany of her desk. With each tap, my shoulders hunched a bit more. "Are you thinking of going to work for Ms. Yoo? Because I won't tolerate disloyalty."

The suggestion immediately put my back up. "Are you threatening me?"

"No, Brinkley, I'm not threatening you." *Tap. Tap. Tap.* "You've been like a daughter to me, and I just want to make sure you're feeling happy and well taken care of here." *Tap.*

Tap. Tap. "Ms. Yoo was ready to strike out on her own, but you're still tender. I can see that."

"I'm not quite as tender as you think." Mark had bruised my heart, but he hadn't destroyed it. I still had good friends who cared about me, and I still had my gallery. I was so much more than a broken woman who needed to be sharpened.

"Brinkley." She reached across the desk and squeezed my hand. "I'm only trying to help you. The women at the hotel who hired you to take down their boss are counting on you. You're going to make a real difference in their lives, and I'd hate to see you shortchange them."

It was the same song she'd been singing for years, but with Emma gone and the men minus Mark still employed, the sisterhood that had drawn me to this line of work had vanished. I wasn't making a difference. Maybe I'd made women feel good temporarily, but what did that really do for them in the long run? Did it give them options for a better career? Did it encourage them to take charge of the situation? Did it counsel them in any way? All the bullshit Margo had used to sell me on H4H had become mere words without action. And all the women I "helped" didn't truly end up better off.

Just like I hadn't really ended up better off by working for Margo.

The satisfaction I got from doling out revenge only made me feel good for a moment, but once that high wore off, the emptiness always set in. It wasn't the job that had gotten me over Aiden; it was Emma and Allie and Charlotte. It was painting and dreaming and making plans for my gallery. It was me, living my life.

Margo had pretended to nurture me when I'd been low and vulnerable. She'd made me believe I needed H4H to heal. But if she really cared, she would've encouraged me to stand on my own.

"I quit." I had no backup plan and no other job to replace this one, but once I said those words, the weight I'd been carrying lifted. Like exhaling after holding my breath for years.

"Excuse me? What did you just say?" Margo sputtered.

"I quit." I stood, and my knees didn't wobble a bit. In fact, I'd never felt stronger. "I'd put in my two weeks' notice, but . . ." I shrugged. "I don't really feel like it."

And just like that, I was no longer employed at Heartbreak for Hire.

CHAPTER 32

>>>———————————————>

How did the unemployed spend their days? Apparently, elbow deep in mint-chocolate-chip ice cream and angry cat. I didn't regret quitting H4H—that had been a long time coming—but I did regret giving up the paycheck before I had another job in the bag.

If I didn't find something soon, the savings account I'd so carefully built up would deplete within months. I needed something that would at least cover my current bills or else my apartment would have to be the first thing to go. It had been an extravagance to live on Michigan Avenue, but I couldn't beat the lighting in the master bedroom. I'd told myself it was an investment in my art.

The next thing to go would be my gallery. I hoped it wouldn't come to that, but as it stood now, I had enough money to either fix it up or make payments. I couldn't do both. One without the other would be pointless. Even though

I was at least a month out from that point, it felt like my dreams were dying before they'd had a chance to bloom.

I'd spent the past two days checking Monster and Indeed for places to send my résumé. And by résumé, I meant the pile of bullshit I'd strung together to account for the last two years, since I didn't think Professional Heartbreaker would endear me to prospective employers and I doubted I could count on Margo for a referral anyway. Pickings were slim under normal circumstances, slimmer when I had to check each opening against the men in management I'd been humiliating for the last two years. Those three or more assignments a week really added up.

Then there was the issue of my degree. As much as I hated to say my mom was right, a bachelor's in art theory and practice qualified me for precisely nothing. I had to look for jobs that only required a degree, any degree, which didn't leave me with a lot of promising options.

I clicked on a link for an administrative assistant at a Bells and Stern accounting firm—the irony amused me—and nearly vomited when I saw the pay. It would take me a month to earn what I'd made in a week at H4H. I hadn't expected to make as much as I had working for Margo, but half would've been nice. Half would've kept me in a smaller apartment in the city and on a steady diet of ramen noodles.

I turned my laptop toward Winnie. "This is what rock bottom looks like."

She hissed and flounced away. She'd been extra cranky with me since I could no longer afford to keep up with the latest in cat fashion. I couldn't even make the creature who depended on me for food and water love me unless she got something in return.

But I wasn't destitute yet. I was just forced to move, kill my dream, and piss off my already murderous cat. Other than that, I was doing fine. Ice cream and Netflix helped. Emma had offered to let me move in with her, but I valued my friendship with her too much to risk it. If I forgot to wash one dish, she'd probably kick me out again. I'd thought Mark was anal when it came to neatness, but Emma had him beat by a mile. She organized her socks by color. The thought made me shudder.

If things got really bad, I could always fold T-shirts at H&M. I'd have to get a studio in the suburbs to survive, but it beat asking my mom for help. Especially because I hadn't spoken to her since Dr. Faber's retirement party. She still blew up my phone every day, but she'd reduced her calls to once an hour instead of once a minute. She refused to take the hint. Even Mark had gotten a semihint, reducing his floral deliveries to every other day. I deleted all of her voice mails without listening to them. I already knew what they'd say anyway.

A knock sounded at my door, and I looked down to make sure I was presentable. Pajama pants I hadn't changed out of in three days? Check. Oversize T-shirt with unidentifiable stain? Check. Hair a matted lump on top of my head? Check.

It was as good as I was going to get. With luck it would be Mark. I stood a solid chance of running him off for good in my current state. But instead, I opened the door to find my mother standing on the other side.

"Why are you here?" I asked. "I didn't chant your name five times into a mirror."

"I've had enough of being ignored." She pushed past me and stopped short as she took in the glory of my decay.

Almond Joy and beef jerky wrappers littered the couch. Coffee mugs I hadn't bothered to take to the kitchen crowded every open surface. A pile of used tissues, which I affectionately referred to as Olaf, spilled off the side of my end table. My insides had manifested in the most depraved way possible. I would've been embarrassed, if I'd been able to feel anything at all.

"What is going on here?" My mom whirled on me. "Are you on drugs?"

"Mark and I broke up, and then I quit my lucrative job of heartbreaking for pay." Might as well lay it all out there. She'd hear about it through Eve's grapevine sooner or later, plus she had no high ground to judge me anymore. "Oh yeah—I was never an administrative assistant. For the last two years I worked for a company called Heartbreak for Hire. Women paid me to take revenge on men they hated. I lured them in, chewed them up, and spit them out."

My mom's posture stiffened. "This is not the time for one of your jokes."

"Not a joke. It's truly what I did for a living. How do you think I afforded this nice apartment, present condition notwithstanding? I broke men for a living. Which, let me tell you, makes finding another job a real pain in the ass."

Her face paled. "You're serious."

"Yep. But that's done now. So if you'll excuse me, I'm busy

job-hunting. Though I might have to resort to selling my used underwear on eBay. Apparently there's a whole market for that sort of thing." I jerked my chin toward the still open door. Her cue to leave, which she ignored.

"Where did I go wrong?" She stared up at the ceiling, as if the ghost of Freud might reach down a mighty hand and give her the answers she sought.

"Is that a rhetorical question? Because if not, I have several answers."

"Do you, now?" My mom raised her eyebrows. "Let's hear them then."

"Setting aside your affair with a married man and lying about my paternity for a moment, how about the fact that I was never good enough for you? Or we could go with that time you threatened to have me kicked out of school because I didn't study your preferred major." I ticked them off on my fingers. "The subtle digs you took after my relationship with Aiden ended, constantly insulting my choices, calling my art a pipe dream. Look at that." I held up my hand. "I just scored a bingo."

"You think I was insulting you? That I didn't think you were good enough?" Her face scrunched with confusion. "I pushed you, yes, but it was always because I thought you were better. Better than Aiden, better than a substandard art degree, better than me."

She'd never once hinted that she thought I was better than her. Quite the opposite, in fact. Where most kids got measured with a Sharpie line above their heads, I got measured in all the accomplishments I hadn't reached by a certain age.

When my mom was eight, *she* was doing long division, so why couldn't I add double digits? At fourteen, *she'd* already read Shakespeare's entire works, so why did I struggle with the language in *Romeo and Juliet*? At eighteen, *she'd* been valedictorian, so why should she be impressed that I'd graduated with honors?

I sighed. "You're only saying this now because I know you're a fraud."

"What do you want from me, Brinkley? If you want to keep punishing me, fine, you're entitled to do so. But I can't go back and change the past."

"Don't stand there and say I'm punishing you like you're a victim." I closed my eyes and breathed. She'd asked what I wanted—maybe it was past time I actually told her. "It would've been really great if you'd been supportive of me. I didn't need you to push me growing up. I needed a terry-cloth towel monkey."

"A towel what?"

I waved it away. "Never mind. I meant I needed you to care, not tell me all the ways I could've done better. I wanted you to say you were proud of me. Not because I'd done something to earn your approval, but because you were proud of me for just being me."

"I am proud of you. I've always been proud of you. Do I think you could improve? I—"

"Ack." I cut her off. "No qualifiers, please. This is me." I gestured to the absolute wreckage of my apartment. "I'm a complete mess. I make mistakes. I'm a damned good artist. Take it or leave it, because this is who I've always been."

She pursed her lips as she took in the paintings covering my walls. This was the first time she'd been in my apartment, the first time she'd seen my work. Insecurity had me knotting my fingers behind my back as she walked over to one of the walls to get a closer look. No one outside Mark, Emma, and the pizza delivery guy had seen the full scope of my work, and now it was under the scrutiny of my biggest critic.

She turned back to me, and I flinched. "These are good."

"I'm sorry, what?" Had she just given me a compliment? A genuine one without a hidden barb?

"You're extremely talented. I had no idea you could do any of this." She gestured toward my paintings. "I'm sorry I didn't support you more. And just so you know, I am proud of you. No qualifiers. You're a much better person than I was at your age."

"Wow. All right then." I didn't know what to do with my mom when I wasn't arguing with her. "Should we hug or something?"

"Yes, that would be quite reasonable." She hugged me. While it was stiff and awkward, like hugging the animatronic mouse at Chuck E. Cheese, at least she made an effort.

If we could keep meeting halfway, maybe we'd be okay after all.

My mom stayed to help me clean my apartment. As we bagged the trash, she asked me more about my art, what my plans were to get it out there. I told her about my gallery. She offered to give me financial help, but we'd just started to get on even footing, and I didn't want to tip the scales again by owing her. Plus, my gallery was something I wanted to do on my own. Even though I was in very real danger of losing it, I could always find a way to keep saving, or maybe find a partner to go in with me on the next phase. That was the silver lining of failure: it offered limitless chances to dust yourself off and try again.

"I appreciate the offer, but I can't take it." I put the last of my crusty coffee mugs in the dishwasher and turned to my mom. "Thanks for helping me pick up. I'm sure you have to get back to your office."

"I do." She paused, her nostrils flaring as if she was about to say something really unpleasant. "But before I go, we need to discuss your education."

I knew this afternoon was too good to be true. "What about it?"

"That two hundred thousand from Richard wasn't hush money from my father. It was actually for child support. I didn't want to accept it at first, out of spite, but when he offered me a lump sum, I took it for you. For school."

I sighed. "I'm not going back."

"No. I know." She huffed out a short breath. "But there was enough money for you to go all the way through to your doctorate. Since you had three years left, I'm going to write you a check for the remaining balance. You won't owe me anything. It's not my money. It's yours."

Holy shit. Three years of grad school tuition, even with the family discount, would be over $75,000. "Mom. I don't know what to say."

"Say you'll take the money and do what you were always meant to do with it." She tucked a loose piece of hair behind my ear, and her eyes widened as she stared at her hand, wondering how it had made such a casual gesture of affection without her permission. "But first, you should really get in the shower. You look atrocious, dear."

"I'll take it." I threw my arms around her, sending us both stumbling.

"Yes. Well. Good." She straightened her jacket, all business, but her cheeks had a happy pink tint to them. "By the way, I've seen your gentleman around campus."

I shook my head. "I told you he's not my gentleman anymore."

"I know, but from the way he's been walking around like the living dead, I'd say he's still very much your gentleman."

I didn't have a response for that. I'd forgiven my mother for her lies, but she'd let me live in her womb for nine months. In a way, Mark's lies had hurt worse because I'd trusted him against my better instincts. My mom was right about one thing: you couldn't go back and change the past.

CHAPTER 33

A few weeks later, I wiped the sweat off my brow as I hauled another podium into place in my gallery. Thanks to Richard's child support, I could fix up the place *and* make my payments without living on cat food. I still needed to move into a smaller apartment—I had to be careful with the money—but I'd deal with that after the opening.

The floors had been refinished two days ago, and all the shelves I'd installed had a fresh coat of paint. I ran a hand over the lacquered red counter, its shiny surface like glass beneath my palm. Yesterday I'd hooked up Square to an iPad that would flip toward customers so they could sign, and I'd rung up a phantom dollar just to make sure it worked.

The technical aspects of my business had all been handled. Now I was on to the fun stuff—the designing and decorating I'd been itching to do.

Emma had stopped by earlier to bring me coffee and catch me up on all the latest happenings with her advertising firm. She'd been stealing business from her old employer, and she found it a thousand times more satisfying than exacting revenge on men who'd had nothing to do with screwing her over. According to Charlotte and Allie, Margo had been having a difficult time trying to simultaneously replace Emma and me, so it had hit her especially hard when they both put in their two weeks' notice. That bit of news warmed the cold dark place in my heart that still enjoyed a little schadenfreude.

We had plans to all meet up for drinks after my opening, but I missed seeing them on a daily basis. The only part of H4H I missed.

"I had a drink with a guy the other night," Emma told me.

I set my coffee aside and hopped up on my new counter. "Tell me everything."

"Not much to tell." Emma averted her eyes. "He's okay. Kind of a goober, but in a good way. He runs an appraisal business. His office is next to mine. When he asked me out, looking all earnest in his three-piece suit and Coke-bottle glasses, I figured, why not?"

Why not indeed. "I like him already. His name?"

"Ugh. I knew you were going to ask me that. His name is Walter."

"Is he eighty?"

She grinned. "He's thirty-five, so obviously his parents hate him." She set her coffee on one of the shelves. "I've got the rest of the afternoon off if you want some help."

"I would love it, actually."

We'd hauled podiums around until I had them all perfectly positioned. Emma held the ivy and lights border I'd bought on discount to frame my ceiling, while I used a nail gun to secure it in place. The soft white lights gave the room ambience. I'd taken a few trips into the suburbs to hit up estate sales for vignette items. In one window I'd set up a chair with an old teddy bear who was missing one of his button eyes. An old tin train set on rusted tracks rested on the floor. Paper hot-air balloons hung from the ceiling, and I'd fashioned an old carousel horse to function as an easel to display my painting of the little girl looking into the toy store.

I'd added a few plants to fill the space, then went out into the street to check out how it would look to people passing by.

"It's perfect." Emma rested her elbow on my shoulder. "You're really building something here. Not just a business, but the start of a new community. I'm so proud of you."

I hugged her. "Thank you. For always being the best."

After Emma left, I continued to work. I had brought a few of my pieces to set around the room. Not for display, but just to have them there. In my space. There'd be no going back or calling myself "aspiring." I'd be putting my work out there for the world to see. I was an artist, and the label didn't scare me anymore.

A man in a corduroy jacket poked his head in my door. "I'm sorry to bother you. It doesn't appear like you're open yet, but I was wondering if that painting was for sale." He pointed at my toy-store display.

"I . . ." I wasn't technically ready, but who was I to turn down a sale? I gave him a warm smile. "Sure. Come on inside."

After a few difficulties with my new credit card reader, the man walked out with one of my paintings, and I'd just made my first sale two weeks ahead of launch. I was walking on puffy clouds in an endless blue sky. This called for a celebration, but Emma had already gone, and I didn't feel much like drinking and making a fool of myself in the city.

I grabbed my phone off the counter and called the one person I wouldn't have a few weeks ago. "Hey, Mom. Are you free for dinner?"

⚔

Opening night. The air rippled with anticipation. Everything I'd been working toward had all come down to this moment. A dream realized.

Tilly's House of Horrors had been helping me with promo all week, handing out fliers with each vial of blood and two-headed skeleton they sold. We had a mutual interest in seeing each other succeed, but it wasn't just about that. Tilly was an art lover and a genuinely kind person. I'd already begun to feel the sense of community in this neighborhood.

My gallery fit in nicely with the fusion restaurants and funky shops in the area. The photography studio that shared the other wall with me showcased beautiful black-and-white pictures of the city. I'd thought about selling photography too, but I didn't have the room, and I didn't want to step on toes. I liked that the businesses around here didn't compete, but rather worked together to ensure the high tides would raise all our ships.

A chef from the culinary school kitty-corner to me had come over to introduce herself the other day and told me I'd be more than welcome to stop by one of her classes anytime to meet her students. I'd have to take her up on the offer soon, if for no other reason than to build more bridges and invest in this corner of Chicago that we'd all carved out for ourselves.

I'd expected to have to do some scouring to find artists who'd be willing to take a chance on me, but it turned out word had spread once I'd secured Ava's pieces. Now the artists came to me. This was how I lifted up women now, by giving them a space to showcase their talent, by creating beauty and a sense of purpose that had nothing to do with tearing down other people.

Previously empty shelves displayed glasswork from local blowers, pottery, beadwork, and ceramics. The real highlight, though, was the podiums I'd spread around the room to showcase Ava's metal sculptures. She'd had a falling-out with her last gallery, so we'd negotiated a much fairer arrangement, 40 percent, where her last gallery had taken a 60 percent cut. Having her work had garnered me write-ups in the *Sun-Times* and the *Tribune*.

And in the windows, with unique vignettes to complement the various scenes, my paintings had been set up for sale. I'd had to pinch myself several times while putting the displays together. But they were real. This was real.

I'd hired my old friend, the waiter with the wine tray from Dr. Faber's retirement party, to serve drinks as people browsed my selections and made purchases. Everyone I loved and cared about had come out tonight. All except one. . . .

Mark had given up his "not calling" quest. I hadn't received flowers in over a week, and while part of me was relieved he'd finally gotten the hint, another part wanted to let go, show up at his apartment unannounced, and throw myself back into his arms. But I couldn't let regret and old feelings consume me tonight. I had to stay strong. My life was too busy and chaotic for a relationship anyway. Getting a business off the ground took serious commitment.

My mom stood beside me, drinking the one glass of wine she'd allow herself in public, and took in the scene. "I have to hand it to you. This is extraordinary."

"Thank you." I gave her an awkward side-hug. We were still working out how to show affection to each other. "And thank you for not finding something to turn up your nose at."

"Really, Brinkley." She sniffed. "I'm not a monster."

"Of course not." We were both curbing our urge to pick fights. "I really appreciate you coming out tonight and showing your support."

I left her to go mingle in the crowd. Emma stood with Allie and Charlotte. She'd dragged Walter along, and he was adorably uncomfortable with the large crowd but looked at Emma like she held the world. I hoped the two of them worked out.

My featured artists had brought their families, people wandered in off the street through the open doors, and the place was packed. Between ringing up sales and introducing myself to the people I didn't know, I didn't have a free second to catch my breath.

As I sold a gorgeous handblown glass sphere in shades of blue and green, something outside caught my eye and I looked up, as if my subconscious had pulled at me.

Mark stood on the sidewalk. He wore an argyle sweater-vest, and in his arms he held Winnie, who was wearing a matching sweater-vest and butting his chin with her head, completely content.

I stopped everything I'd been doing and went outside. "What is this?"

He set Winnie down but kept her tethered to a cat leash. "I know I said I'd stay away, that I wouldn't call or contact you, but every day I wake up and it's like I'm being stabbed in the heart. I can't even escape it in sleep because I dream about you every night. I miss you. I miss us. Please, Brinkley, give me another chance."

"You bought a matching sweater for my cat?" That surprised me more than seeing him standing outside my gallery on opening night.

"I love you more than I hate clothes on animals."

"That's . . ." I didn't know how to finish that sentence. It shocked my system to see him outside my gallery. I'd almost gotten to the point where I only thought about him every five minutes. But he'd still betrayed me, and I couldn't just forget about it. "That's not enough for me."

I started to walk away, hoping he'd put my cat back where she belonged, when he said, "I left Northwestern."

I faced him. Hardly daring to say anything until he explained himself, I narrowed my eyes. "Why?"

"Because you were right about me." Winnie wound around his legs, and he attempted to untangle her cat leash while he talked. "I was self-destructing, and it blew up in the worst way when I lost you. I withdrew the article and quit."

"Okay." He had my attention. "So what are you going to do now?"

"Just this week I was hired as a middle school teacher on the South Side. I'm going to run a metal detecting club after school." He took a step forward and clasped my hands in his. "I never would've admitted that's what I really wanted if you hadn't pushed me to face who I could be, not who I thought I was supposed to be."

Truth be told, I'd been a goner from the moment I saw he'd put on a matching sweater with my cat. But this—this was the Mark I'd fallen in love with. The man who had a passion for teaching and a dorky hobby that fueled his soul.

"It's about damn time." I threw my arms around him.

He stumbled back as he picked me up and spun me around. Winnie hissed at our feet. His deep exhale of relief caressed my hair, and I pulled back, staring up at those beautiful storm-cloud eyes I'd missed so much.

He cupped my face, running his thumbs along my jaw. He stared at me as if I were more precious than the glass sphere I'd just sold. Pushing up on my toes, I caught his lips and kissed him hard enough to make my toes curl.

I rubbed his chest with my hands. "You know what this means, right? I'm going to make you and Winnie wear these sweaters for my holiday card this year."

He laughed. "You say that like there isn't a matching one

in your size hanging in your closet as we speak. The only thing hanging in your closet, actually, since you keep all your clothes on the floor."

I raised an eyebrow. "How did you get the key to my apartment anyway?"

"I had some help." He looked over my shoulder, and I spun around.

My mom raised her glass to us with misty eyes. That little sneak. I'd given her a spare key for safekeeping weeks ago, but I supposed I could forgive her. I'd gotten pretty good at that.

Turning back to Mark, I kissed him again. I couldn't get enough of touching him, feeling his solid arms around me. This was what home felt like. This was my life.

The place where I was always meant to be.

ACKNOWLEDGMENTS

>>> ───→

First, I'd like to thank all of my readers! I had an absolute blast drafting this story, and I hope you enjoyed going on this journey with Brinkley and Mark.

To my incredible editor, Sara Quaranta, working with you has been the absolute best. I can't thank you enough for your insight, expertise, and passion for this story and these characters. This was an incredible experience, and I'm so thankful to be a part of this team.

A million thanks to my amazing agent, Rebecca Podos, who has been my cheerleader and champion through the highs and lows of this wild business. When I came to you and said I wanted to start writing adult fiction, your enthusiasm and support gave me the push I needed to turn this dream into a reality.

Huge thanks to production editor Alysha Bullock, managing editor Caroline Pallotta, managing editorial assistant

Allison Green, art director Lisa Litwack, publicist Michelle Podberezniak, marketer Anne Jaconette, interior designer Michelle Marchese, subrights director Paul O'Halloran, copyeditor Joal Hetherington, cover designer Vikki Chu, and the entire team at Gallery Books.

To Jen Hawkins, this one is for you.

To my coven, Andrea Contos, Annette Christie, Auriane Desombre, Kelsey Rodkey, Rachel Lynn Solomon, and Susan Lee, thank you for always being there with light and laughter. You pick me up even on my most down days, and I'd be lost without all of you. And thank you for also having pretty awesome first names too. ;)

Kellye Garrett and Roselle Lim, that card is still going.

To my husband and girls, I love you. Thank you for your never-ending love and support.